JUST ONE MORE DAY

SHARI LOW

First published in Great Britain in 2026 by Boldwood Books Ltd.

Cover Design by Alice Moore Design

Cover Images: Shutterstock

A CIP catalogue record for this book is available from the British Library.

Paperback ISBN 978-1-83518-500-1

Large Print ISBN 978-1-83518-501-8

Hardback ISBN 978-1-83518-499-8

Trade Paperback ISBN 978-1-80656-270-1

Ebook ISBN 978-1-83518-502-5

Kindle ISBN 978-1-83518-503-2

Audio CD ISBN 978-1-83518-494-3

MP3 CD ISBN 978-1-83518-495-0

Digital audio download ISBN 978-1-83518-498-1

This book is printed on certified sustainable paper. Boldwood Books is dedicated to putting sustainability at the heart of our business. For more information please visit https://www.boldwoodbooks.com/about-us/sustainability/

Boldwood Books Ltd, 23 Bowerdean Street, London, SW6 3TN

www.boldwoodbooks.com

To the incredible team at Boldwood Books. I am forever grateful...
And to the readers who buy my books, thank you beyond words for allowing me to tell these stories.
With all my love,
Shari x

To the incredible team at Boldwood Books. I am forever grateful...
And to the readers who buy my books, thank you beyond words for allowing me to tell these stories.
With all my love,
Shari x

ON JUST ONE MORE DAY, WE MEET...

Bernadette O'Brien – Devoted nurse at Glasgow Central Hospital ED (Emergency Department), loving mum, now reverted to her maiden name of O'Brien after divorce and death of her ex-husband, eminent cardiac surgeon, Kenneth Manson.

Jack Donovan – Owner of a successful haulage company in Ireland, widower, found late-in-life love with Bernadette.

Nina Kerr – Kenneth and Bernadette's daughter, married to Gerry; their children, Casey, 12, and Milo, 10, are the lights of Bernadette's life.

Stuart Manson – Bernadette and Kenneth's son, a criminal justice lawyer who lives with his partner, Connor.

Caleb Henry – Bernadette's friend and favourite colleague, a fellow ED nurse at Glasgow Central Hospital.

Val Murray – Bernadette's pal, widow, mum, gran and force of nature.

Lila Anderson Atkins – Former mistress of Bernadette's ex-husband, Kenneth Manson. Now living in Edinburgh, married to another renowned cardiac surgeon, and living proof that beauty is only skin deep.

Marge Drummond – Mum to Estelle, widowed after a long, happy marriage to Ian, the love of her life. Kenneth's Manson secretary for three decades, prior to his death.

Estelle Drummond – Marge's daughter, a wedding dress designer with a small but exclusive roster of clients. In a long-term relationship with boyfriend, Craig.

Yvie Danton – Much loved nurse on the elderly ward at Glasgow Central. Notorious strawberry jam thief.

Keli Clark – Yvie's friend and huge-hearted fellow nurse on the elderly ward.

Amber Collins – Mum of Alfie, 5, and Sid, 4, divorced, owner of a busy flower shop, Amber Bouquets, occasional catastrophiser. Has glued her heart back just enough to embark on a new relationship.

Ewan Collins – Amber's ex-husband and father of her sons. Eternally regretful that he broke their family.

Diana Atkins – ex-wife of Edinburgh-based surgeon Murray Atkins.

Murray Atkins – Surgeon and friend of Kenneth Manson for many decades prior to his death.

Sir Lester Kelaney – Esteemed President of the Scottish Society of Surgeons and Marge's boss in the early years of her career.

Clara Kelaney – Sir Lester's very elegant wife and mother of their three daughters.

Danielle Strang – Former model and erstwhile intimate friend of Kenneth Manson.

Annabel Stevenson – Member of Scottish Parliament, who is much better at choosing policies than choosing men.

PROLOGUE

10 FEBRUARY 2021

The Scottish Chronicle Newspaper
Obituary

It is with deep sadness that the family of Dr Kenneth Manson, MBChB (Bachelor of Medicine, Bachelor of Surgery), FSSoS (Fellow of the Scottish Society of Surgeons), announces his sudden passing on the 5 February 2021.

Throughout his dedicated service and esteemed career as one of the country's most respected and eminent cardiac surgeons, Dr Manson was relentless in his pursuit of surgical excellence and exemplary patient care. He leaves behind a grieving family, and a wealth of friends, colleagues and former patients.

In a prescient foreshadow of his untimely death, Dr Manson was asked during a recent guest lecture at the University of Glasgow what he considered his eulogy should be. His reply was, 'Think of not just the life he lived, but the lives he saved.'

Dr Manson's funeral will take place on Sunday 21 February at 10 a.m., at Glasgow Cathedral, followed by a private gathering for invited guests at the St Kentigern Hotel.

In lieu of flowers, please consider a donation to the British Heart Foundation.

5 YEARS LATER

21 FEBRUARY

8 A.M.–10 A.M.

1

BERNADETTE O'BRIEN

As Bernadette gradually transitioned from a dream-filled sleep to the semi-awake awareness of a new chilly morning, her gaze didn't fall on the empty space beside her in bed. Or the light from the lamp post outside the window that was casting a beam through the still-dark morning. Nope. The first thing her eyes settled on was the pair of high-grade elastic, waist-to-knee, extra-firm control knickers that were draped over the chair in front of her dressing table. And her first thought was that the prospect of getting them on was almost as terrifying as the dream she'd just had.

Determined not to relive another moment of it, she picked up her mobile phone from the shabby chic, white wooden chest of drawers beside her cream padded headboard. Her daughter, Nina, would tease her that, like much of this house, the bedside chest was definitely shabby, but perhaps not so chic, but Bernadette didn't give a damn what anyone thought. This little two-bedroom cottage on the outskirts of Glasgow's West End was the first and only home she'd ever bought by herself and it was so much more than just bricks and questionable décor choices.

When she'd come over from her home city of Dublin as a newly qualified nurse, she'd shared a rented flat with friends, until she'd married Kenneth Manson and moved into his family home, only a couple of miles but a whole world away from where she lived now. This little slice of heaven had been her first purchase after she left Kenneth almost ten years ago, after thirty years of marriage. She'd furnished the whole place by herself, from thrift stores and second-hand furniture websites, and she adored every last nook, cranny and chalk-painted wonky table leg. It was all hers and, as far as she was concerned, it was perfect. More importantly, it was peaceful. And after a lifetime of marriage to Kenneth, that was worth more than all the swanky furniture in the world.

As she did every morning, she pushed herself up in bed and dialled Nina's number. 'Good morning, love. Well, how are you feeling? Excited about tomorrow?'

Nina spoke loudly to be heard over the familiar noise of merriment in the background. Bernadette's grandchildren, Casey and Milo, were twelve and ten, and their favourite games all involved a volume control turned to high. Bernadette didn't mind one bit and Nina was a master at tuning it out. 'Oh, Mum, I can't wait, honestly. Are you looking forward to it?'

Bernadette's answer was automatic. 'Of course. You know how much we love Gerry. And your marriage and those two gorgeous children are worth celebrating.'

Tomorrow, their whole family and friends were gathering for Nina and Gerry's vow renewal, on their fourteenth wedding anniversary. Bernadette had been surprised when her daughter had shared her plans – Nina wasn't usually one for big events or romantic displays of affection – but, well, this generation celebrated so much more than hers had. Baby showers. Gender reveals. Hen weeks abroad. Pregnancy announcement parties. Babymoons. Push presents. Nursery school graduations. And now, the first vow renewal in the family. Bernadette wasn't judging. Any excuse to get the people she loved together was fine by her. If there was a bonus, it might even wipe away some of her memories of Nina and Gerry's original wedding. Kenneth had been so suave and handsome as he'd walked his daughter down the aisle and at the reception afterwards, he'd been the perfect father of the bride: hospitable, charming, debonair and an all-round personification of success and achievement. At least, that's how it had seemed. But the truth? It was all a sham. Kenneth Manson was an eminent cardiac surgeon and George-Clooney-esque pillar of the community on the outside, but on the inside, he was a controlling, insidious, emotionally abusive, unfaithful man who had made Bernadette's life a misery. That day, he had constantly hissed criticism and abuse at Bernadette: her outfit wasn't up to his standards, she wasn't saying the right things, her make-up was running when she cried, she was embarrassing him... On and on until Bernadette was just counting the minutes until she could go home and quell the churning anxiety in her stomach. It had been that way for decades, and she'd tolerated it for reasons she chose not to relive now. Although, she still sometimes wondered if she would have left if she'd known that at that time, he was already having an affair with a woman in her twenties called Lila, who'd eventually showed up on their doorstep on the day Bernadette had finally walked away from the marriage a few years later.

Bernadette also found out later that much as Nina loved her father and was sheltered from the worst of his faults, she'd been made well aware that Kenneth didn't approve of her choice of husband. He'd foreseen a fellow doctor for his beloved girl. Perhaps a wealthy banker. Someone of note and influence. He definitely didn't count on a working-class electrician stealing her heart, but Nina had been proven right because, all these years later, they were still going strong. Nina was working full time again as a psychiatric nurse on a mental health ward at Glasgow Central, the same hospital where Bernadette had spent her whole career. And Gerry had left his job as a spark for a housing association, set up his own company and now had a thriving business that had afforded them a lovely home and a couple of holidays a year.

Bernadette knew that Kenneth's narcissistic resentment, jealousy and snobbery would have hated that. He'd also have been spitting that their son, Stuart, had forged a successful career as a criminal justice lawyer and was still settled and content with Connor, his partner of a decade now.

Kenneth had made Stuart miserable right into his early twenties, forcing him to live a secret life, too terrified of his father to admit that he was in a relationship his dad would disapprove of, while pursuing a career he didn't want, because Kenneth had insisted his son follow in his footsteps to become the next great Manson surgeon. Her son had found the courage to defy Kenneth on both counts. Eventually, Bernadette had taken her own path too.

Thinking back to that time in her life made Bernadette shudder. There was nothing about marriage to Kenneth Manson that she wanted to remember, so she was absolutely in favour of making as many wonderful new memories with her family as possible.

'And I've got my outfit all ready.' Bernadette's gaze went back to the knickers, but then veered to the hanger on the front of the wardrobe, where clear plastic covered a cream velvet shift dress adorned with tiny black crystals around the neckline. It was perhaps the most glamorous and expensive dress she had ever bought, but tomorrow's occasion would be worth it. Besides, Nina had persuaded her to splash out, and when they'd added the accessories and a floaty black velvet jacket, Bernadette had felt lovely in it. She was pretty comfortable in her body, well aware that there were more important things in life than a flat stomach or boobs that still pointed forwards, but if a pair of magic pants restored her arse to its natural position, and a lush jacket camouflaged the bingo wings, then she was all for it.

'Glad to hear it. You'll look gorgeous... Milo, darling, stop hitting your brother with that banana. What was I saying? Oh yes, you'll be gorgeous, Mum.'

'I can assure you, no one will be looking at me when you're there, my darling,' Bernadette laughed. 'I can't wait to see your dress. I still wish you'd let me come with you to pick it.'

Nina's breathing had got a little faster and Bernadette could picture her wrestling a banana from the little hands of her mischievous grandson.

'I know, but I want this time to be a surprise, even for you. I promise you'll love it. What time is Jack arriving?'

A sigh was out before Bernadette could stop it. Jack Donovan. Her boyfriend of several years, and yes, it still felt strange calling him that at their age. 'Manfriend' didn't sound right. 'Lover' made her toes curl. And 'partner' wasn't strictly accurate, given that they lived in different countries and didn't actually share anything other than deep love and great fun when they did manage to snatch time in the same place. Bernadette adored him.

They'd met after Bernadette had shared an eventful flight to St Lucia with Jack's sons on the way to a destination wedding. It was three years after her divorce and only a few months after the death of her awful ex-husband, and the scars of her marriage had left her with no intention of entering another relationship. She'd vowed to guard her freedom. To preserve her independence. But to her surprise, she'd clicked with Jack and since then, they'd been wholeheartedly committed to each other, but not how or where to live their lives. Jack was in Ireland. She was in Scotland. Neither was ready to move. And for now they both just accepted that if they were meant to be together, that was something they'd resolve in the future. Only, for Bernadette, that 'future' was getting closer every day.

'He had to work today. I did explain that he's supposed to be off on a Saturday, but he gave me the, "Haulage is a seven days a week business" argument, so I gave up. He's getting in on the 6 a.m. flight tomorrow morning, so he'll be in plenty of time for the ceremony. It's not ideal, but it was the best he could do.' Jack's haulage company was his life's work – the business that he'd set up as a young man and devoted his entire working life to growing. Neither of his sons were interested in taking over, so he'd been upfront that he'd work there "until the day I can no longer get out of bed and lace up my boots".

'I'm sure it'll be fine, Mum. Anyway, I'd better go...'

'Nina, are you sure there's nothing I can do to help today? I've got plans tonight...'

'Oh really? What's going on tonight then?' Bernadette could hear the teasing in her daughter's tone. 'Wild night out with the Aching Bones Club?'

'I'll tell my lovely pals you said that...' The Aching Bones Club was Nina's nickname for Bernadette's close circle of friends: Val, Sarah, Alice, and a few others, all menopause joint-ache survivors and usual companions for Friday and Saturday night visits to the cinema or one of her favourite little bistros when Jack wasn't here.

Nina groaned. 'Oh Jesus, don't – Val will be in here like a shot. I'll need to hire security.'

'You will indeed.' Bernadette artfully avoided the question about her plans for this evening. She wasn't going to spoil Nina's joy by bringing up the significance of today's date. And she definitely wasn't going to share how she marked this date every year. There were some things that her daughter just did not need to know. Instead, she focused back on her original offer. 'But I'm at a loose end today, so I could come watch the kids, give you time to get pampered, or—'

'Thanks, Mum, but I've already got everything covered with my pals. They're coming over later, and they've got a full itinerary arranged. It's going to be fabulous! I'll see you tomorrow. Love you.'

Bernadette didn't even get to reply before the call ended, leaving her staring at the phone. It wasn't in her nature to wallow, or feel sorry for herself. She was a 'glass half full' person all day long... but she couldn't help feeling a twinge of sadness that Nina had planned this whole day with her friends and Bernadette had no part to play in it. She'd offered several times to get involved, but Nina's answer was always the same. 'You have enough on your plate, Mum,' she'd insisted, and Bernadette's arguments had fallen on deaf ears.

The truth was, she didn't have enough on her plate at all. Yes, she had her job at the busy Emergency Department in Glasgow Central Hospital, and no she still didn't understand why they'd renamed it after a lifetime of being called A&E. She also had the support group she ran for women who were leaving or had already left abusive relationships. And she had friends that she loved dearly. But with Jack being across the sea, and this limbo stage they were in... lately, it just hadn't felt like enough.

And the Kenneth that occasionally visited in her dreams knew that. Last night he'd been taunting her, telling her that she'd never find love again. That Jack was lying to her. That she was being played for a fool. There was so much irony there. Those were his actions, not Jack's. And even now, five years after Kenneth Manson had passed suddenly from a heart attack, he could still make her wake up with a feeling of dread.

That's why tonight was important. It was a gathering. A source of moral support. An affirmation that she wasn't alone in the struggles she'd had with Kenneth. A collective of women who'd shared some her experiences with him.

Bernadette took a sip from her coffee and glanced out of the French doors to the garden. There was still a frost there, and it was to be freezing all day, so maybe not a morning for a walk. She'd kept the whole day free in case Nina needed her, and in the hope that Jack might get here early, but it was a no on both counts. So what to do? It was too late to call any of her lovely pals at such short notice. Yet, her restless soul couldn't bear the thought of sitting at home all day, thinking about Kenneth, thinking about the past, thinking about tonight.

She was glad of the distraction when the ring of her phone broke the silence.

'How's my very favourite ED nurse doing today? Does saying you're my favourite contravene some HR policy? Did I just end my career before I scratched the surface of my full potential?'

Bernadette's laugh was his answer. 'Only if I report you, but I can be bribed with wine and biscuits.'

Caleb Henry was one of her favourite nurses too. They'd become firm friends from the very day she'd moved back to the ED department after a two-year stint in the ICU, and she adored him. Barely out of his twenties, he had the kind of cool head in a crisis that was invaluable in their line of work, and in Caleb's case, that also came with compassion, expertise and a wicked sense of humour that made her howl.

'Deal. I'll tape a packet of Hobnobs to the front of your locker. Anyway...'

The last word was said with a sigh, some hesitation and then drawn out. Bernadette knew that could only mean one thing.

'The answer is no,' she blurted. 'Not even for you.'

'But you don't know what I'm asking.'

'Oh, but I do. The ward is short-staffed. I'm needed on my weekend off. They've asked you to call, because everyone knows I treasure your existence. And you're taking one for the team despite feeling awful about it because you know I have Nina's vow renewal tomorrow. Did I get any of that wrong?'

'You're mildly terrifying when you do that. Have you thought about a career as a psychic?'

Bernadette popped two slices of bread in the toaster and pushed down the lever. 'Nope, I'd hate to give up the long shifts, the inadequate pay and the ill-fitting uniforms of my nursing career.'

This time it was Caleb who laughed. 'I understand the appeal. Okay, I'll tell the boss I tried. If he asks, say I begged you. I want him to think I'm assertive. But you're quite right – I didn't want to call you but every time the new ward manager asks me to do something, my spine falls out. Much as I miss you, I was hoping you'd say no because you've got far better things to be doing today. You go and have an incredible day. You deserve it.'

'Thank you.' Bernadette knew she should leave it at that. Take the win. But decades as a nurse with a heartfelt devotion to her job, her patients and her colleagues got in the way. That, and the fact that she'd already ascertained that she was staring down the barrel of a boring day. Before she thought better of it, the words drifted out. 'Just how short-staffed are you?'

'Erm, admittedly, it's brutal. Three down this morning. Norovirus is taking us out like coconuts at a fair.'

Bernadette knew exactly what that meant. Frazzled staff. Long waits.

Furious patients. Concerned families. A whole lot of heartache. She sighed. Stuff it. At least if she went into work, she'd feel useful and needed. 'Okay, I'll be there as soon as I can.'

'Don't do it, Bernadette.' His voice was low and insistent now. 'Stick to 'no'. Enjoy your day. Go chill before Nina's big day tomorrow.'

'Nope, I'm not leaving you to deal with that when I'm perfectly able to come in and have no other plans. But I think you just cost yourself another packet of biscuits,' Bernadette chuckled, giving him no further opportunity to object. 'I'll see you soon.'

Her toast popped as she hung up, and she grabbed some butter and jam from the fridge, her status now flipped from 'aimless' to 'woman in a hurry'.

What did this say about her life, she wondered as she scraped the knife across the toast, that the only real option to pass the time today was to go into work. That was a claxon alarm signalling something she'd been contemplating more and more over the last few months – she needed something more in her daily existence. Needed to be fulfilled. Content. Busy. Challenged. Excited. And right now, FaceTimes with Jack just weren't enough to tick those boxes. She missed him and she wanted more.

How many times did she tell Nina and Stuart that if they weren't happy about something, they had to change it? Well, it was high time that she took her own advice, even if that meant getting over her understandable fears of commitment, of change, of relinquishing independence, of trusting her judgement. On the day she'd left Kenneth, she'd sworn to herself that she would never give up anything for a man again – not her independence, her financial autonomy, her freedom or even a permanent place in the other side of her bed.

But maybe it was time to admit that she'd had enough of living alone and snatching happiness where she could. She loved Jack. He loved her. She was sure she'd got it right this time. If that meant making changes to be with him, then maybe it was time to do something about it. He was only going to be here for one day on this trip, so she was going to have to make a decision and implement it. And no, there was nothing traditional about the little idea that had been tugging at her heart for the last few weeks, but perhaps that was a good thing. Wasn't it?

Tomorrow, after all the celebrations were done, she was seriously considering asking Jack Donovan to marry her. Maybe. Perhaps. Possibly.

But tonight, she had to lay Kenneth's ghost to rest once and for all.

2

MARGE DRUMMOND

'Here you go, Marge,' the nurse said, as she put down a plate of toast and a mug of tea on the table that stretched across her bed. 'Jeanie was about to bring it in, but I didn't want to involve her in our conspiracy.'

Marge Drummond managed a grateful smile that widened as Charge Nurse Yvie Danton glanced around her, as if checking for cameras, then pulled a mini jar of strawberry jam from the pocket of her scrubs trousers.

'And I managed to get this. Swiped it from my Carlo's restaurant when I stopped in for coffee this morning. If he finds out about this treacherous act of theft and cancels our wedding, you'll have it on your conscience.'

'It'll be worth it,' Marge croaked. Her voice hadn't returned to normal since her surgery and the complications afterwards that had forced the medical team to put her on a ventilator for three days. That had all happened a few weeks before, and it had been touch-and-go, but she'd made it. This time.

'How are you feeling today, Marge?' Yvie asked, after a quick glance at the clipboard at the end of her bed. 'Did you sleep?'

Marge managed a hoarse whisper. 'I feel like all I do is sleep.'

'Well, maybe we can get you into the chair and take you for a grand sightseeing tour of the corridors on this floor of Glasgow Central Hospital today. I'm on with Jeanie today and then Keli is coming in on the late shift, so if one of us manages to get a break we'll come sneak you out.'

Marge had already learned that Yvie and Keli were best friends both in and out of work, and that they both adored Jeanie, the assistant on the ward.

'Did I hear my name getting mentioned there? You'd better be saying I'm the engine that keeps this place going or I'll be contacting my union.' Right on cue, Jeanie, the nursing assistant, chief caterer, master gossiper and oracle of all knowledge and scandal within the walls of Glasgow Central Hospital, popped her head in the door.

Marge used all her lung power to get out a breathy, 'Morning, Jeanie. That's exactly what we were saying.'

'Aye, just as well or I'd be grassing her in about the extra jam she sneaks you every morning. Don't think I don't know everything that goes on in here.'

'I've no idea how she knows that,' Yvie said, deadpan. 'I think she's got this whole place bugged.'

Marge felt her cheek muscles muster up her best attempt at a grin, but even the short conversation had left her exhausted. The banter, the sarcasm, the humour and the kindness of these women had kept her going every day of the last four weeks that she'd been in here and she was beyond grateful for it. The NHS had its very own mountain of problems, but the staff on this ward showed her every day why the people in the health service were the very best of it.

But even with the company of these gems, early morning was her least favourite time of the day, because that's when she woke up and saw yet again that this was her reality now. It wasn't all just a bad dream. Or a dreaded premonition of hard times to come. The worst times were already here.

As someone who had never smoked a day in her life, she still raged at the unfairness of her diagnosis. Lung cancer. A rare kind. The surgery had been the third operation to remove a section of her lung and more lymph nodes, but when they'd opened her up, they'd seen that the cancer in her lung was far more advanced than they'd realised. Worse, tests had shown that it had spread to her bones, to her brain, to every bloody place. So that was it. They'd thrown everything at it, but despite the surgeries, chemo, radiotherapy, the bastard disease wasn't giving up its grip. The next move wouldn't take her back to her much-loved home in the west end of the city that she'd lived in since her twenties. It had been a little cottage flat back then, but after she'd married Ian they'd bought the property upstairs and converted it into a lovely semi-detached home in a building that had been built back in the days before this hospital even existed. No. She wasn't going back there. They'd be moving her soon, but it would be down to the palliative care ward, just as soon as they had a free bed. This was end days. But even though the hours of nothingness stretched in front of her, she was still grateful for every moment, every conversation, every laugh these women gave her.

Jeanie was inside the room now, wiping down the bedside table, plumping Marge's pillows, straightening her sheets, working around Yvie, who was going through the well-practised routine of taking Marge's statistics and marking them on the chart. The pride they took in their work was in every action they carried out while Jeanie chatted. 'I bet this isn't quite the same as the swanky place that you worked in, Marge, was it?'

The corners of Marge's mouth turned up as she shook her head. No. This was nothing like the Royal Scottish Private Hospital, the institute on the other side of the city where she'd worked for the best part of thirty years as secretary to Kenneth Manson, one of the best surgeons of their generation. She'd actually known Kenneth for even longer than that, as they'd run in the same circles before he'd poached her from her role of secretary to Sir Lester Kelaney, President of the Scottish Society of Surgeons, to work for him instead.

She'd been in awe of Kenneth Manson back then, well aware of his genius and his charisma and immune to his legendary arrogance, so when he'd finally attained his own private practice at the Royal Scottish Private Hospital, she hadn't hesitated to take up his offer of a position at the desk outside his office. From there, she'd managed every aspect of his work life, ignored the foibles of his personal life, appreciated his surgical excellence, and admired his rise through the hierarchy of Scottish medicine, right up until the day, five years ago, when he hadn't shown up for his 7 a.m. surgery. Marge had known immediately that something was wrong. Kenneth Manson, she'd learned over the years, had many, many flaws – but he never missed a surgery.

Kenneth's death, just a few years after his divorce from the wonderful Bernadette, a woman he didn't deserve, was both tragically sudden and a great loss to the medical community. It had also given her the impetus to retire, something he wouldn't even hear of while he was alive. 'I couldn't do it without you, Marge. Don't make me start again with someone new. No one else would put up with me,' he'd say, with all the suave, self-deprecating charm that made him one of the most well-respected men in the city. And probably one of the most manipulative too – but weren't most successful men like that? Of course, she'd given in to him and stayed at her desk.

Neither of them would ever have predicted that he'd give up on life first. The irony of the cardiac surgeon who didn't see his own heart attack coming. They did say that doctors made the worst patients and in Marge's experience that was true.

She drifted back to Jeanie's question. 'No, it's a bit different,' she told her honestly.

Another irony. If her illness had been diagnosed while she still worked with Kenneth at the private hospital, the terms of her contract included health insurance that would have allowed her to have been cared for there for free. Instead, her symptoms had developed just a couple of months after she'd handed in her notice, on the day after Kenneth's funeral. Just another twisted stitch in the tapestry of her life.

The door to her room opened again, and her daughter, Estelle, came in. Her gorgeous Estelle. Her quietly artistic only child had grown up to be creative, confident, athletic and so different from the woman Marge had been at thirty-five. Back then, Marge had been modest in her fashion. Pristinely dressed and well-groomed at all times. Never left the house without her hair done, her lipstick on and shoes that matched her handbag.

But Estelle? In she came, her light brown, highlighted hair pulled back in a high ponytail, face free of make-up and dressed in... what did she call it? *Athleisure* wear. Stretchy flared trousers – apparently 'yoga pants' was the official title – and trainers, with a sweatshirt that fell off one shoulder and had holes in the cuffs for her thumbs to stick out. The reasons for that were beyond Marge, but she didn't ask, just happy to have her daughter here, whether she was wearing office attire, athleisure garb or a pink polka dot bikini. Although, the latter would risk her being ejected from the building. As always, Estelle had a sketch pad under her arm, a permanent presence since she was a teenager with an obsession for sketching beautiful gowns. That passion had seen her through a fashion design degree at the Glasgow School of Art, where her talent had been honed and elevated. An internship had led to a ten-year stint as a designer at a bridal fashion house, until she'd taken the step of setting up her own company, specialising in the kind of stunning bespoke gowns that fairy tales were made of. Marge couldn't be more proud, and she chose to believe that her late husband had been by Estelle's side for every step she'd taken since he passed.

Estelle's smile was infectious. 'Good morning, ladies. Lovely to see you this morning.'

Both Yvie and Jeanie returned the greeting, while Estelle went round to the opposite side of the bed from where Yvie was standing and leaned in to give Marge a kiss.

'Good morning, Mum. Did you sleep well?'

Even if there had been a rock band playing outside her door, three fire alarms and a SWAT team raid during the night, Marge would have given the same answer. She could already see the deep lines of stress around her daughter's eyes, and the concern that no amount of faux cheeriness could mask. If Estelle could fake this, could pretend to be cheery, then the least Marge could do was match that sentiment and be relentlessly positive as she forced out her words.

'I did, darling.' She didn't. 'And I feel properly rested...' She didn't. 'And all the better for seeing you.' That last one was true. 'No Craig, today?'

Estelle's boyfriend often popped in if he was dropping Estelle off, and sometimes stayed a while, depending on his work schedule.

'Not today, Mum. He's gone off to do some work at his brother's house in Edinburgh for a couple of days – they're fitting a new kitchen.' Craig had a joinery business and was always helping out family and friends too. He'd even installed a whole new set of beautiful bookcases in Marge's lounge a few years ago. Definitely a keeper.

Estelle sat down on the blue armchair with the washable surface on her side of Marge's bed. She'd spent countless hours there in the last month, sometimes working on her laptop or on her sketch pad during the day, other times curled up under a blanket in the evenings. Marge would often insist that she go home, but Estelle would always say, 'A little while longer, Mum.' Then Marge would fall asleep and it would be morning again.

This might not be a swanky private hospital, but she was grateful for the private room because it came with open visiting hours, allowing Estelle to come whenever and as often as she wanted. Of course, Marge knew why she'd been moved out of the four-bed ward next door. Over the years, she'd seen many patients and their families being given their privacy and dignity when it became clear that time was running out. On the day they'd moved her into this room, she'd been both relieved and devastated. But she wasn't going to give in to that despair when Estelle was here.

'Here you go, Mum, I brought you a ginger slice. Your favourite. Got one for me too and I plan to hoover it up like a Dyson.'

Jeanie was clearly jealous of Estelle's breakfast choices. 'Och, these young ones can eat anything and not put on a pound, eh Marge? What I'd give to have a metabolism like that again. I've gained half a stone just being in the same room as that cake.'

Estelle laughed, as she pulled her legs up under her on the chair.

Her daughter ran every day and did Pilates or yoga five times a week – three things that Marge had never taken to, despite Estelle dragging her along many times. She much preferred a bit of Zumba or salsa. Of course, that was before her lungs grew TBD. The Bastard Disease.

'Ah, but I only eat like this on a Saturday, Jeanie. It's my one cheat day.'

'Cheat day? I like the sound of that. But only if it involves me and Brad Pitt. My Arthur would never need to know.'

And with that, and a cackle, she went off to cheer up the patient in the room next door.

Marge's mind latched on to what Estelle had just said. 'But your cheat day is normally a Saturday, darling. Did you change it this week?'

Estelle put her hand over hers. 'It is Saturday, Mum.'

'It is? I get so mixed up with the days in here. It's so easy to lose track.' She didn't add that the reason for that was because every day was the same.

Something else was causing another tug of confusion in her brain as she tried to work it back. Once upon a time, she'd been the most organised person on earth, storing calendars, itineraries and schedules in her acutely methodical mind. Now time just seemed to slip past.

So today was Saturday. It was February. A memory. On the first day of the year, when she opened her new calendar. Circling a date in red. Just as she'd done every year for the last four years. Could that be...

'Darling, what date is it?'

Estelle paused to think about it, before answering. 'It's the twenty-first of February.'

The panic set in before Marge even spoke.

The twenty-first of February. Tonight, Marge had somewhere she should be. Somewhere she went on today's date every year. It was the anniversary of a gathering that had changed her life, one that protected secrets she should have told Estelle about many years ago, but Marge had been too cowardly, too scared to reveal the truth to the one person in the world that she loved more than life itself. This was her last chance to let Estelle meet the family who would look out for her after Marge was gone – people Estelle didn't even know existed.

Today was the day that all her truths had to come out.

And Marge just hoped that her daughter would forgive her.

3

AMBER COLLINS

Amber yawned as she stretched one arm out from under the Spiderman duvet and sent up a silent prayer of hope to the gods of sleep deprivation. Just five more minutes. That's all. Now that the boys were four and five, they were so much better at sleeping through the night, but last night had been an exception. Alfie had woken up twice for absolutely no reason other than he wanted to check his dinosaurs were still where he'd left them and Sid had come into her room at 5 a.m. to ask if it was time to get up. She'd assured him that it wasn't and ushered him back to bed, but he'd insisted she stay with him until he fell asleep. No doubt the correct parenting strategy in a choice between saying no or giving in to his demand would have been to calmly and gently extricate herself so that his early-morning rises didn't become a habit. But hey... spending the rest of the night in a single bed with Sid and Spiderman, then waking with a dead arm because a child's head had been pressed into her elbow for the last two hours, was a small price to pay to avoid 5 a.m. tears and conflict. Besides, she could stare at that little face beside her, with the long dark eyelashes and his dad's dimple on his chin, all day. She could just use her good arm for all required tasks this morning until the feeling in the dead one came back.

After a few moments of peaceful bliss, the pull of a cup of coffee overruled her futile wish for more sleep, and, using ninja-like skills of balance and the gravity-defying bendiness of a limbo dancer, she managed to extricate herself from under Sid's head without waking him, then make it to a standing position before tiptoeing out of the room.

First stop was back into her own bedroom, planning a shower that was long enough to shave her legs before the boys woke up. As her head cleared, she reminded herself that it was Saturday. And not just any Saturday. Ewan, the boys' dad, was collecting them this morning for a sleepover and then she would... 'Bzzzzzzzz.'

She was just walking past her bedside table when the phone on top of it buzzed, cutting off her train of thought.

Second choice of the day. Ignore it or pick it up.

It wasn't really a choice. She'd left her second in command, Millie, in charge of her shop, Amber Bouquets, today and much as she was the most calm, organised and creative florist that Amber had ever worked with, something out of her control might have happened. There could have been a leak. A burst pipe. A national overnight flower shortage. A car could have ramraided their shop window and destroyed their entire stock of hydrangeas. She really needed to stop watching true crime shows on Netflix because her imagination lived permanently on the dark side these days.

The iPhone buzzed again as she disconnected it from the charger and lifted it up with her good arm to see... Oh, no. Bugger. Damn. Crap. This was worse than a crime against hydrangeas. There were a dozen messages. At least five missed calls. And now, two things were happening at once. Her doorbell downstairs was ringing and her befuddled brain was taking in the time at the top of the screen – 9.15 a.m. Nooooooooo! She hadn't slept past 7 a.m. since 2019! And why today of all blooming days?

Her groan was just another thing to add to the myriad of noises that were suddenly emanating from all over the house, roused by the doorbell. Sid was shouting, 'Muuuuuuuum.' Alfie had apparently woken up and rejoined his dinosaurs, because there were Jurassic Park-esque sounds coming from his room. And the bloody phone was ringing again with a name flashing on the screen. Ewan. Her husband. Ex-husband. Crap.

'Downstairs for breakfast, boys!' she hollered, as she began galloping downstairs in stunt woman fashion, taking them two at a time. Each thud accompanied with a wail of 'Bugger.' 'Bugger.' Bugger.' 'I'm coming!'

She finally reached the bottom, snatched open the door, very aware that last night's make-up was still on her face, her hair resembled a leylandii, she was wearing pyjamas and... her one good arm crept across her chest as she realised that she was swinging low because she hadn't got to the 'putting on a bra' part of the day yet.

'You didn't need to dress up for me,' were the first words out of Ewan's mouth, which might have been mildly amusing if he wasn't leaning against the door frame, phone to his ear, sporting a grin that bordered on mocking.

'Is there a moratorium on being irritated by everything your ex-husband says and does?' she fired back, but her heart wasn't in it. Besides, she'd always had a soft spot for him in a beanie and a puffa jacket. It reminded her of all the ski trips they took when they were young, madly in love, before children and prior to him deciding to break every last shred of trust between them.

'No, I believe you can carry that on until the end of time,' he answered, wiping his boots on the mat.

Amber suddenly felt the effects of the cold draught from the door on her braless boobs. Dammit. They could now double as somewhere to hang his puffa jacket. She folded her arms and hoped he hadn't noticed. 'Excellent, that's what I thought. But I'll lay off the barbs this morning if you overlook the fact that I've slept in and the boys aren't ready. Sorry. They kept me up half the night. I'll also give you extra points if you help me get them dressed and stop Alfie from feeding his breakfast to a Tyrannosaurus Rex.'

Ewan's chin dimple stretched as he grinned. 'If I'd known that was all it took to make you hate me less, I'd have bribed the boys to make you sleep in before now.'

He came in, hung his Carhartt jacket on the rack at the door, kicked his boots off and removed his beanie as he walked towards the kitchen, pausing to collect Sid, who was halfway down the stairs, in his SpongeBob pyjamas, hair going in seventeen directions.

'Good morning, buddy,' he said, kissing his son's head as he scooped him up.

Sid rubbed his eyes, probably unsure if he was still dreaming. 'Daddy!'

That set off a stampede as Alfie heard the greeting and tore down the stairs, climbing right on board his brother's excitement bus.

Amber felt a pang of something in her chest, but she didn't have the energy to try to name it.

When they'd first split up, all she'd felt was anger. Fury. Betrayal. Disgust.

But somewhere in the two years since then, she'd come to accept that she couldn't live that way forever, not when they had so many years of history and two boys to parent for the rest of their lives. And not when he was the only family she had in the city, so her entire support system was now striding towards her kitchen. She'd thought about moving back to her native Inverness to be nearer her parents, but that was a whole other gift wrapped box of disfunction that she didn't want to open. Her mother was on her third marriage. Her dad on his fourth. Her entire childhood had been spent shuttling around from place to place, never quite knowing who the step-parent of the month was going to be, or how they would treat her, or how long they would last. Much as she loved them, the truth was that the only reliable thing about either of her parents was their relentless self-absorption, so not exactly the type of folks who would swoop in and be stable, consistent, involved grandparents to Sid and Alfie. And other than step-siblings that came and went with her parents' divorces, she'd grown up as an only child, so there was no-one else to depend on. That's why, despite going through relentless stages of rage, resentment, disappointment, grief, and devastation when their marriage broke down, she couldn't bring herself to take the boys away from Ewan. Because much as he'd broken her trust, he adored their boys and he was a great dad to them. It hadn't been easy, but eventually she'd let go of the hurt and the fury and somehow, they'd found their way back to friendship. Although, it came with a fairly healthy amount of sarcasm and a determined effort to ignore the fact that seeing him here with the boys, back in the kitchen that he'd built from scratch, standing on the floor he'd spent a whole weekend laying so that he could surprise her when she got back from her hen trip, caused a tightness in her throat that was hard to ignore. That was who he was then. It wasn't who he became after eight years of marriage and two children. No. That guy was the one who could take her heart and crush it. Friendship was all that he deserved now. But that didn't mean she couldn't enjoy this moment and be grateful for the extra pair of hands to help with the morning chaos.

In ten minutes, Ewan had whipped up scrambled eggs, while she'd nipped back upstairs to remedy the braless situation, then returned to make toast and chop the boys' fruit, before serving it up to them, as they sat happily at the breakfast bar – Alfie chatting to two of his prehistoric creatures, while Sid drew a picture of an unidentifiable object. No doubt he'd announce what it was at some point, and they could nod knowingly.

Nutrition delivered, Amber rustled up a couple of coffees on the Tassimo machine Ewan had bought her on their last anniversary before they split up. *No*, not split up. That was two simplistic. Too sanitised. *Before he broke them*. Yep, that was closer to the truth.

Amber handed his mug of milky cappuccino over and they both leaned against the kitchen counter, within reaching distance of the breakfast bar in case of spillages or disasters.

Ewan nodded appreciatively. 'So, any plans for today then? God, when did I start sounding like your hairdresser making small talk?'

Amber felt herself flush. There was no way she was sharing her itinerary for the day with him. Conversations about romantic entanglements on either side were strictly off limits. She didn't want to know what he did in his spare time. And she had no intention of sharing what she'd be doing today either.

'My hairdresser never makes small talk. I tell her so much about my life, she knows when I'm due a smear test. Oh, and she's not your biggest fan.'

That made him laugh. 'I could have guessed that. If you can give me her name, I'll make sure she never has scissors anywhere near my hair.'

'Probably a wise move,' Amber concurred, but she couldn't help but be amused.

He let out a sigh. 'You know...'

'Oh, no. I recognise that tone. Serious. Whatever it is, I don't want to know.'

'I saw Estelle last week.'

Amber could almost hear the steel doors of her mind slamming shut.

'Like I said, I don't want to know.'

Estelle. Her best friend since they'd met in their first year at art school. The sister she'd chosen for herself, a bond that filled the hole created by her turbulent family background.

'Amber, you need to forgive her.'

He wasn't giving up. Bollocks. Every time she let him in even a little, he somehow managed to take a chisel to another piece of her heart.

She picked up a cloth and began washing down the breakfast bar as a distraction. 'I really don't.'

'Amber, you know it was all on me. She's not responsible for what happened. She thought she was doing the right thing.'

'The right thing?' She turned to face him and lowered her voice so that the boys wouldn't pick up on her words. Not that they'd understand what they meant, but they were about to be said in the same tone she used when they'd drawn on the walls with felt pens last week, so they'd get an inkling that she was peeved. 'The right thing would have been to tell me. It would have been to stop covering for you...'

'She didn't...'

'Oh? So my best friend *didn't* find out that my husband was having an affair and decide to keep that to herself?'

'It wasn't like that...'

'It was exactly like that!'

Final straw. Camel's back broken. Amber inhaled. Exhaled. Glad the boys were distracted with a tussle over a triceratops.

'I'm not going to argue with you, Ewan. Conversation done. Thanks for helping with breakfast.' She turned back to the boys, smiley face and sing-song voice reinstated. 'Right, my handsome ones, let's go get ready to go to Daddy's house for the weekend. First one to brush their teeth gets the biggest hug ever.' They were still at the age where that was a prize to fight for, so the two of them took off, with Amber tearing behind them. Teeth were brushed, hugs were given – she called it a draw so they both won the prize – and they were back downstairs ten minutes later with their overnight bags in their little hands. They had their own rooms at Ewan's townhouse, just ten minutes away, with clothes and toys there, but they still insisted on taking their favourite teddies and books back and forwards with them.

At the door, Ewan helped get them into their little parkas, boots, hats and gloves, before pulling all his outwear back on and then kissing her on the cheek. 'Sorry. I didn't mean to piss you off.'

'Daddy!' Alfie exclaimed. 'That's the F word!'

'No darling, that's the P word,' Amber tried to explain.

Alfie shook his head wearily. 'Ah, p... uck.'

Ewan immediately put his hands up in a protest of amused innocence. 'Wasn't me.'

Amber struggled to keep a straight face. 'Wasn't me either. The teenagers next door forget their audience sometimes. Anyway...' She leant down and squeezed them both. 'I'll see you tomorrow night and I love you both more than elephants love buns. Be good for Daddy.'

'We will.' With two slobbery kisses, they were gone, leaving behind a knot in her chest that came every time she had to say goodbye to them.

She gave herself a moment, leaning against the inside of the door, processing the transition between 'mum' and 'single woman' in record time because... She checked the clock on the wall and uttered the correct F word under her breath. She was late.

Taking the stairs two at a time again, she galloped upwards, then flew into her bedroom. Robe. Shower. No time to wash hair. Or shave legs. Underarms only. Another F word. Quick dry. Deodorant. Ouch. Body cream slathered on. Damn, it was on the carpet. Rub with foot. No time to paint toenails. Slap on foundation. Bit of mascara. Ouch again. Can only see out of one eye now. Turn head upside down and blast hair with hairdryer. Scrunch in some product to make it look less like the after effects of an electrocution. Lip gloss. Remove hair that was now stuck to lip gloss. Quick perfume spray. Ouch again. Both eyes now injured. Pull on bra and cream knitted lounge set that an Instagram influencer persuaded her to buy. Manage to open one eye to see if she looked like said influencer. Nope. Damn. More like a throwback from a granny's knitting pattern book. Too late to change. Doorbell ringing. Fly downstairs. Checks reflection in mirror. Too late to change anything. Deep breath. Shoulders down. Act laissez-faire and casual. Open the door for the second time this morning, looking a little more polished than she had last time.

'Hey, gorgeous.' The man she'd been seeing for the last two months greeted her, before he stepped forward, put his lips on hers and kissed her breath away.

The last two years had been the toughest of her life. She'd lost her marriage. She'd lost her best friend. She'd lost the future that she'd thought she would have with her beautiful family, the one where she grew old with Ewan and Sunday lunches were a family affair with their sons and grandchildren. Today she was just going to forget about the past. Forget about regrets. Forget about her heartache. Let go of all the things that has wrecked her faith in love.

Today, she was going to give this new relationship a chance and see where it took them.

4

FIVE YEARS AGO…

Bernadette – Sunday 21 February 2021

Bernadette checked her reflection in the mirror on her bedroom wall and sighed. She hated to wear black. She always felt that her skin was too pale for it, and the auburn red hair that had been on half the kids in her family when she was growing up in Ireland was too stark a contrast against the gloom of her ebony skirt and jacket.

Not to mention that she would rather be anywhere else in the world, and be doing anything else in the world, than going to her ex-husband, Kenneth Manson's funeral.

Last night, sitting around the old oak table in Bernadette's kitchen, Nina had been in pieces as she'd put the final touches to the eulogy she was giving this morning. Their daughter was the only one from the family who was willing to do it. Bernadette felt it wasn't her place, now that their divorce was behind them. And as for Stuart…

He had held his coffee mug in both hands, as if the heat of it was a comfort, as he'd said, 'Mum, I have nothing good to say. He never accepted anything about me. Not my relationships, my sexuality, my career choices… He was a bully and a cheat who was as vicious to you as he was to me, so why would I stand up there and say what a great guy he was?'

Bernadette admired his honesty, but felt the familiar tug of guilt that she'd allowed her ex-husband to make her son feel that way. She would always regret not leaving Kenneth sooner. Why had it taken thirty years? Her only defence was that she'd thought she was doing the right thing, because Kenneth had made it clear that if she left him, he'd fight her for custody, and he'd told her repeatedly that he was such an upstanding pillar of the community, he'd win. She just hadn't been sure enough, or perhaps brave enough, to take the risk. So, instead, she'd stayed and tried to give Nina and Stuart the best childhood they could possibly have. Now that they were adults, the verdict on her decision was split. For Nina, it had been the right thing to do, but not for Stuart.

It would have been easy for Nina to be upset with her brother's harsh words, but she understood. She'd been the apple of her father's eye, the one who looked like him, enjoyed his company, only ever got the best of him, but who'd also spent her whole life defending Stuart against Kenneth, being the buffer between them. Bernadette had long accepted that Nina's love for her father was complicated – Nina saw all the negatives that Stuart experienced, yet for her it was balanced to a degree by the goodness she saw in in her dad and the love he'd bestowed on his favourite child. It was understandable.

That's why writing the eulogy had been so painful for her daughter and Bernadette had done her best to support her and be positive about the words Nina would say. There would be two other speakers – Murray Atkins and Sir Lester Kelaney. The former was one of Kenneth's oldest friends, a fellow cardiac surgeon, based in Edinburgh, who'd graduated just a year or two after Kenneth, and like her former husband, had risen to become highly respected in their field. Bernadette didn't know him well, but on the couple of occasions she'd met him, she'd felt that Murray and Kenneth had a strange relationship – brothers in arms, but ruthlessly competitive at the same time. She suspected it was difficult to have two narcissistic Messiah complexes in the same room.

Sir Lester Kelaney, on the other hand, was a more subdued, much revered gentleman, and an old mentor to Kenneth. As top dog at one of the Scottish medical community's governing bodies, Bernadette had met him many times at posh functions and events over the years. Like Nina, Sir Lester had always chosen to focus on Kenneth's good qualities: his charm, his fierce intelligence and his surgical brilliance. Kenneth's skills in the departments of schmoozing the right people were always in full swing when Sir Lester was in the room.

But they wouldn't be today. Was it wrong that Bernadette felt there was some sort of justice in that?

Bernadette had long let go of her hatred of the narcissistic sociopath that she'd married, but that didn't mean she'd forgotten a single moment of the life they'd lived, the world that was made of eggshells she'd had to walk on. The one where she'd had to make excuses for his rudeness and his disdain for anyone he thought beneath him – which was every other person he ever met.

The world in which she woke up every morning and never knew if she was going to get the charming husband at the breakfast table or the one who would fly into a rage because his fork wasn't in the correct place.

Who would tell her how she revolted him yet refuse to let her go.

Who told her she was insane when she accused him of having the affairs he'd entertained all through their marriage.

Who said she was weak when it took more strength than he would ever have to stay with him.

Now, this morning, was her one last obligation to Kenneth. One final day of pretending that he was a better man than he'd ever been. She'd spent a lifetime doing that, for the sake of Nina and Stuart, so she could manage a few more hours.

Her black patent clutch purse was on the cream boucle armchair in the corner of the room, so she picked it up before pausing at the door, and taking a breath. This was the last moment she'd be alone today. She could already hear voices from the kitchen. Nina. Gerry. Stuart. Connor.

Gerry and Connor must have arrived in the last few minutes, but Nina and Stuart had both stayed here last night – Nina in her spare room and Stuart on the sofa bed in the living room. It was the first time in over a decade that they'd all slept under the same roof, and Bernadette had been thankful for it. Even now, and despite the circumstances, having both of them close to her made her feel peaceful – something she'd craved throughout her marriage. Peace.

The first time she'd truly experienced that feeling was on the day she'd left Kenneth. She closed her eyes as snapshots of that day flitted through her mind.

It was just the two of them. He'd come down to breakfast and was soon in a rage at some perceived slight. Bernadette had blocked it out, but as far as she could remember, it was something to do with his breakfast not being how he wanted it. Or maybe it was because her phone rang and broke his rule about no phones at mealtimes. In all honesty, it could have been about a hundred different things, but it followed the same pattern: he flew into a fury, thumped the table, unleashed a diatribe of scorn in her direction and she held her breath until he finally walked out of the door, off to be a superhero and save lives.

Bernadette had already planned out the day. She'd been carefully packing the things that meant most to her, happy to leave most of her belongings behind. All she'd wanted were photos, her late mother's jewellery, some clothes and anything else that had sentimental value.

Kenneth had been barely out of the street when her friend, Sarah, had pulled up as planned, and they'd begun loading the car, Bernadette's hands shaking with every black bag they threw in the back.

When they were done, they'd gone to Nina's house, so that Bernadette could break the news to her in person. There had been tears, but there had also been understanding and support, and for that, Bernadette would always be grateful.

When she'd told Stuart later that day, he'd reacted with relief and encouragement, both of which had helped to quieten the panic that was rising over how Kenneth would react.

Afterwards, he'd gone through all the stages of narcissistic loss. The fury. The disbelief. The belittling. The scorn. Then came the flip, as he switched tack and began doing everything he could to win her back. All his pleading and declarations of love and regret might have brought some kind of satisfaction if Bernadette hadn't known him too well. If there was one thing Kenneth couldn't bear, it was to lose – and Bernadette was a very real, very public loss. His ego couldn't stand it. He didn't want her back because he truly loved her – he wanted her back so he would win, and Bernadette didn't take the bait. Not for a single second had she considered it because her freedom had been the biggest gift she'd ever given herself and she would never surrender that to a man again. Not ever. She couldn't even imagine meeting anyone again, but if she did, it would be for friendship. Fun. Her independence had been hard a fought battle, and she couldn't imagine a world in which she'd ever give that up again.

As for Kenneth, was it her rejection that ate him up inside? Was that anger and internal rage the thing that had killed him at not even sixty years old? He was super fit – cycled to work every day, worked out in the gym five times a week, ate a clean, balanced diet with no cheat days – at least not of the nutritional kind.

The other kind? Well, that was a different story.

Another flashback to their last day together. She'd gone back to the house later that night to collect more things and he'd come in and found her there. Nina and Stuart were with her, and for once, Kenneth had delivered a tirade of abuse in front of them. Head held high, Bernadette had walked down the hallway and opened the door to leave, when she saw that her path was blocked by a stunning young blonde woman. Bernadette was trying to remember who spoke first, when Nina's voice snapped her back to the present.

'Mum, are you ready? The car will be here soon.'

'I'm just coming, love.'

She checked her watch. Just after 9 a.m. The funeral car was due to arrive in fifteen minutes to take Nina and Gerry, Stuart and Connor, and Bernadette to Glasgow Cathedral for the service. Bernadette had resisted the idea, saying that as the ex-wife, it didn't feel right to be in the chief mourners' car, and several of her friends, Sarah, Alice, Val, had offered to take her, but Nina had insisted. 'Mum, we're all there is. This is it. We have no other family, so who would have an opinion on it?'

She'd still swithered, until Stuart had interjected. 'Mum, I don't want to have to look for you in the crowd. Tomorrow will be hard enough, so I want to know you're beside me.'

So here they were. Final chapter.

Another deep breath as she summoned every ounce of the strength she was going to need to get through today. This wasn't for her. It damn well definitely wasn't for Kenneth. It was for Nina and Stuart. And that would always be enough for her to pull her shoulders back, grit her teeth and be the support that they needed. Enough for her to rise above the knowing looks and stares of pity that would undoubtedly come from the attendees who knew of Kenneth's many infidelities. Enough to reject her friends' offers to come and support her. She didn't need anyone because she was strong enough to do this on her own. And knowing that confidence would infuriate the man who'd spent a lifetime telling her she was weak, made her pull her shoulders back just a little bit more.

Downstairs, she went into the kitchen, and saw that Nina and Stuart were already at the table, the same one she'd sat around with them last night. It felt odd. Incongruous. Since she'd left Kenneth and moved in here, this kitchen had been her place of sanctuary, of freedom, of safety and of so much joy. Her pals were regular visitors and this table had held countless mugs of tea and more than a few buckets of wine too. It had been the centre point for giggles and gossip and so much love from the women in her life. Hopefully this would be the last day that it saw tears too.

The lovely Connor put four mugs in the dishwasher, just as Nina's husband, Gerry, came in from the hall. 'That's the car here. Time to go.' Bernadette watched as he reached his hand out to Nina, holding her steady as she got up from the table, her face a mask of grief and sorrow. It didn't matter a jot to Bernadette that he wasn't the high-flying academic that Kenneth had envisaged for his daughter. Gerry was the kind of man her daughter deserved: kind, steadfast, loving – and Bernadette was grateful for him. Maybe Kenneth's malevolent influence had taught their offspring what to avoid in a partner, because Connor was a gem of a human being too, someone who loved her son the way he deserved and who'd become a frequent visitor and a much-loved member of the family. Bernadette reached out and squeezed his hand, conveying a million thanks for being there for them all.

Bernadette hugged Nina before she and Gerry headed out of the kitchen, towards the front door. Connor was behind them, giving her a couple of seconds with her son. He was twenty-six years old and so stoic, so smart, yet all she wanted to do was to hold him close. She settled for another hug and a couple of words of encouragement.

'We'll be fine, darling. We've got this,' she whispered, and he nodded, with a sad smile of thanks.

'I know, Mum. I just want it to be over.'

'Me too, son.'

He reached out his hand and she took it, realising that he was the one comforting her now.

As she locked the front door behind them and climbed into the long black car, Bernadette wondered if Kenneth was looking down on them now. On the wife he'd been so relentlessly cruel to. On the son he'd demeaned and diminished. On the daughter whose marriage he'd disapproved of. And she could almost hear him raging at the prospect of having absolutely no control over anything they did after today.

One last day. That was all he was getting. And the most important thing was that he couldn't cause her, or anyone else, another stab of pain.

As she stepped out of the door of her home, she had no idea that she was about to find out that she was wrong.

10 A.M.–NOON

5

BERNADETTE

Bernadette was rushing out of the door and had got as far as her front path when a little white Jeep came roaring up the driveway towards her, making the pebble stones fly in every direction as it braked to a halt.

A helmet of blonde hair emerged from the driver's door, followed by a white furry jacket, with arms that threw themselves around Bernadette. Val Murray, one of her closest friends and an absolute diamond of a human being, was never shy about making an entrance.

'Hello, ma darlin'. Glad I caught you. Are you off out? Don't tell me if you're going off on a three-day shagathon with that handsome big man of yours – it'll only make me jealous. Have I ever mentioned that he reminds me of Liam Neeson?'

Bernadette couldn't help but chuckle. 'Only a hundred times or so.'

'Ah right. Repeating myself is allowed at my age. It comes with saying whatever I damn well please and leaving the house with my slippers on.'

Bernadette glanced downwards just to check and was relieved to see a screaming pink pair of moonboots. Val's usual slipper choice of white furry mules were no match for this weather.

'Anyway, no shagathon, I'm afraid. Can't afford the chiropractor I'd need afterwards. And Jack isn't arriving until tomorrow morning because he's working today, so I'm picking up an extra shift at the hospital.'

That clearly perplexed her pal. 'But I thought you were off today?'

'I was, but they've called me in because they're short-staffed and I had nothing else on.'

'Oh.' Bernadette wasn't sure she'd ever seen Val lost for words, but her friend recovered quickly. 'Right then. Och, well, I was just coming to see if you wanted to come for a wee pamper day. I'm going to Jessie's salon to get my hair done...' Jessie was another of Val's wide circle of chums, and she owned a salon over in a little village called Weirbridge. Bernadette had been going to her for a couple of years now and adored her. '...And she has a free slot right after me.'

'I could well be doing with it. Would you look at the state of my roots.' Bernadette lowered her head to make the point. Her greys were coming through like weeds. 'I truly wish you'd pitched up here an hour ago, before I agreed to go into work.' She gave Val another squeeze. 'Thanks for thinking of me, but I need to dash. You're still coming to the vow renewal tomorrow morning, aren't you?'

'Of course. Wouldn't miss it. Are you sure you can't get out of working and come have a bit of fun with me today? Your roots will thank you.' As she said that, Val looked a bit crushed, and Bernadette felt terrible. Val was one of those women who put a cheery face on every day of her life, and if there was a problem, she'd suck it up and focus on everyone else. True salt of the earth. But seeing her looking so disappointed, Bernadette wondered if anything was wrong. There was no time to pry, but she made a mental note to speak to her tomorrow and find out if anything was going on.

Bernadette gave her another hug. 'I wish I could, but I can't let them down now. I'll see you tomorrow, lovely. Have a smashing pamper and tell Jessie I send my love.'

'Will do. You be careful driving out there today. Those roads are brutal with ice and you drive like a Formula One racer with his helmet on backwards.'

And there it was – normal service resumed. Val doling out care, cheek and humour in the same statement. Bernadette was still chuckling when she started the car and followed Val's Jeep down the drive.

It took twenty minutes to get to Glasgow Central Hospital from home, and Bernadette had made the journey so many times, her Fiat 125 could do it all by itself. However, as an ED nurse, she saw way too many accidents arising from drivers not paying attention, so she kept her eyes fixed on the road, as she said, 'Hey Siri, call Stuart.'

'Calling Stuart mobile,' Siri responded, before spitting out a load of beeps as it dialled. Bernadette tried to work out where her son would be at this time on a Saturday morning. Probably at the gym or out for brunch somewhere cool and trendy. He and Connor lived in the West End of the city, and they both liked to make the most of their weekends – which was clearly the case this morning, because the call went straight to voicemail.

A second call to Jack did exactly the same. Thank God Val had pitched up this morning because everyone else in her world – with the exception of Caleb at work – was making her feel decidedly unwanted. It brought her back to what she'd been thinking about earlier. She had to make changes in her life. She just hoped that Jack felt the same and wanted more than they already had too. Although, given that he always seemed to be too busy for her lately, she was beginning to wonder.

Maybe if she moved back to Ireland that would change. But it was a risky strategy. Could she really give up everything she had here – a rewarding job, her lovely house, the close proximity to her family – for a man?

Hadn't that already backfired once before?

She'd met Kenneth when she'd come over to Scotland as a junior nurse, looking for a bit of adventure, but only intending to stay for a year or two. It was a solid plan, until the moment the incredibly handsome doctor walked onto her ward, and she was smitten at first sight. Even then, she hadn't thought for a second that someone like him would be interested in her, but he'd swept her off her feet and... what was that expression Nina used the other day? It came to her. He'd love-bombed her to smithereens. Adored her. Made her feel like the only woman in the world. Like she could do no wrong. Like he couldn't live without her. Like they were going to have the most wonderful life ever. And that's exactly what had happened. Until it stopped.

It was only a few months after the wedding, when she was in too deep to turn back, that he'd lost his shit for the first time. Then the verbal abuse had started. And the demeaning comments. By the time she was pregnant with Nina, she was walking on eggshells around the controlling, intolerant, manipulative, uncaring man that she'd learned he was. And yet she'd stayed for many more years of that. She'd long ago decided that regretting that time was pointless, but it had definitely made her wary of committing again.

She returned to her earlier thought. Surely it was time to stop being afraid and trust Jack. And, more importantly, trust herself. Wasn't it?

As she pulled into the car park at the hospital, her phone beeped, and she waited until she'd parked before she checked it, hoping it was Jack finally replying to her.

Nope. A friend. Diana. Someone that she saw once a year, on the same date.

Today's date.

> Hey, just wanted to say I'm looking forward to tonight.

Bernadette fired off a quick reply.

> Me too. Usual time and place. See you then. Xx

She waited for her reply to go off into the ether, then checked for any other messages, expecting similar texts from a couple more of the attendees tonight. When there was nothing else in the inbox, she stared at the screen for a few moments, wondering if she could manifest a reply from Jack just by sheer mind power alone.

Apparently not.

As she got out of the car, Bernadette could feel her face settle into a frown and hated the emotions the uncertainty with Jack was bringing up. The insecurity. The tension. She immediately began giving herself a stern lecture. *Bernadette O'Brien. You are a fifty-nine-year-old woman and this is pathetic. Control your own life. You're in charge. Stop waiting for him to call you, reclaim your power and know your worth. Oh, and stop reading those Instagram buzz posts because you're beginning to speak like a self-help manual.*

Ten minutes later, after a quick change into her scrubs, she walked into the Emergency Department, and could immediately see why she'd been called in. The waiting room was already packed, every member of staff was busy, and going by the tense expression on Caleb's incredibly handsome face, he hadn't had his coffee this morning.

Not that you could say it out loud these days, but he was definitely the department's poster boy. Over six feet tall, biceps like melons and a male model jawline. He also gave rugged cowboy-esque vibes, which was hilarious because he didn't do outdoors. He did, however, do wide, way-too-handsome grins in her direction.

'I want it stated for the record that I disapprove of you being here because you should have said no and enjoyed your day off. But now that you're here... thank you, you fricking hero, for coming in. I will never love anyone more than I love you right now... Unless someone takes the drunk woman in bay number four, in which case I'll forget who you are and love them more.'

Bernadette gave him a nudge with her shoulder, which only reached his elbow, because Caleb was almost ten inches taller than her. 'Good to know that loyalty still exists.'

He laughed, before gesturing towards the whiteboard on the wall and switching into professional mode. 'Okay, so every bay is occupied, we're already on a three-hour wait for non-emergencies, and Stevie is in X-ray today and it's already backed up.' Stevie was female, and Caleb's best mate. She was also one of Bernadette's favourite people and dating a real-life Hollywood star, an actor called Ollie Chiles, who was in a huge TV hit, The Clansman, a show about Scottish warriors from bygone times. Bernadette went over to Val's every Thursday night so they could watch it together and it was the highlight of their week.

'I'll buy you a huge cake on our break. It's the least I can do,' Caleb promised, as he pulled a bloodwork test kit from the drawer and then went off back to whichever patient he was dealing with.

She had another quick stare at the board that detailed every patient, their location and status, taking it all in. To anyone else, it would look like a jumble of letters and numbers, but Bernadette had been doing this for so long, she got a handle on it all immediately. Being strong, confident and focused in her professional life came naturally to her. Why couldn't she take that confidence and skill and apply it to her personal life?

She already knew the answer to that. Somewhere along the line, it had seeped into her psyche that proper, functioning, loving, balanced relationships were incredibly rare. And worse, it was so easy to walk right into destructive partnerships that seemed great at the start, but then turned into something else altogether. Didn't the people she was meeting tonight prove that?

Switched-on, smart women, who'd all fallen for lies and manipulation.

Like them, she'd made that mistake. And what if lightning really could strike twice?

Was it the significance of today's date that was putting all her nerves just a little too close to her skin today? Or was it the fact that there was so much scar tissue around her heart that she wasn't ready to open it again yet? Or should she just take the bloody plunge and tell Jack how she felt and what she wanted?

Why wasn't any of this adulting stuff easy? And shouldn't she have worked it all out by her age?

She was as sure as she could be about Jack, but what if she was wrong again? Why take that chance? If only there was an instruction manual to all of this. Or a roadmap. Some kind of sign as to what she should do. Yep, that was what she needed. Some kind of divine sign from the heavens. Although, she very much doubted that she was going to get answers to anything by doubting herself, her relationship, and her personal decisions while she was standing in a packed ward with someone drunkenly singing 'Wonderwall' from behind one of the curtains.

Her professionalism stuck a temporary pin in her personal turmoil, as she sprung into action. Deciding to lighten Caleb's load, she gathered up the chart for bay number four and made her way across the war zone, trying to ignore the rising sense of impending doom. As she pulled back the curtain, she saw a clearly intoxicated woman dressed all in white, a lopsided veil on top of her head, a smashed bouquet of flowers lying on the floor beside her, her bruised, swollen ankle elevated on a pillow, pulling a bottle of vodka out of her bag.

'I decided I didn't want to get married, so I did a runner,' the woman explained, a tad unnecessarily.

Bernadette sighed. Bollocks. It was definitely a sign.

She just wasn't sure if she wanted to believe it.

6

MARGE

Marge only realised that she'd dozed off when she woke up and saw that the light had changed a little in the room. That happened a lot now. She'd close her eyes for a second, and then there would be a time jump – minutes, sometimes hours that she'd missed. It was just another one of life's cruelties. Her time was running out, yet sleep was snatching it from her with no warning or apology.

And worse, she lost even more time because she had to rewind her mind to wherever it had been before she drifted off. She flicked back through the Rolodex of her brain until it landed on the correct page. The date. Yes. That's where her thoughts had been. Today was the date that she had somewhere to be. Where people could help her with the last thing she had to do while she still had time.

She shifted her gaze to the side of her bed, where Estelle was sketching on her design pad, lost in her work, completely oblivious to the fact that Marge was awake, and with no cognisance whatsoever that today was going to change her life.

'Estelle...' she whispered and watched as her daughter lifted her head and smiled.

'Hey, Mum. You drifted off...'

'I know. I'm sorry.'

Estelle leaned forward and covered her hand with hers again. 'You don't ever need to be sorry.'

Marge wanted to tell her she was so wrong. She had so much to be sorry for.

'My phone...?' Marge asked the question, her throat hurting as she forced the words out. This was why she couldn't do this alone. Couldn't say all the things that Estelle needed to hear.

'You want your phone now?' Estelle checked.

Marge nodded, then managed, 'Please.'

Estelle had a quick scan of the bed, then got up and went over to the bedside cabinet. Nothing on top, so she opened the top drawer. 'Here it is, Mum, but it's dead. Do you want me to charge it?'

Marge nodded, then watched as Estelle pulled a charging cable out of the same drawer and plugged it in. Okay. As soon as it had enough charge, she could make calls, put a plan in place.

'Do you want anything, Mum? A drink? Something to eat? I could cut a piece off the cake I brought in for you?'

Marge shook her head. 'Thank you, darling, but I'm fine.' Food hurt to swallow and seemed so pointless now. She could barely taste it – another casualty of the chemo, or the radiotherapy, or the surgery. She wasn't sure of anything anymore.

Estelle got comfortable on the chair again, her legs pulled up under her, the same way she'd sat since she was a child.

Marge took the kind of low slow breath that she needed before she pushed out words. 'Estelle, you don't have to spend all your days here.' Another breath. 'It's not fair. I want you to enjoy your life.'

'Mum, there's absolutely nowhere else I want to be. Just here. With you.'

It should have been a comfort to hear that, but the opposite was true. It was the thing that Marge worried about, that she fretted over most. Only couple of years ago, Estelle's life had been busy and full of fun. There was her boyfriend, Craig, and of course there was Amber, Estelle's best friend for as long as Marge could remember. The girls were inseparable, socialised together, went on holiday together, spent all their time together. But then there had been a fallout and Marge had been so sure they'd get over it, but they never had. She could only hope that they would find their way back to each other because Estelle was going to need a friend to support her after Marge was gone.

'You know, you murmured Dad's name when you were sleeping,' Estelle said, smiling.

'I did?'

Marge smiled and closed her eyes again, hoping the dream or the memory would return. She was about to open her eyes again, but then she saw him. Ian was waiting right there for her, and he looked exactly the way he had on the day they had first met over thirty-five years ago.

'Excuse me, I have an appointment today with Professor Kelaney?'

Marge discreetly swallowed the aspirin that she'd just popped under her tongue, and greeted the visitor with her usual warm professionalism, despite the queasiness she was feeling. The previous night, she'd been at a reception for the recently graduated surgical class, and had been persuaded by Kenneth Manson to drink way too much champagne. He was already tipped as being a future star. They'd met at several functions over the previous couple of years, and she'd long ago realised that he was incredibly difficult to say no to. Now she wished she'd stuck to one glass of bubbly, because she was paying for it this morning.

She focused on the visitor who was now standing in front of her desk, wearing a very smart navy suit and a Paisley pattern tie that was just the right side of muted for a business appointment. He wasn't a tall man, perhaps five feet ten or so, but with his brown curly hair and cute face, he reminded her of that actor from When Harry Met Sally. *Billy Crystal. Yes, that was it.*

'Of course. Can I have your name please?'

'Ian Drummond. I'm interviewing for the chief accountant position.'

'Please take a seat and I'll let Professor Kelaney know you are here.'

'Thank you.'

Marge's first thought as she watched him make his way to the brown leather Chesterfield sofa next to the floor-to-ceiling Georgian windows was that he had a kind smile. Her second was that her boss at the Scottish Society of Surgeons, Professor Kelaney, hated doing interviews almost as much as he hated 'bean counters', as he called them, so this was bound to put him in a terrible mood. Just what she needed when she was already feeling under the weather.

She wasn't wrong. The interview barely lasted half an hour, before it was over and Ian was passing her desk on his way out, his expression a little downcast.

'Good luck,' she said, trying to make him feel better. 'I hope you're successful.'

'Thank you.' That kind smile again. He kept on walking, and Marge popped a Polo mint into her mouth. It wouldn't help with the nausea, but at least it would mask any traces of last night's overindulgence. The last thing she needed was Professor Kelaney questioning her professionalism. So that probably meant putting her head on the desk and having a hangover nap was out of the question.

'The thing is...'

She was so surprised by the interruption that she almost choked on the Polo. She hadn't even seen the interview candidate backtrack to her desk.

'I don't think the interview went very well. In fact, I can pretty much guarantee that I won't be back, given that his disposition had all the warmth of a polar expedition...'

The Polo slid into her left cheek as she smiled.

'And I promise I don't make a habit of this, and, actually, have never done something so spontaneous before...'

Marge could not for the life of her work out what he was trying to say, unaccustomed to any kind of personal chat in the halls of this ancient old building.

'But would you like to have a drink with me sometime?'

Her response was instant. 'Oh no...'

He immediately put his hands up in surrender. 'Right. Sorry. I shouldn't have asked. Very unprofessional of me. I shouldn't have put you on the spot like that. I'll just go and this time I'll make it all the way to the lift.'

'No! I mean... Sorry!'

'That's quite okay. Like I said, I shouldn't have asked...'

Marge was suddenly aware that this was descending into one of those farce comedy sketches where everyone got the wrong end of the stick. On top of that, it was all very odd. Would she normally accept a drinks invitation from a stranger she met at work? No. But then, hadn't she already learned that she had a weak spot for intelligent men in suits?

'Yes!'

Confusion crossed his face. 'Yes, I shouldn't have asked? Or yes, you'll have a drink with me?'

Even if her original answer had been a rejection, the way his brows rose and the twinkle in his eye would have made her change her mind. Besides, Professor Kelaney would be passing by on his way to his next meeting shortly, and she didn't want him to see her having informal chats and giggles with a potential employee. He definitely wouldn't be impressed.

'Yes, I'll have a drink with you. Sorry. The reason I said no initially was to the drink, not the date. I have a slight hangover, not something I'm accustomed to, so I was going to suggest a coffee instead.'

The twinkle in his eye gleamed a little brighter. 'That's a relief. I don't think I could take two soul-crushing rejections in the same day.'

'I wouldn't dream of inflicting that on you,' she teased a little. 'But I do need to get back to work...' She shot a glance at Professor Kelaney's door. It was still closed. For now.

'Of course. Coffee it is. Name the day and time.'

Today was out of the question. After work, all she wanted was to get home and go straight to bed until the queasiness wore off.

'How about Saturday morning? I like to go to a little coffee shop on Hyndland Road called The Sanders. We could meet there. Say 10 a.m.?'

Before he could answer, Professor Kelaney's door opened and he marched towards them, his stride swift and businesslike. Ian immediately spotted the red flush creeping up her neck. That always happened to her when she was panicking, anxious or embarrassed. She wasn't sure which one fitted the bill right now, but he countered it by making a fake excuse for the fact that he was still in the building.

'Ah, yes – thank you for the directions. I'm sure I'll find my way there.' With that, he nodded to the professor and left.

Professor Kelaney watched him go. 'Bit chatty for an accountant, don't you think?' he asked her.

'Really? I didn't notice.'

Only she had noticed. And every single thing she'd noticed about Ian Drummond, she liked.

That's when she heard the sound of a door opening...

No. Wait. The light made her pupils contract, as her eyelids fluttered. The sound of the door opening wasn't from back then, it was here and now. In her hospital room. And she wasn't twenty-something-year-old Marge, she was this one, the broken one...

'Did I fall asleep again?'

She saw that Estelle had her sketch pad on her knee again.

'You did.'

'I'm...' She was about to say sorry, when she remembered their exchange from earlier. No need for apologies, Estelle had told her.

What else had they talked about? Her phone. Yes, that was it.

Before she could think that through any further, her attention went to the door, because it was indeed open and Nurse Yvie was waiting there.

'I have a visitor here who'd like to say hello. Do you feel up to it Marge?'

Marge tried to run through her mind again. Had anyone else said they were coming up today? She didn't get many visitors. There was no family left and her whole life had been long hours at work, then going home at night to Ian and Estelle. At least, until Ian had left them. It would be almost fifteen years ago now and it had shattered every piece of their hearts. That was the thing that had been weighing on her more than ever this week. When this was done, when Marge was gone too, then Estelle would be alone.

'What do you think, Mum – are you up to company?' Estelle asked, bringing her back to Yvie's question.

Marge crossed her fingers that somehow it was the one person she wanted to see. 'Yes, I am.'

7

AMBER

Amber lay back on top of her duvet and exhaled like a racehorse that had just crossed the finish line. That is, if the racehorse was a bit out of practice, a tad out of shape, and worried that her boobs were sliding into her armpits and may never be seen again. She was quite accepting of the changes that two children and two rounds of breastfeeding had made to her body, but this whole thing with Ray was still very new and she was trying to give off sexy and confident vibes, as opposed to 'tuck my boobs in my waistband' vibes. Hopefully he'd be distracted enough by her unshaven, Velcro-like legs to notice any of her other flaws.

'That was incredible,' he murmured, running a finger up and down her bare stomach. Okay, so either he'd enjoyed it, or he was a great actor, and for the sake of her fragile first-shag-since-divorce confidence, she was going to choose to believe him. Although, she did wonder how long it would be before he had to go pee, because she wasn't sure how much longer she could hold her stomach in without causing muscle spasms.

'It was,' she agreed, trying to nonchalantly pull the duvet out from under her body, so that she could flip it over her torso and release the abs. Instead, she somehow managed to get it wrapped around one leg, so now she resembled a snail, halfway emerged from a shell and confused as to where to go from here.

Not that she regretted a single second of what had just happened, but it was just a bit of a culture shock, after being with no one else other than Ewan for the last ten years. Or, to be more accurate, Ewan for eight years and then a no-sex zone for the last two years since the divorce.

Against her conscious will, the mischievous part of her brain decided to compare the two. Sex with Ewan had been amazing at the start. Slightly less amazing but still highly enjoyable after they were settled into their relationship. And then, a tad more habitual, but still worth doing, after the kids had come along. Although, apparently, he didn't feel the same, because somewhere along the line he'd decided to turn his attention elsewhere. Her revulsion at that thought snapped her right back to the present. Ewan's affair had already taken up way too much time in her head and she never wanted to think about it again.

But back to the moment. Sex with Ray had been... different. Exciting. Energetic. And, if she were honest, a bit intimidating. Ewan hadn't been a big talker, and Ray had insisted on telling her every single thing he was about to do to her and how everything was making him feel. There were a couple of points when she wasn't sure if he was making love, or reading out the warning page from the instruction manual for the air fryer. Oh that's hot. So hot. You're turning me on. Press right there. That's it. Right there.

He absolutely knew his way around her body though – no surprise given his medical background and the fact that he'd been doing this a lot longer than anyone else she'd ever slept with. At first, she'd wondered if the twenty-odd-year age gap would be an issue, but she'd decided to be open-minded for three reasons: he was a doctor and, weirdly, that was sexy to her; it was the first time a customer in her shop had ever asked her out; and even in his smart suit, she could see his wide shoulders, chunky biceps and would have bet her last orchid that under that shirt there was a six-pack. Looking at his naked abs, she confirmed that she'd been right.

Now that she'd satisfied that curiosity, her next question was, what did they do now? After sex with Ewan, she'd either fall asleep, put earphones in and watch Real Housewives of Anywhere on her laptop, or, if he was snoring, she'd go downstairs, make a cuppa and call Estelle for a blether.

If circumstances were different, she'd definitely be in the bathroom, with the tap running, so that Ray couldn't hear her on the phone to Estelle right now, giving her a blow-by-blow account of what had just happened. And yes, they would have had a pre-planned code word prepared in case Estelle had to come and rescue her because Ray was a weirdo, a disappointment, or he'd already given her the ick.

Sometimes she wondered whether she missed Ewan or Estelle more. The two most important people in her life, gone at the same time. Amber still wasn't sure she'd ever be able to put her heart back together after that.

'You're deep in thought,' Ray commented, still tracing her clenched stomach.

Oh crap – that was worryingly close to 'what are you thinking?' and she was fairly sure that replying honestly with 'I was just pondering the loss of my husband and best friend' might be a bit of a passion killer.

'Sorry, I just… I was thinking I haven't had a morning like this in a long time.' It was close enough. 'And I was wondering what we do now?' She'd tried to deliver that with coy, teasing flirtatiousness, but she was pretty sure she missed the mark and just came off as clueless. Thankfully, he didn't seem to mind.

'Well, I was thinking…' He pushed himself up on one elbow and then leaned over and kissed her, slowly, passionately. She hadn't been deprived of oxygen for that long since she tried to get the hang of scuba diving on a holiday to Fuengirola in 2016. He then moved above her and left no doubt as to exactly what he thought they should do next. Bloody hell. And was it wrong that her first thought was to wonder if he'd popped a Viagra when he pulled up outside in his flash car? She hadn't had sex twice in quick succession since… since… maybe ever.

Still, she happily went along with it, because, if nothing else, she could distract him long enough for her to unclench her stomach and buttocks, then re-clench when they were back in his eyeline.

Viagra or not, she appreciated both the stamina and the second run through the instructions for the air fryer. She was now fairly certain she could rustle up chicken nuggets without checking the settings. Push there. Pull like that. Turn over. Nearly there. Almost ready. Yeah, that's hot.

And it was. She was having a perfectly lovely time. She just wasn't sure that it was… fulfilling. Deep. Comfortable. Or even fun. It all seemed a bit sterile and he hadn't seemed to notice or care that she hadn't got to the orgasmic bit on either attempt.

Maybe she was doing it wrong, given that she didn't have his wealth of experience or his variety of partners. On their first date, a couple of months before, they'd covered all the factual stuff. She'd shared her relationship history – a few boyfriends, then marriage at twenty-three, which seemed so young now, but back then she'd thought she knew everything.

Ray, on the other hand, had been married twice, had several long-term relationships in between, and she was under no illusion that he'd been active on the dating scene, based on the flower orders he'd placed with her alone.

When they concluded – ding ding – round two, she'd learned her lesson from the first spin round the block, so this time, she made sure to flip up the edge of the duvet so it was in the right position to pull over her mum tum. She told herself this would pass after they got more familiar with each other. In a couple of months, she was sure she'd be wandering around naked, with absolutely no trace of self-consciousness.

Wait, did that mean she thought they'd still be together in a couple of months? She'd told him right at the start that casual sex wasn't her thing, so over the last two months, they'd got to know each other over a few lazy brunches when Ewan had the kids. Then there had been at least one dinner every week. And daily FaceTimes. And so many texts she was almost late getting a 'congratulations on your triplets' bouquet with three balloons to a woman on the baby ward at Glasgow Central last week and, let's face it, if anyone deserved a bunch of winter blooms, it was a woman who'd just pushed three humans from her body. Anyway, all the romantic foreplay had clearly won Amber over, because when he'd asked her if she would consider dating him exclusively and taking their relationship to the next level, she'd heard herself agreeing. Twenty-four hours later, here they were – naked and definitely next level.

Ray interrupted her thoughts with kisses this time, then pushed himself up on one arm again. It was clearly his party trick. 'I'm going to go grab a shower. Care to join me?'

She was about to refuse when the little voice in her head that was frustrated with her lack of oomph and adventure these days spoke up and told her to shift her naked arse and give it a try. Live on the wild side. Make the most of this sexy adventure. Embrace new experiences. Clearly, a double shag in the daytime hadn't been enough to shut the voice up. But it had a point. She'd never showered with anyone. Not once. In their early years together, she and Ewan had lived in a flat, where the shower was barely big enough for one of them. When she was pregnant, they'd both found it hilarious that the only workable shower solution was for him to hose her down in the bath.

After that, the kids came and... well, showering became one of the only precious times that she could play music and spend ten minutes uninterrupted by a small child demanding food, water, play or cuddles.

'Sure,' she heard the adventurous little voice in her head answer for her.

He climbed out of bed, then reached for her hand, before leading the way. There hadn't been time to properly tidy the ensuite, so she kept her fingers crossed that he wouldn't spot her greying bra on the top of the laundry basket, or the two bottles of bubbles left over from when the boys used her shower the other day. The main bathroom in this house only had a bath with a hose, so they much preferred to shower in Mummy's bathroom. It was cheaper than taking them to a soft play, much more fun, and it ticked the box of getting them clean, so she was all for it.

Ray reached in and turned on the water, then stepped first into the long, narrow shower cubicle before turning to face her and holding out his hand. 'Coming?'

Too late to back out now. She stepped forward, and he pulled her into his body, kissing her again as he stepped backwards so that they were both going towards the large square rain shower and...

Amber wasn't quite sure what happened next. It was all so fast. One minute they were kissing as they moved, and the next minute, he began to drop. At first, she got the wrong impression and thought her adventurous voice had got her into something that she and her woefully ungroomed legs definitely weren't ready for, but then she realised that he'd slipped, and the sound he was making was a yelp of surprise, as he continued to fall, almost taking her down with him. She tried to hold him, save him, but lost her grip on his wet arm, and that's when he banged his head against the tile wall and slumped like he'd been shot by a sniper.

She wailed, reached over him, slammed the water off, then flew down to his level.

'Ray. Ray!' Panic was rising. Thankfully there was no blood, but he was out cold and she had absolutely no medical experience other than a first-aid course when she was captain of the netball team in the last year of high school.

It was enough to know how to check his pulse. Still breathing. Okay. At least she hadn't killed him. Oh bugger, this was such a mistake. What had possessed her to do this? She'd had sex one time since the divorce – or technically twice – and she was now close to being the subject of a true crime podcast.

Still frantic, she sprinted out of the shower, grabbed her phone, dialled 999, begged for an ambulance, then raced back to him as soon as they said it was on the way. She checked his breathing again – still fine. Tried to rouse him, but no response. She held his hand for a few moments, then realised that not only was it pointless, but she was still butt naked and there were probably rules against flashing a paramedic, so she really had to throw on some clothes.

'Ray? Ray? I'll be right there in the bedroom so just... I don't know... groan if you need me.' She felt the need to reassure him because she'd heard unconscious people could still hear what was being said to them. Or was that people in a coma? Damn, why hadn't she paid more attention to Chicago Med?

Unsurprisingly, there was no response, since he was still out cold, so she rushed into the bedroom, grabbed the first clothes that came to hand then threw his stuff into a bag: wallet, watch, phone, and clothes which she saw now had all been carefully folded and placed on the chair beside the bed. She made a note to question the slightly worrying pre-sex folded neatness, if they made it out of this without serious injury or a suspected murder charge.

Back in the bathroom, she kept talking to him while jumping on the spot as she tried to pull jeans onto her wet legs, then clipped on a twisted bra and dragged a sweater over her damp hair. 'Ray, Ray. Please wake up. Ray, please. Wake up. I'm so sorry.'

For years, she'd been reading about the long wait times for ambulances, but by some absolute miracle, only a few minutes had passed when she heard banging on her door. She rushed downstairs to let them in. 'He's up here,' she blurted, then led the two paramedics with kitbags, one male, one female, upstairs, taking two at a time again.

In the bathroom, they quickly assessed the damage, and Amber almost cried with relief when Ray left out a low moan. He wasn't going to die in her shower. Or at all, hopefully. There hadn't been a time in her life when she'd ever contemplated that thought would be in her head. Or that her bathroom would be host to two paramedics, one naked man and, she saw now, a definite erection that the medics were too professional to mention. That probably answered the Viagra question she'd pondered earlier. Her face flushed to the colour of the sexy red knickers she'd worn for the occasion.

She stepped back to let them work, then watched as they slipped a yellow collar around his neck, then gently manoeuvred a drowsy Ray out of the shower and onto the bathroom floor. She grabbed her dressing gown from the door and covered his still-erect dignity with it as they tried to communicate with him, while he was drifting in and out of consciousness. One of them went back out to the ambulance and returned with a stretcher. Gently, carefully, they eased him onto it, then carried him out of the door. As Amber followed behind them, fear gripping every nerve in her body, she glanced back at the shower and immediately saw the culprit. He was ten inches tall. Bright yellow. Squirted water from his mouth. Answered to the name SpongeBob Square Pants. He was also Sid's very favourite bath toy.

'Are you coming with us?' the paramedic asked, and Amber realised she hadn't thought about it, but there was only one answer.

'Yes. Yes, of course.'

At the bottom of the stairs, they paused to let Amber go ahead and open the door for them, then steered the stretcher outside. It must have been the snap of cold air, or perhaps the motion of the stretcher on the gravel path, but he suddenly came round again and began to mumble.

More relief. And thanks. And gratitude to the heavens. Until...

The words he was murmuring caused her to pause. Had she heard that? No. She must have got it wrong.

He said the same words again.

And Amber's soul left her body.

Because she was entirely positive that he'd just mumbled something about calling his wife.

8

MARGE – SUNDAY 21 FEBRUARY 2021

As she glanced around the crowd of solemn faces in the foyer of Glasgow Cathedral, Marge couldn't help but think that Kenneth would be happy with what he saw.

After much discussion with Kenneth's daughter, Nina, and his work colleagues, the funeral was taking place on a Sunday to accommodate the busy schedules of the assembled mourners, because if this were a weekday, there would be very few intricate, life-saving cardiac surgeries taking place in the central belt of Scotland this morning because every top heart surgeon that immediately came to mind was here. As were dozens of renowned specialists in other fields, several of the board members from the Scottish Society of Surgeons and she could see at least two peers of the realm.

According to the order of service that had been given out as the mourners entered the foyer, Sir Lester Kelaney was giving a eulogy. Oh, Kenneth would love that. And he'd be thrilled to see a few politicians, city councillors, and even... was that...? Yep, there was Jonas Connolly, Scotland's newest addition to the House of Lords. Kenneth had performed lifesaving surgery on one of Lord Connolly's grandchildren, earning eternal gratitude from the peer and his family. In fact – Marge cast another subtle glance around – there were probably at least a dozen people here who owed their lives to Kenneth's brilliance. Such a sad, tragic irony that his death, and his absence from the profession, may ultimately lead to more lives being lost.

Kenneth Manson was many things to many people, but to her, he was the man that she'd worked alongside for three decades. As his secretary and executive assistant, she'd sat outside his office, met all his patients, fielded all of his calls, kept his diary and organised almost every hour of his life. She'd arranged the cocktail parties that he hosted as networking events, she'd managed his professional finances, and yes, it was a cliché – even bought his wife's birthday and Christmas presents.

Without thinking, she pulled a cotton square hanky from the pocket of her thick wool coat and dabbed at her nose.

'Are you okay, Marge?'

The whispered voice in her ear was full of concern, and Marge was grateful for it, especially as the young woman beside her had stepped in to save the day at the last minute.

She'd been planning on coming alone, but her daughter, Estelle, had insisted on joining her. 'I know how much he meant to you, Mum, and I can't stand the thought of you being there alone,' she'd said over coffee and croissants the previous week. Estelle always dropped by on her way to yoga on a Saturday morning, and Marge treasured those starts to the weekend. Sometimes she came alone, but most mornings Estelle's best friend, Amber, would be with her. It was their standing joke that Marge had given birth to one daughter but ended up with two, because the young women had been joined at the hip for years and Marge adored them both.

Marge had tried to resist Estelle's offer to come to the funeral, but Estelle had been so insistent, she'd conceded in the end, realising that the more she dug her heels in, the more her daughter would match her energy. Estelle was kind, she was generous, she was smarter than Marge would ever be, but she was also stubborn as a mule and fiercely protective of Marge, probably because the two of them had been on their own for so long.

The plan had been set... until nine o'clock this morning, when Estelle had called in a panic. 'Mum, I rolled my ankle when I was out running this morning. I'm so sorry. I'm on the couch with an ice pack on it and I can't put any weight on it. That's what I get for being bloody healthy on a weekend. I should totally have stayed in bed. Anyway, Amber was already at the Cathedral doing the flowers, so she's going to come get you and accompany—'

Marge had realised what her daughter was about to say and cut her off. 'No, no – that's not necessary. I'm happy to go on my—'

Just at that, the doorbell had rung, and there was Estelle's best friend, dressed head to toe in black.

'I believe you ordered a funeral companion?' Amber had said, before wincing. 'Too soon? Sorry, I make terrible jokes when I'm in sad situations.'

Marge had smiled to put her at her ease. 'Not too soon. But honestly, Amber, you really don't need to...'

'Oh, but I do. I'd hate my mum to have to go to a funeral on her own. Especially someone she was close to. I'm happy to do it. And it's the least I could do after you recommended me for the flowers. It's the biggest job of my year so far. I just got done with the final touches at the cathedral – that's why I'm already dressed like this.'

Even in the solemnity of the day, Marge was pleased to know that Amber's business would benefit from the occasion. When Nina had asked her for help in planning the invitations and attendee list for the funeral, Marge had offered another couple of solutions too, and one of them had been the flowers for the cathedral. Kenneth's daughter had taken her suggestion on board, and now that they were here at the cathedral, Marge could see that it had been a good choice – the flowers were indeed stunning.

However, Marge's gaze was prevented from lingering on them, because the attention of everyone in the foyer suddenly turned to stare out of the huge open doors, where the funeral cars were now pulling up.

Marge swallowed, her throat tight, her chest even tighter, as she watched the hearse come to a halt, then six gents in traditional funeral suits – Marge assumed they worked for the funeral directors – stepped forward. They efficiently but respectfully removed the coffin from the back of the car, then, with a nod to the family, who had now alighted from the second car, they began to make their way up the steps, coffin on shoulders, gazes straight ahead. Marge took in the pale, tight expressions on the faces of Nina and Stuart, and her heart broke for them, and for Bernadette, who walked between them, holding their hands.

In accordance with tradition, the mourners stood aside, letting the coffin and family pass, then followed behind them into the empty church. Not wishing to claim any kind of false importance, Marge, with Amber beside her, slid into a middle pew, letting others go ahead of her to the front.

'Shit, I haven't switched my phone off,' Amber whispered, before thrusting her hand into her bag and pulling out her mobile, then pressing a button on the side. 'Oh, I'd have been mortified. Could you imagine the minister's face if "You Are My Sunshine" started playing? Sorry. Doing that inappropriate conversation thing again.'

Marge didn't mind. In fact, she realised now she was glad to have someone objective there, someone who wasn't emotionally involved. It was helping her to detach, to keep it together, and she wasn't sure if she'd have been able to do that if she'd been alone. Especially now that the minister was opening the service with sad words of sympathy and loss, and promises of redemption.

Marge's gaze drifted once more to Kenneth's family, and her chest tightened again. Bernadette stood stoically between her adult children and Marge admired her greatly, although they weren't friends – Kenneth had been incredibly particular about keeping his work and personal life separate, so their only communication occurred when Bernadette called in or when Marge phoned Kenneth's wife on his behalf.

As for Nina and Stuart, Marge had met them dozens of times over the years, bought gifts for them, arranged work experience and even, once or twice, in bygone days, picked them up from school or sports if Kenneth was supposed to do it and he was held up in surgery or otherwise engaged. Now that they were adults, she wondered how they viewed their late father. Like many of his ilk, his work had been all-consuming and Marge couldn't possibly count how many times he'd asked her to call and tell his family he'd be late home, or wouldn't make it to a special event.

And then there were the times that his absence wasn't down to a work commitment, but to something more personal and illicit. Marge had always done as he asked, but not without a tug on her conscience. She told herself she was protecting them as much as she was protecting Kenneth, but that didn't mean that she'd approved for a single second of his behaviour or of the position he'd put her in time after time. Kenneth Manson was many things: brilliant, dedicated, strong, compassionate to his patients, supportive to his colleagues, but he wasn't perfect and it had been part of Marge's job description to mask those flaws. Now, there would be no more moments of admiration for the boss she'd worked with for decades and there was no longer a need to cover for his failings.

The hardest part of Marge's job had been turning a blind eye to Kenneth's dalliances, and it was a moral dilemma she'd wrestled with many times over the years. But at the end of the day, the truth was that she'd overlooked his infidelities, compartmentalised them, so that she could continue to work with him. She wondered if that was something she would come to regret. But then, Marge knew she wasn't perfect either. She'd made her own mistakes – as Kenneth knew all too well. Their relationship was a trade off. An understanding that had remained between them for a lifetime. And one that would shock many members in this hallowed congregation to the core.

As Sir Lester Kelaney took his place behind the pulpit, Marge put her head down, deciding to stick with emotional detachment, so that she didn't show any kind of response that would draw attention. She kept the same posture as Nina took Sir Lester's place and delivered a beautiful, heartfelt tribute to the man that Marge knew had adored his daughter beyond anyone else.

It was only when Murray Atkins, the final speaker, opened with a witty anecdote about Kenneth's fierce competitiveness that Marge lifted her head. As the congregation laughed, she doubted if they understood the deep-rooted significance of the story, but Marge caught it straight away. Something in Murray's posture. A slight reverberation in his voice – loss? Grief? Or perhaps malice? Maybe even triumph? Murray and Kenneth had been friends for decades, which made the truth even more unpalatable, but Marge knew that Kenneth had had a brief, meaningless but entirely secret affair with Murray's ex-wife, Diana, while they were still married. And Murray, that the man up there praising his old friend, knew all about it.

It would be unfathomable to most normal people. Why would someone give a eulogy for a friend who'd betrayed him? But Marge already knew the answer. Men like Murray and Kenneth would never turn down an opportunity to hold court with the people in this room. She'd met many brilliant surgeons in her life who were truly decent people, but there were some who were just different – men (and yes, it had all been men in this category so far) whose psyches were made grandiose and their egos swollen by their ability to snatch life from the jaws of death. They had different standards to normal people. Different values. Different perceptions of what mattered and what didn't, what was right and what was wrong. Kenneth had been in that category – a complicated genius driven by his ego. Now she wondered if his old friend was too.

As Murray veered off into another anecdote about his times with Kenneth, delivering it with a pitch-perfect balance of respect, humour and self-deprecation, Marge allowed her stare to wander and immediately proved her own point.

Murray's ex-wife, Diana, was sitting further along her row, tears falling onto her jacket that was unmistakably Chanel. She'd been an expensive fling for Kenneth. Marge remembered the Hermès scarf, the Tiffany ring, the weekend at the five-star hotel on the shores of Loch Lomond.

A loud sniff took her gaze a few rows forward. Annabel Stevenson, a politician in the Scottish government, had been expensive too – a trip to Paris under the guise of a medical conference. Although, Marge was fairly sure that conferences didn't take place in a suite at the George V. That one had ended badly when Annabel had discovered that Kenneth was still very married and she'd freaked out over the potential damage that could cause her career.

Another shift in direction. In a pew to her left was former model, Danielle Strang, a lovely woman he'd met about a decade ago at a Christmas ball, which led to an entanglement that had lasted until that summer.

And then... Marge almost gasped as she caught sight of a face she would have been happy never to see again as long as she lived. Lila Anderson. Much younger than Kenneth. Probably not much older than his daughter, Nina. At one point, Marge had thought that affair would have been the one to bring it all crashing down and it almost did. It certainly, as far as she knew, played a part in the end of Kenneth and Bernadette's marriage. The others Marge had some compassion for – she could tell by their actions that the women didn't have a full picture of Kenneth's married life. But Lila? No. She was dangerous. Nasty. Vicious. Marge made it a point never to disparage another woman, but if she were to break that rule, she would call Lila a first-grade bitch. For the seven years of their affair, Marge had put up with her demands and her spoiled brat behaviour. She'd been forced to cover for Kenneth when Lila had shown up at his office and they'd suddenly locked the door, the sounds coming from inside making it clear what was happening on the other side of the wall. Lila Anderson was the closest Marge ever had to a nemesis, and she couldn't believe she had the absolute audacity to show her face here today. Marge just hoped that Bernadette didn't spot Lila in the crowd.

The minister was wrapping up the ceremony now, saying the goodbyes, and notifying the congregation that Kenneth's body would be taken for a private burial, but that they were all invited to join the family at a hotel in the city for the wake. Marge had known that in advance of today. The burial was taking place tomorrow, with just the family present, because the gravediggers didn't work on a Sunday. Even God had a day of rest.

Marge felt Amber slip her arm through hers and realised that they'd been asked to stand to sing the closing hymn. Kenneth's favourite. 'O Come All Ye Faithful'. Of course it was. Because it was always the most righteous and duplicitous that completely missed the irony of their choices.

As she joined in, singing quietly, she watched as the coffin passed her by, a solemn procession of mourners behind it. Nina. Stuart. And, of course, lovely

Bernadette. Then the speakers... Murray Atkins. Sir Lester Kelaney. Followed by other VIPs as they filed out row by row from the front.

And as she sang and watched the procession, Marge felt a slow burn of shame rising up her neck.

For thirty years she'd been keeping all of Kenneth Manson's secrets. But this morning was the starkest reminder that she had a couple of her own.

NOON–2 P.M.

9

BERNADETTE

At the nurses' station in the middle of the Emergency Department, Bernadette glanced up at the whiteboard again, deciding this was the medical equivalent of Whac-A-Mole – but for every one that they got rid of, two more appeared in its place. Two things weren't helping – the ice on the roads and pavements outside, and the fact that the Saturday morning school sports fixtures were still going on across the city's pitches, which inevitably resulted in a wave of sprained ankles from adolescent football players, blunt-force traumas from hockey players, and way too many broken bones, head wounds and concussions from the rugby squads. On top of that, there was a slow, walking-dead procession of people who'd woken up after their Friday night out and discovered the tiny cut or bump they had after a drunken fall, fight or collision was actually a gaping wound or an injury that needed medical attention.

'Tell me why I chose this life?' Caleb asked, coming up behind her. 'I could have been anything. A lawyer. A politician. The bloke that sells deckchairs at the beach clubs in Ibiza...'

'Ah, but you wouldn't have met me if you'd done that. I avoid lawyers, don't trust politicians and I burn like a barbequed chicken in the sun, so I never go near the beach,' Bernadette shot back, all of it true.

'Or me.' That came from Stevie, a radiographer in the X-ray department and Caleb's best friend, who'd just joined them, and was now handing a chart over to Bernadette.

Every time Bernadette saw her, she thought of Stevie Nicks, the iconic songstress that her colleague had been named after and bore a striking resemblance to. Although, the original Stevie Nicks didn't generally wear scrubs and had definitely never been in the ED of Glasgow Central Hospital.

'I was coming this way anyway, so I brought this. Your runaway bride. Ankle fracture, ligament damage, a growing hangover and a huge case of marital remorse. And you might want to put security on standby, because I just heard there's a drunk bloke in a morning suit and top hat roaming the corridors, shouting for his bride. He must have come in another entrance and worked his way through the hospital.'

Bernadette shook her head. 'Caleb, son, I might change my mind about Ibiza.'

Caleb gave her a weary thumbs up. 'I'll have my swimmies packed by morning and meet you at the airport.'

A beep from the desktop radio, the communication system the paramedics used to alert them to incoming patients, interrupted the conversation, and Caleb attended to that, while Stevie got back to work too, but not before saying, 'Bernie, we're hoping to take our break at two o'clock, if you can get away at the same time and join us.'

'I'll try, lovely – but only if you promise to dish some scandal about that man of yours.'

Bernadette had treated a fair few famous faces over the years, and most of them – if she were being honest and indiscreet – were egotistical arses, but Stevie's Glasgow-born actor boyfriend, Ollie Chiles, truly seemed to be a good one. And in a weird, small-world coincidence, Val was friends with his mother, Moira Chiles, and said she was an absolute gem – which was close to sainthood in Val Murray's book of praises.

Alone for the first time since she'd started three hours ago, Bernadette took advantage of the moment to quickly pull her phone from her scrubs pocket and check the screen. Still no reply from Jack. Still nothing from Stuart. Nina hadn't changed her mind and asked her to help with preparing for tomorrow's vow renewal. But there was a notification to say there were two texts in the group that she'd set up for the ladies she was meeting tonight. That chat lay dormant all year long, and then burst into life on the twenty-first of February every year as they confirmed attendance.

The group had been established in 2021, and in the four meetings they'd had since then, no one had missed the gathering, and Bernadette had no reason to think anyone would cancel on them tonight. She was about to check the messages, when a harassed junior nurse came hurrying towards her, sporting a troubled expression.

'Bernadette, can you help me out? I've got a patient in bay 11 – head injury, possible concussion, extremely agitated and saying that he's discharging himself. He's also asking to see the consultant on call, so I literally don't know if he's coming or going, but I don't want him leaving before we X-ray him to rule out a skull fracture.'

Bernadette immediately put her at ease. As the most senior nurse on the floor, she was always prepared to take on the more challenging and belligerent patients because she had almost forty years of experience in dealing with them and didn't want the more junior staff to have to put up with it. Especially as it was a growing epidemic these days. Back when she'd started, there would be the occasional abusive drunk or outrageously obnoxious family member, but now it seemed like every single day they had people demanding to speak to management, shouting about their rights and giving the staff utterly unwarranted abuse. Bernadette completely understood why more and more people were leaving the service.

'No worries, Letisha, I'll have a word.'

'Thanks, Bernadette.' The young nurse handed over the chart and was about to go in the other direction when she stopped. 'Oh, and he's ranting about being a doctor. I should probably have led with that.'

Bernie felt an immediate conflict of emotions. There was an acknowledgement and respect for the fact that the patient was a fellow medical professional, and then that positive feeling was immediately bumped out of the way by irritation because a doctor should know bloody better than to harass and make life difficult for a junior nurse who was only doing her fecking best. Then came an instant judgement that this man – like many of those celebrities she'd treated – was an arse. She'd had her fill of men like that in the past and no intention of putting up with their crap now.

Taking a breath, she steeled herself, mentally clipped on her bulletproof bra, and marched over to bay 11, pulled the curtain open far enough to step in, surveyed the scene and almost gasped aloud as she saw the familiar face that was lying on the bed.

'Murray!' Hers was a shocked but warm exclamation.

'Bernadette?' His was almost a groan. That was a surprise, because on the few occasions they'd met over the years, she'd always had a perfectly cordial relationship with Murray Atkins, one of her ex-husband's oldest friends. Or maybe that should be peers. Long-term acquaintances. Bernadette had always thought that, like most narcissists, Kenneth didn't have the emotional capacity for true friendship. And she'd occasionally wondered if he and the very charismatic Murray Atkins were two of a kind: ruthlessly driven, self-aggrandising, brilliant perfectionists, with unlimited charm and zero empathy or conscious thought for anyone but themselves.

Although, in the next couple of seconds, a couple of reasons for his less than enthusiastic reaction to their reunion emerged loud and clear.

The first was sitting on the chair in corner of the room. A younger woman, maybe in her early thirties, her brows knitted with concern. His daughter? Bernadette racked her brain. Nope. Murray had no children. And she knew that because, oh bugger the coincidence... The text she'd got this morning from Diana. Diana was Murray's ex-wife. Information began dropping into place. That meant that the last time she'd seen Murray Atkins was five years ago today, at Kenneth's funeral. He and Diana had avoided each other that day because they'd recently divorced and couldn't stand the sight of each other. Jesus, what a mess.

More information dropped in. A memory. Something Diana had said the next time Bernadette had spoken to her, on the first anniversary of Kenneth's funeral. An update on Murray's marital status that had both shocked and mildly amused her, but didn't fit with the scene that was playing out in front of her right now.

Cue the second possible reason for Murray's reticence to greet a blast from the past with a sunny, welcoming smile – other than the obvious reality that he was in a hospital ward with a head injury. She took in his bare feet. The bare legs sticking out from under his gown. The bare shoulder visible at the neckline. He'd come in with a head injury – so why on earth was Murray naked under that gown?

And why was he in a very evident state of arousal, one that he was trying desperately to conceal? Oh, in the name of the holy erection, this was mortifying.

Bernadette maintained her warm, calm professional manner. 'I would say it's lovely to see you, but given the circumstances...' She offered a gentle smile. 'Okay, let's see what we have here.'

She took a step towards him, but he put his hand up.

'Look, Bernadette, I just want out of here. Draw up the discharge papers and I'll sign them, otherwise I'm walking out the door. I'm perfectly fine.'

She decided it wasn't the moment to point out that if he walked out of the door right now, bollock naked and aroused, he'd end with a charge of indecent exposure and an entry on a register – not ideal for one of the country's top doctors.

'Let me make a deal with you,' she said, ignoring his reluctance as she reached the bed, where she used her torch to check his pupil dilation. 'The nurse who dealt with you...' She tried not to say that in a chastising way. 'Is concerned about a possible skull fracture, so I don't want you leaving here in case she's right and then I'll have that on my conscience. I don't need to tell you the potential complications if something is missed. But I can see that you're busy and don't want to be here, so let me go and speak to X-ray and see if I can get you fast-tracked...' She knew that would play to his ego. 'And if so, we'll get you over there, checked out and then have you out of here in no time. I'll be right back.'

She didn't even give him time to object, before turning to leave. On the way out, she gave a well-practised smile of reassurance to the young woman in the corner. Another tug of recognition. She'd definitely seen her before. But then, in her decades of work in a busy hospital, she'd met thousands of people and stored their faces in her memory bank. It was quite possible that the woman had come in with appendicitis in 2012. Or maybe she was someone who'd been in Nina's year at school. They could be around the same age. Murray. Fricking. Atkins. What the hell was he doing?

Turned out she didn't have to go through to radiology to check the processing times, because Stevie was back at the nursing station writing something on the whiteboard. When she'd finished, she put the pen down and turned her way.

'Bernadette, are you okay?'

Bernadette stumbled over her words. 'Yes. I think. Just a bit... surprised.

Letisha asked me to see a belligerent patient and it turns out he's a doctor, an old friend of my ex-husband.'

'Not the first time we've had a difficult doctor around here.'

'That's very true, so that wasn't the surprise. It was more the person he's with. A woman. And going by their body language, her expression, his state of undress, and what looks like an advert for the staying power of Viagra, I'm pretty sure they're more than just friends.'

Stevie's eyes widened and there was an unmistakable flicker of amusement, before she cleared her throat. 'And is that a problem?'

'I think so. Because I know his ex-wife and last I heard, he'd just got remarried to another mutual acquaintance. So that woman in there... I've no idea who she is, but she's definitely not his wife.'

10

MARGE

Nurse Yvie stepped aside and, with a flourish of the hand, ushered the visitor into the room.

'Presenting Wilma Cunningham,' Yvie said, with an elaborate bow.

'Honest to God, Marge, that lassie thinks she's a comedian,' Wilma quipped, with faux disapproval, as she swept past the amused nurse and came straight over to Marge's bed, arms outstretched.

It wasn't the person that Marge had been praying to see, but this was a wonderful consolation prize.

'Oh Wilma, you're looking smashing,' Marge told her truthfully as the other woman wrapped her in a gentle hug. The pain and tightness in her throat had eased a little, thanks to her daily medication, and she was finding it easier to speak. She knew from experience that it wouldn't last, but she was grateful that it gave her a chance to talk to this most welcome arrival. 'And what a transformation. It's great to see you looking so well.'

Marge meant every word, but if she were being entirely truthful with herself, somewhere deep inside, she did have a twinge of envy. Wilma had been chronically ill when they'd met, and now look at her. She'd got better. And Marge never would. That thought sent unexpected tears springing to her lower lids and she blinked them back. Not now. This wasn't the time to crumble.

A glance at Estelle's puzzled face distracted her long enough to compose herself. As Wilma released her and plonked down on the edge of the bed – a breach of the rules that Nurse Yvie appeared to be ignoring – Marge found the strength to make the introductions.

'Estelle, this is Wilma. She was in the furthest away bed on the ward next door when I was first admitted.'

A flicker of recognition, then a wide smile from her gorgeous daughter.

'Of course. You do look wonderful now.'

Marge wasn't surprised that there had been no instant recognition on Estelle's part. The ward next door was a four-bed unit and Wilma had been diagonally opposite her. However, on that ward, visitors were only allowed in for two hours twice a day, and Wilma always had several of her seven adult children surrounding her at visiting times, often with the curtains pulled, because they were smuggling in fish and chips to try to tempt their mother to eat. That had caused another pang of envy in Marge's soul. She'd have loved to have a big family like that. Not just for herself, but, more importantly, for Estelle. The thought of her daughter being alone to deal with Marge's death was more painful than this disease.

'Thank you, love. I was on death's door when I met your mum, but it's almost four weeks since my operation now and I'm still a bit sore, but other than that, I've never felt better.'

Estelle was clearly interested in her good fortune and Marge understood why. Good-news stories, especially ones that defied the odds, were like gold dust to the families of terminally ill patients. They offered the one thing that the science, or even the swankiest hospital, couldn't always deliver – hope.

'That's wonderful to hear.' Estelle leaned forward, her smile a little apologetic. 'Can I ask what surgery you had?'

'Of course. Honestly, I'm so relieved that I survived the bloody thing, I'd put it outside on a billboard if I could. It was a kidney transplant, love. Touch-and-go for a while before the surgery. All of my other six were tested, but they weren't suitable donors, then it turned out my boy, Malcolm – he's the second youngest one – was a match. We only discovered it at the last minute, because he ran into a bit of legal trouble in Thailand last year and was detained there for an unexpectedly prolonged period of time. I swear, if my shite kidneys don't kill me, the worry of my Malcolm will. Anyway, he just got home last month and now all is forgiven because he gave me half of one of his kidneys –

which is enough to keep me going for a while longer. I was a week down in ICU after the op, and then they put me on ward 54 with a load of younger women because that was the only free bed. They barely said a word – all of them scrolling on their phones all day. Not like all the chats we had up here.'

Wilma wasn't wrong about the chats. Olive and Theresa in the other beds weren't much fit for talking – Olive had dementia, and Theresa was a quiet, reserved woman who spent most of her time with her earphones in, listening to audiobooks that she'd tell them all about over dinner. But Marge and Wilma would blether all day, or rather, Wilma would gab, and Marge would listen, because with seven children, eighteen grandchildren and four former partners, the other woman had an infinite stream of stories to tell. Marge was happy to hear them all because they passed the time, kept her entertained, and, most of all, they made her think.

In fact, it had been the thinking that had led her, in the middle of the night, to one awful, stomach-churning worry.

Wilma's life had been saved by a kidney transplant from her son. What if Estelle ever needed someone who shared her DNA? Marge was the only person she had in her life, and when she was gone, Estelle would have nowhere to turn. At least, nowhere her daughter knew of.

The truth was, there were still people out there who shared her genes, people who could help if they chose to. Estelle had options that she knew nothing about. Could Marge really go to her grave with that on her conscience? Or could she summon up the courage to be honest, even if it hurt the person she cared about most on this earth?

Never shy to chat, Wilma was now giving Estelle a blow-by-blow account of her illness, her surgery and her recovery, barely drawing breath between sentences. Marge was grateful for it because it allowed her mind to wander back to the last time she'd had the courage to be honest. It was not long after she'd met Ian, and it was one of the most difficult conversations of her life. Marge felt herself drifting back there, watched as his handsome face came into focus again, his smile, his kind eyes.

They were sitting in a garden... The little patch of grass at the back of the cottage flat she lived in then... It was a sunny day. He was holding her hand. She'd decided that she had to tell him what was on her mind because she couldn't keep it to herself for a moment longer. He deserved the truth, even if it meant he would leave her. As a tear began to run down her cheek, she'd opened her mouth to speak. 'Ian, I need to tell you...'

She didn't get another word out because the ground quite literally trembled. Marge opened her eyes to see that Wilma had stood up, causing her bed to shake.

'Anyway, Marge, I'll leave you in peace, because I can see you're tired, pet.'

Before she could respond, Marge felt a dampness to the side of her face, and realised that a tear had slid down there in this life too. She wiped it away, hoping Wilma hadn't spotted it, but fearing she had. This wasn't a time for sadness. Especially not when her friend had a new lease of life, something wonderful to celebrate.

'I am a little tired,' Marge said, hoping that would cover up her sorrow.

However, Wilma was staring at her with such concern and compassion that Marge knew the other woman could feel her pain.

'I can see that, love,' Wilma told her. 'If it's all right with you, I'll pop back in to see you next week...'

Marge reached her hand out. 'I'd like that very much.' She didn't add that she might not be here next week. She could see in Wilma's eyes that the woman knew that already too. 'Thank you so much for coming. I can't tell you how much I've treasured knowing you, Wilma.'

The other woman covered up a loud sniff by reaching up her sleeve for a hanky, then pretending to sneeze into it. They both knew what was happening, and Marge sensed that behind Estelle's smile, she could see it too.

'It's been grand to know you too.' Wilma's chin was wobbling now, so she gave Marge a final squeeze of the hand, and then bustled out of the door, repeating a cheery, 'I'll see you again soon, Marge,' as she went. Marge wasn't sure who she was trying to convince, but she was going to choose to believe her.

'That was lovely, Mum. Such a nice lady. And what an incredible story. It makes you think, doesn't it.'

Marge had no idea where this was going. Was Estelle going to raise the subject of her own non-existent gene pool now? Was Marge going to have to blurt it all out, admit to all her lies, without the correct support structure in place? No. She wasn't ready. She needed other people here for that. She needed the one person who knew, who understood, who would be here for Estelle long after Marge was gone.

'Estelle, is my phone charged yet?' she asked, remembering their earlier conversation.

'It should be, Mum, let me check.' Estelle got up from her chair and went back round to the bedside table, then picked up the phone and looked at the screen.

'Yep, it's charged. Do you want it now?'

Marge nodded, as she felt a tiny tug of relief. It was time to stop hiding the truth. And yes, she was heartbroken at the pain that this would cause, but the alternative could be so much worse. 'Yes please. Could you dial a number for me?'

'Of course, Mum.' Estelle was already putting in Marge's password. She'd been making calls on her behalf regularly over the last month, when Marge didn't have the strength, the will or the voice to do it.

'Thank you. I just need you to call my friend, Bernadette.'

11

AMBER

Amber wondered if Ray's concussion could be contagious, because she was suddenly experiencing a crushing headache, rising anxiety and definite symptoms of confusion. How the hell had this become her day? A couple of hours ago, she'd been having an afternoon quickie with her new boyfriend and her biggest concerns were her stretch marks and her unshaven legs, and now she was in Glasgow Central Hospital and unless she was imagining it, there was an undercurrent of something very strange going on.

It had started when Ray had come round in the ambulance, realised what had happened, where he was, and where he was headed, and become totally agitated, to the point where he'd demanded they pull over and let him out. Thankfully, he'd passed out again before the paramedics were forced to make an emergency stop or tie him to the stretcher. The medics had already asked his name when they'd been treating him back at the house... 'Ray Atkins,' she'd told them, before correcting herself. 'Actually, his full name is Murray, but Ray for short.' He'd told her about his nickname the first time they'd met face to face. 'Call me Ray,' he'd said, leaning on the counter of her flower shop. 'All my closest friends do.' He'd said it with such a cheeky smile that she'd thought it was cute. Funny. Or maybe she'd just been swayed by the fact that he'd ordered a hundred quid bouquet for his mother.

'And is this his home address?' the paramedic had gone on.

'No, he lives at...' That was when Amber had realised she had no idea of the answer. She'd never been to his home. All she knew was that it was in Edinburgh. God, she really hadn't done her research.

He'd woken up again just as they'd arrived at the ED, and had been absolutely furious when they'd wheeled him to a bay instead of bowing down to his wishes to be released. The whole time, Amber had just followed behind quietly, carrying the bag with his belongings, but it struck her now that she hadn't actually told him that she'd brought his things and he'd been too furious to notice.

It was only thanks to the frankly heroic patience of the first nurse who'd treated him that he was still here, because she'd insisted on a preliminary check of his injuries and she'd stood her ground while he spoke to her in what was, quite frankly, a disgracefully entitled, arrogant way. Much as she'd like to blame the concussion, Amber was coming to realise that if they made it out of here in one piece, her short-lived romance with this man was very definitely over. She hated people who treated others unkindly. It happened regularly in her shop, when customers would act like she was beneath them, just because she was providing a service. There was one very posh lady from Kelvinside who had been coming in for years for weekly bouquets and had yet to utter a 'please', a 'thank you' or even learn her name. Amber and the rest of her team had nicknamed her Cruella and decided she was probably a serial killer in a past life. Or possibly in the present one too.

Amber had fully expected the young nurse to call security and have him ejected, but she'd stuck with him, until he'd threatened to leave again and demanded to see her superior.

That's when things had taken an even stranger turn. The older nurse who'd come in... Amber pursed her lips as she thought back to the moment she'd seen her. The woman had red hair, a kind face, a soft smile and Amber had been absolutely positive in that moment that she'd seen her before. Maybe a customer at the shop? Or a woman who went to the same Pilates class? Or perhaps this was the nurse who'd treated her the time she'd come in here after a near-amputation of her pinky when her pruning shears had slipped. Thankfully they'd managed to save the tip, but it now pointed left when the rest of her digits were going right.

It had immediately been clear that Ray knew her. She'd called him Murray, so obviously not one of his 'closest friends', and he'd called her Bernadette, and his attitude had changed completely. He'd gone from outright belligerence to a more respectful, but firm, negotiation stance, and if this were a movie on TV, Amber would have punched the air and given a 'hell, yeah' for the way that the senior nurse had handled him. She'd clearly had some experience of this kind of behaviour because she'd swayed between reassurance, kindness and a firm, no-nonsense demeanour to get exactly what she wanted – a point being proven by the fact that Murray's naked arse and now, thankfully, only semi-erect penis, was still in this bed.

Her gaze went to the bag of his possessions in the corner behind him. She'd considered giving him his clothes, but she didn't want to make it any easier for him to flee the scene in case he later collapsed from undiagnosed complications, and she would have that on her conscience. And she wasn't going to be responsible for him having a penis-meets-zip incident. There had been enough damage done today.

Was catastrophising another sign of second-hand concussion?

Now he was lying in bed, clearly fuming, and Amber realised she had no idea what to say to him, given that their entire conversational history so far had been flirtatious, getting-to-know-you, surface-level stuff or – after this morning – some explicit chat about his sexual preferences that she would probably think about every time she popped chicken nuggets in the air fryer for the rest of her life.

Should she leave? She thought about it, but his car was still back at her house, so he'd need to come back there to get it. Cue an inevitably toe-curling reunion. Also, leaving someone in their time of need was pretty ruthless, especially when she'd been snogging the face off him just a few hours before. Besides, the only thing worse than having a medical emergency the first time you have sex with someone new was realising that the potentially life changing incident was all down to the malevolent presence of a five-year-old's SpongeBob Square Pants, so she did feel more than a little responsible.

'Can I get you anything?' she asked him, more for something to say than because she wanted to actually help. He'd practically ignored her since they'd got here, and the few words he'd said to her had been snappy, so she wasn't exactly up for playing Florence Nightengale. 'Water?'

'No.' There was a pause, before he caught himself and added a somewhat grudging, 'Thank you.'

Another pause. Then he suddenly grasped his wrist.

'My watch...'

She decided not to mention that it was with the rest of his stuff in the bag in the corner.

'You took it off right before you got in the shower. You know, before we...' The words stuck in her throat, where they were incinerated by the red-hot heat of regret that she suspected they were both feeling now. If only she had a rewind button.

He obviously felt the same because he changed the subject. 'This is ridiculous. I'm bloody fine. I'm a doctor, for fuck's sake. I'm perfectly capable of making my own diagnosis. Can you go and find Bernadette and ask her to hurry the fuck up?'

Wow, who was this man? The Ray she'd been romancing for the last two months had been sweet, and kind, and attentive and oh so debonair. This guy was a complete dick. And no, she wasn't going to go track down that lovely nurse and tell her anything. She decided to distract him with banal conversation.

'You and the nurse... Bernadette... know each other then? Did you work together?' She knew he worked in an Edinburgh hospital now, but maybe he'd worked in Glasgow too at some point. Again, note to self. Do a tad more research before getting to bendy naked stage.

'What? No,' he brushed her off. 'She used to be married to Kenneth Manson.'

Amber felt like she'd been slapped. 'Kenneth... the funeral...'

'Yes.' He was now looking at her like she was stupid, as if there was something completely obvious here that she was missing. And he was right. It all suddenly clicked. That's why she recognised Bernadette. Years ago, she'd done the flowers for Kenneth Manson's funeral and then, thanks to a weird twist of fate, had ended up accompanying Marge to the service because Estelle had rolled her ankle that morning.

That seemed like a lifetime ago and just the very thought of Marge and Estelle made her stomach tumble. She had so many feelings about her former friend, but none of them could even come close to taking priority right now, because other pieces of the jigsaw were sliding into place and she was hating the picture they were making.

'Why do you look surprised by that? I assumed you knew her, given you were at his funeral,' he snapped.

That wasn't a new piece of the jigsaw. In fact, it had been the reason that they'd connected and the spark for their relationship. She should have known nothing good would come from a relationship with someone she'd first met at a funeral.

He'd been a customer of Amber Bouquets many times over the years, but always placed his orders on the phone or online, until just a couple of months ago, when he'd come in to pick up the exceptionally expensive bouquet for his mother's birthday. She'd recognised him almost immediately as the man who'd given the eulogy at the Manson funeral and she'd told him so, kicking off a conversation that led to his double back somersault in the confines of her shower this morning.

Murray 'call me Ray' Atkins hadn't recognised her, of course. She hadn't even spoken to him at the service, as her focus had been on making sure Marge was okay.

Marge. Amber missed her almost as much as she missed Estelle. For the second time today, she thought how there was a time that she'd be straight on the phone to Estelle right now, telling her all about the batshit crazy day she was having.

But that was before they'd fallen out, after her best friend had betrayed her. Not now.

'I *was* at the funeral,' she agreed, dipping back into the conversation, 'but I didn't know anyone except Kenneth's secretary, Marge, and I was only there with her because her daughter couldn't make it. I was a funeral stunt double.' She tried to rack her brain for any further information. Marge had given her a brief rundown of the chief mourners at the time. 'And am I wrong in thinking that Kenneth and...' she paused, as she pulled the name back up, before repeating, 'Kenneth and Bernadette... they were already divorced back then, weren't they? Didn't he have an affair? I'm sure my friend, Estelle, told me that.'

'I thought you said you were no longer friends with her?' he asked, the muscle on the side of his jaw visibly throbbing.

Another piece of the jigsaw. When they'd reconnected in her flower shop, he'd asked her lots of questions about whether she was still in touch with Marge. Of course she'd said no, explaining that she hadn't seen her in years, which was technically true. He'd taken that in, continued chatting, then, after that, eventually asked her out.

'I'm not.' Why was he biting her head off? True, they were in a slightly stressful situation and he clearly didn't want to be here, but this was such a disproportionate response and, quite frankly, it was pissing her off.

She was saved from her rising irritation by Bernadette, who had just reappeared around the curtain. 'Okay, good news for you, Murray. I've spoken to radiology and they're sending someone round to get you now. They'll just be a couple of minutes.'

At first, Amber thought he was going to reject the suggestion, but he kept his mouth snapped shut. This woman clearly had magical powers.

Bernadette picked up his chart from the table beside his bed. 'While we're waiting, I just need to take some more details because the admitting nurse didn't have a chance to get everything we need.'

There was a hint of a reprimand in there, but he ignored it, because everyone here knew that the poor junior nurse who'd first attempted to take his details had been run out of the room before she could finish her job.

'Okay, I've got full name. Date of birth?'

He rhymed that off and Amber realised that he'd shaved a couple of years off when he'd told her his age. Yet more evidence for the dickhead prosecution.

'Address?'

He opened his mouth to speak, then stopped, a flinch of something Amber didn't recognise crossing his face. Then he switched to a swarthy smile and tone of voice that she definitely did recognise, because it was the one he'd been wooing her with for the last two months. And did anyone still say 'wooing'? That was another question she'd have asked Estelle if they were still friends.

'Amber, would you mind getting me that water after all?' he asked her. 'There's a vending machine just outside the doors, if I remember correctly?' He directed the second part of that question to Bernadette, who was now nodding.

'Yes, just as you go back into the ED reception. The doors are locked, but if you let the nurse at reception know who you're with, she'll let you back through.'

Amber got the hint, saying, 'Erm, sure,' as she got up and opened the curtain just wide enough to let herself out. She should have crossed the ward in the direction of the doors, but something made her stop. Maybe curiosity. Or a premonition. Or the realisation that he'd already lied, coupled with a desire to get the full picture. Whatever the reason, she stopped, stood absolutely still, and listened as he rattled off an address in what she knew was a very posh part of Edinburgh.

Bernadette spoke again, and even on the other side of the curtain, Amber could hear something loaded in her words.

'Next of kin?'

There was a pause that stretched. And stretched. Then a little longer. Before the man she'd just shagged sighed, and then reeled off a name that surprised her. Actually, it was more than surprise. This one probably fell into the 'shocked the knickers off her' category. Not that she was ever removing her undergarments for a bloke again after today. The NHS couldn't afford it.

But still... It was all she needed to hear. Another piece of the jigsaw clicked in. Make that two pieces, because she also remembered his murmured words when they were loading him into the ambulance.

She followed Bernadette's instructions and made her way to the doors, where a smiling triage nurse pressed a big green button to let her out. She considered just keeping going, but she'd left her handbag behind, and besides, she needed more than a partial confirmation of her suspicions. That's why she bought a bottle of water, then, helped by the receptionist as directed, went straight back into the Emergency Department. By the time she reached his bay and went back through the curtain, Bernadette was gone. Excellent. That meant she could get straight to the point. She inhaled. Tried to keep her voice steady. Spoke in the same tone she'd used once before when she challenged a man she'd caught lying to her. Back then, Ewan had come clean. She wondered if this one was about to do the same.

'Ray, I need to ask you something. Are you married?'

12

LILA ANDERSON – SUNDAY 21 FEBRUARY 2021

Since she'd walked into the wake at the function suite of the very grand St Kentigern Hotel in Glasgow a few moments ago, Lila Anderson had been waiting for someone to wrestle her to the ground and have her ejected. Thankfully, back at the cathedral, the traditional post-funeral line-up – whereby the family members stand in a line outside the church, and the mourners stream by, giving their condolences to each person – had been dispensed with, probably because of the chilly temperatures, the light rain, and the need to avoid keeping about two hundred VIPs waiting in the cold. That meant everyone had made their way back to the hotel in swift fashion, flooding the function room and overwhelming the person at the door who was checking the names on the guest list. Lila had just held her head up and swooped by as if she belonged here – which, in her mind, she definitely bloody did. She had been an intimate part of Kenneth Manson's life for over seven years – the mistress who had catered to his every whim, who'd believed all the promises that he would leave that cow, Bernadette, for her. Of course, that wasn't exactly how it had all worked out, and Lila felt her face flush to the colour of the soles on her Louboutin stilettos every time she thought about the night that had wrecked everything. Before her mind could slip back to the past, she distracted herself with a very necessary drink.

Without even a glance at the waitress holding the tray, she scooped up a medicinal glass of white wine and wandered over to a high, round, bistro-style table in the corner, where she could keep a relatively low profile while sussing out everything that was going on. As an added bonus, it had a mirrored wall right behind it, so she got the opportunity to check out her reflection and the satisfaction of confirming that she was looking incredible. She was a hundred per cent positive that there wasn't another woman in the room that could come close. Her white-blonde bob was swept back in an elegant chignon, and her Chanel Red lips were a stark contrast to the grey smoky eyeshadow she'd diligently applied this morning. Not too much. Just enough to be utterly striking, while remaining effortlessly classy. Her Louboutins were the perfect accessory to her black Dolce & Gabbana skirt and jacket. In a twist that added to the satisfaction of the moment, she'd remembered this morning that Kenneth had bought the outfit for her in Milan, on a trip they'd taken there under the guise of a work thing. He was a guest lecturer at some university over there, but they both knew he'd only agreed to it so that they had an excuse to get away for a wild weekend – one of the many they'd enjoyed in the seven and a half years that they were together.

Almost eight years. More than one fifth of her life, spent waiting for that man to leave his wife. But she'd thought it would be worth it because despite their twenty-odd year age gap, she'd truly loved his fierce intellect, his sexiness, and yes, his arrogance too. And the gifts and the lavish trips were an added bonus. Of course, she hadn't been stupid enough to dedicate herself fully to him in that time – there was no way she was spending birthdays and Christmases alone, and she needed at least three two-week-long holidays a year, so she'd had other relationships too. One boyfriend had even proposed to her, but of course she'd refused. She and Kenneth both knew that her dalliances were merely place holders until he left his wife.

At least, that's what she'd thought. It still made her want to scream that the sick, twisted bastard hadn't come good on his promises. The aftershocks had come like tremors after an earthquake that night. After losing patience with waiting for Kenneth, she'd finally gone to tell Bernadette about their affair, only to find out that the mousy little thing had actually – slap her arse and call her duped – already left Kenneth. There had been a brief moment of elation at the prospect of her job being done. Kenneth was free. He could be with her. They could ride off into the sunset. Right up until the duplicitous bastard announced that he'd never been serious and didn't want her. She was strictly 'bit on the side' material. Not a wife. And he'd never changed his mind about that. Instead, according to the grapevine, since his divorce, he'd spent his time shagging a selection of glamorous women while trying to win Bernadette The Frump back. What. A. Fool.

Meanwhile, she'd had a couple of videos go viral on social media, leading to a high-profile relationship with the captain of a French football team, and a stint on a reality TV show called Heartbreak Hotspot – a Love Island-style dramafest that put six men and six women who'd had their hearts broken on an island in the sun. For a month or so after she'd been voted off, Lila had been a publicity sensation – and yes, it had got her a free boob job and an invitation to the BAFTAs – but that had soon worn off and she'd been dumped yet again – this time, by the general public, who'd moved on to the next celebrity obsession and left her to dwell in obscurity.

Since then, she'd been forced to make a living as the membership sales manager at her father's very prestigious golf club. Naturally, she was great at it. Coercing middle-aged men into parting with extortionate amounts of money was a talent that could also be utilised in the workplace.

She cast a side eye towards Bernadette, who was now sitting on the other side of the room, oblivious to her presence. There would never be a day when she would understand why Kenneth could possibly want a fifty-something-year-old woman who was dressed in polyester, instead of a thirty-something goddess in Dolce & Gabbana. Maybe he was on drugs.

As the memory of his rejection began to kill her vibe, she shook it off and scanned the room. It was definitely a stellar gathering and she recognised at least a dozen well-known faces. She also recognised at least one other woman that she knew Kenneth had shagged, before they'd got together. Not that he'd admitted that, of course. All she'd had to work on were rumours and the way certain women acted when they were in his company. The important thing was that not one of them came even close to Lila in looks, brains or class.

Was that what had motivated her to come today – one last two-finger gesture up to Kenneth, in case he was looking down on them right now?

Look at me, you absolute idiot. Look what you turned down. What you could have had. Losing me should be the biggest regret of your life.

She usually prided herself on acute self-awareness, but the truth was that she wasn't quite sure what had made her come. Or maybe there were just so many reasons.

This should have been one of her life-defining moments. If Kenneth had chosen her, then she'd be the one in the centre of this sympathy party right now, and all these people would be consoling her. Not to mention she'd be a damn sight richer that she currently was. Last time she checked her bank balance, she was nudging into her overdraft, so she just didn't look any more. She'd worry about it the first time her credit card got declined.

She also wanted to be here because, as far as she was concerned, after giving him eight years of her life, she belonged here. If all she was going to get out of this was a few glasses of wine, some free hors d'oeuvres and a place in a room filled with the kind of people she aspired to be, then she'd take it.

And the final reason... Urgh, these intrusive thoughts were definitely killing her wine buzz again. Being reminded of just how much Kenneth had taken from her made her stomach ache more than her last round of liposuction (this size 8 figure didn't come easy). But the sad, pathetic, unpalatable truth was that he was the love of her life. There. That was it. In fact, he was the only love of her life. She'd never loved anyone before Kenneth or since. Not even the football player who'd been her rebound fling, or the Heartbreak Hotspot bloke who'd proposed a week after they met and then bailed when the publicity died down and he'd decided that, at twenty-four, he didn't want a woman in her thirties. Great. Rejected and old.

Again, she shook off the negative vibes, vowing to enjoy every second of the best revenge against the men who'd discarded her. Right now she was in a room with the Scottish glitterati and that meant a plethora of wealthy, well-known people to network in. Kenneth always was the jealous type so she just hoped that he was watching, full of seething regret, in the afterlife.

As the waitress passed by, Lila swapped her empty glass for a full one, then hastily turned to face the other direction, because she spotted Marge, Kenneth's very own personal Rottweiler, make her way over to Bernadette. Fuck. If anyone was going to get her tossed out of here, it was that old boot. One of Lila's favourite things about her relationship with Kenneth, other than the sensational sex, the gifts, the lavish meals and the flash holidays, was that she'd got to torment that sour-faced battleaxe on a wonderfully frequent basis. She'd once strutted into Kenneth's reception area, completely naked under her coat, and watched with absolute glee as – despite Marge's obvious disgust and vocal objections – Kenneth told Marge to cancel all his appointments and then took her into his office and shagged her on every surface. And Lila had made sure she was gloriously noisy.

'Not every day you see a beautiful woman smiling at a funeral.'

She'd been so lost in thought that she hadn't even seen Murray Atkins coming from the other direction.

'It's not every day that a handsome guy hits a beautiful woman with a pick-up

line at a funeral,' she replied, with just the right amount of sass and coyness. This wasn't her first rodeo. If there was a humanitarian award for attracting members of the opposite sex, she'd have her name on more trophies than Gandhi, Mother Teresa and the Dalai Lama combined.

'Touché,' he responded, putting his glass down on the high table in front of her and making it clear this wasn't a drive-by pick-up.

'Nice speech earlier. Did you mean it?' Lila asked, teasing, one eyebrow raised and a smile on her red lips as she playfully provoked him.

'I meant at least some of it,' he conceded, and Lila was impressed that he didn't try to bullshit her. They both knew too much for that to work.

'Ah, that's good, because I definitely only believed some of it.'

Lila could sense that he was enjoying this exchange as much as she was. And why not? He'd been one of Kenneth's friends and peers whom they'd socialised with often and they both knew the unspoken truth was that even though Murray had been married back then, he'd been attracted to her, wanted what Kenneth Manson had. The underlying rivalry and competitiveness between the two men had been obvious to her, so she'd found it amusing, toyed with him occasionally, flirted a little – just enough to make Kenneth jealous. Back then, she'd never seriously considered going further. But now?

They were both consenting adults. Both attractive. In fact, she was pretty sure he'd never looked better. She heard he'd recently divorced, and she could see it had worked wonders for him. Like Kenneth, he had the body of someone who trained every morning at 5 a.m. His hair was grey but beautifully cut. And his teeth were no strangers to a whitening procedure. Maybe a bit of Botox in there too. She tried to think who he reminded her of. The actor, Richard Gere. Yep, he definitely had sexy Gere vibes. And she never tired of watching Pretty Woman, *despite the fact that it was around the same age as she was. She loved an old classic – in films, cars and men.*

'I definitely didn't expect to see you here,' he volleyed back, in the same teasing tone she'd used. 'Last time we met…'

'The Dome. Edinburgh. Five years ago. The night before Christmas Eve.' She filled in the blanks so he didn't have to, but the memory made something in her smile soften. That had been a wonderful night. She and Kenneth had gone to Edinburgh so that they could have an anonymous festive night out, just the two of them. He'd told Bernadette he'd be sleeping on the sofa bed in his office, as he occasionally

did, because he had back-to-back surgeries. Complete lie. They'd checked into The Balmoral, spent the whole day shopping in Harvey Nicks and he'd bought her a divine Yves Saint Laurent bag as a gift. She'd dressed top to toe in red, and they'd gone for dinner in the splendour of the Dome restaurant, drunk cocktails, feasted on steaks, and they'd just ordered Irish coffees when Murray and his wife had walked past their table.

Kenneth had immediately jumped to his feet, and shaken Murray's hand, then kissed his wife on each cheek. Lila had met Murray many times over the years, but never with his wife. Now she saw why. The woman was beautiful, but she clearly wasn't impressed by bumping into them, and eyed Lila from her Tiffany earrings down to her Jimmy Choos.

Murray's voice brought her back to the moment. 'Yep, it sure was. I believe that was about two hours before my wife confessed that she'd banged him a few years before that. While we were married, but prior to him meeting you, of course.'

Lila wasn't sure if that last bit was true, but for the purposes of her ego, her equilibrium and the flirtatiousness of the moment, she decided to go with it. He had no reason to lie. Kenneth had never mentioned any kind of fling with Diana Atkins, but then, honesty and full disclosure had never been two of his greatest strengths.

'You know we're divorced now?' he went on, spelling it out in case she had any doubt. That almost made her laugh, given that it had already been pretty firmly established that being married clearly wasn't an obstacle in her attraction to a member of the male species. 'There was no coming back from her confession that night,' Murray added. 'He was one of my closest friends.'

'And yet you forgave him? I do believe you stood up there today and told the world how great he was.' Even for her, the double standard was shocking.

But Murray just shrugged. 'Cutting him off would have been detrimental to my career and so much more. Besides... You can't blame a guy for capitalising on an opportunity.'

Lila actually felt her veneers clench at that one, although, yet again, she admired his honesty. It was the old boys' network in plain sight. This guy was exactly like Kenneth. Ruthless. Blunt. Arrogant. Rich. Successful. And absolutely easy pickings to be played at his own game. He wasn't the only one who could look out for his own best interests. She was an expert in that field too.

He leaned towards her, lowered his voice. 'For what it's worth, Kenneth told me how things ended with you two, and I told him he was crazy not to choose you.'

'You did?' Coy again.

'I did.' He held her gaze, sending a signal that she was receiving loud and clear. He wanted her. And maybe she wanted him too.

Yes, she truly hoped her recently deceased former lover was looking down on her right now. Because if he was, he'd see that she'd just discovered that Kenneth Manson, RIP, could still do something for her after all.

2 P.M. – 4 P.M.

13

BERNADETTE

Bernadette had thought there was absolutely no chance of getting a tea break today, but Caleb had persuaded a couple of the nurses on the late shift to come in early. It helped that there was also a slight lull in the number of admissions, now that the Saturday morning rush was over, the Saturday night madness was yet to start, and the worst of the ice had thawed. Freezing-cold days could go two ways – there would usually be a rise in the number of injuries from falls and road traffic accidents, but that was often balanced by a drop in the general accidents, because people were wrapped up under a blanket on their couch because it was too blooming cold to go out.

Whatever the reasons, she had made it to the cafe and she was sitting across from Stevie with a much-needed mug of soup. What. A. Day.

'Results of Murray Atkins scan in yet?' she'd asked Stevie, as soon as they sat down.

'Nope, but he was furious that we weren't strictly honest about putting him to the front of the queue.' It had been a slightly mendacious plan, but giving him preferential treatment went against every scruple Bernadette possessed. Living with a volatile narcissist for thirty years had taught her a thing or two about handling and defusing them with very subtle manipulation, so that's exactly what she'd done. She knew if she got him round to the X-ray department and stalled him there, then he couldn't leave, because he'd be on his own, and would feel that he could be taken in for X-ray at any second. Bernadette had been very clear on the plan with Stevie – only bring him in from the X-ray waiting area when it was legitimately his turn to be seen, and her friend had wholeheartedly agreed.

'He's an obnoxious git, though,' Stevie went on. 'And he needs a crash course in manners. While he was still waiting, he bollocked my junior radiographer, and then he snapped at George the porter, who absolutely slayed him and told him to get a grip of his attitude. I thought Atkins' head was going to explode, which wouldn't have been great given the reason he's in here. Anyway, the scans are done and everything looks normal, but I'm just waiting for the consultant radiographer on call to check them as a secondary precaution. He'll be in at 4 p.m., so Mr Atkins should have his results and be out by 5 p.m. Not bad service, considering how short-staffed we are and how insanely busy it's been today.'

Bernadette nodded thoughtfully as she held her soup with both hands, grateful for the heat. 'Agreed. I'm not sure he'll see it that way though.'

'Who won't see what a certain way?' Caleb asked as he joined them and put his quinoa salad and bottle of green juice on the table. He was fond of saying his body was a temple and he wasn't wrong.

Bernadette moved her four-finger KitKat out of the way to make room for the banana he was now pulling out of his pocket. 'Our friend Mr Atkins in bay 11.'

'Give me the scoop – what's the deal with him?'

Bernadette shrugged. Today had been exhausting and she didn't want to go into all the details in the valuable twenty minutes of her break. Besides, she hated gossip, and as much as Caleb and Stevie were friends as well as colleagues, her professionalism stopped her from sharing the details or her thoughts, especially in a public place like this. The staff canteen in the hospital had been closed thanks to cutbacks a few years ago, so now the staff shared a cafe with the general public. Thankfully, it was deserted right now, because they were right in the middle of visiting hours, so any family and friends would already be up on the wards.

'All I'll say is that he was a good friend of my ex-husband, so I know that the woman who is with him isn't his wife. I wonder if that has exacerbated his agitation because he's clearly been difficult with everyone today. Although, from what I've heard, he doesn't have the sunniest disposition at the best of times.'

'Honestly Bernie, you're such a dark horse. So do you know his wife? Should we be making an anonymous call?' Caleb was teasing, but just the thought of that scenario made her squirm.

She chose her words carefully. 'I've met her once. Or, actually, twice. But the second time we didn't speak – it was at Kenneth's funeral, and I saw her across the room with Murray.'

She didn't add that she knew Murray's ex-wife, Diana, better. Again, the details of her friendship with Diana would open a whole can of worms that she didn't need to share right now. Not the time or the place. And she didn't want Caleb to splutter his green juice across the table.

There was a huge part of her that was wishing she'd stayed at home today. She could have read a book. Watched an old movie. Or – and this would have been the favoured option had she been given all the facts this morning – gone to the hairdressers with Val and undoubtedly had an absolute whale of a time. Another huge part of her was glad of all this drama, because at least it was a distraction from the fact that she'd checked her phone not long before she left the ward and Jack still hadn't returned her calls or messages. What was going on with him? Was his affection waning just as hers was ramping up to potentially make this a more permanent arrangement?

When they'd met four years ago, she was the first woman he'd had a relationship with after the death of his much-loved wife a few years before. Her divorce was not far in the rear-view mirror, and she'd sworn off men for life, so their romance had been a delightful surprise for them both. Yes, it had always been long distance, but there had always been a vague notion that it wouldn't be that way forever, that one of them would move to be with the other when the time was right. Now that she thought about it though, Jack hadn't mentioned that in a while. Had their relationship fizzled out and she hadn't been perceptive enough to notice? Or was she just worrying herself for nothing and he was waiting for her to be ready to suggest taking the next step to be together?

'What's up, Bernie? You're frowning,' Caleb observed.

'Ah, nothing.' She wasn't going to burden them with her problems, because as she'd pondered earlier, shouldn't she have this stuff figured out by now? 'Right, time to get back,' she announced, changing the subject. 'I don't want to be leaving the others stretched already. And I'd better make sure Murray Atkins hasn't started a riot yet, demanding attention.'

'No worries, Bernie. I'll send the final scan report round just as soon as I've got it,' Stevie promised.

'Ah, thank you – you're a wonderful woman. Caleb, I'll see you back there. Just want to nip to the loo first.'

Bernadette got up from the table and put her soup mug on the tray of dishes in the corner, then left the others to finish their lunches.

After a quick pitstop at the ladies', she ended up getting back to the ED nursing station at exactly the same time as Caleb. She quickly opened the drawer to check her phone again and frowned. Only one missed call, but it was from lovely Marge. Kenneth's former secretary was one of the people she met up with on the anniversary of his funeral every year, and Bernadette just hoped she wasn't calling to cancel, because she always looked forward to seeing her. They'd never been close friends – Kenneth had always kept them apart, for what she later learned were very good reasons – but they'd had some very honest, heartbreaking conversations since he'd passed away, and Bernadette felt Marge was someone she could count on. Hopefully Marge felt the same.

'Okay, let's get cracking here,' Caleb said, focusing on the whiteboard again, catching up with what he'd missed while they were in the canteen. Bernie popped her phone back in the drawer. Two of the other nurses were going off on their break, so she didn't have time to call Marge back right now, but she'd buzz her as soon as her shift was over. If it were anything urgent, she was sure Marge would have left a message or texted.

'Okay, I'll take bays six and fourteen. They've been waiting longest,' Caleb offered, grabbing the respective charts that had been left on the admissions rack by the triage nurse.

'Okay, I'll take...' Bernadette was just checking the times on the board, when a click click click and a loud woman's voice interrupted her focus. Without thinking, she turned to see the cause of the distraction and spotted a visitor to the ward, over at the entrance, having what looked like a very serious conversation with the triage nurse. Bernadette couldn't hear, but she could guess exactly what was going on there and it involved demands to see one of the patients. 'Oh Jesus. Jesus. Jesus.' Bernadette exhaled, suddenly rediscovering the power of verbalising prayers, because only some kind of heavenly intervention was going to sort this one out.

Caleb had stopped what he was doing and was staring at her, perplexed. 'What is it? Don't tell me the drug dealers are back, because I haven't got the legs to chase them today.'

Bernadette shook her head. 'No, son, it's much worse than that.' She popped the charts she was holding back onto the rack, her priorities suddenly changed. 'Caleb, see that woman over there, I need you to stall her, distract her, do whatever you need to do to buy me a couple of minutes.'

'Why do I feel like I'm in an episode of *Grey's Anatomy*? I have always wanted someone to say something like that to me.'

'Well, this is your moment,' Bernadette told him, her gaze never leaving the door, where the woman was still remonstrating with the triage nurse.

Despite his enthusiasm, Caleb needed more information before accepting the task. 'Why, who is she, and is she dangerous?'

There was no way out of this. Bernadette didn't have a clue if there really was a potential problem on the horizon. Perhaps her take on this situation was completely wrong and it was all a harmless misunderstanding. Although going by the furious expression on the woman's face, Bernadette had her doubts. She also had no idea how the woman had got past security and the receptionist outside in the waiting area. But if there was anyone who could do that, Bernadette had absolutely no doubt it would be...

'That,' she said, with a long, slow sigh, 'is Murray Atkins' wife.'

14

MARGE

Marge felt like she was watching a film. An older movie. Set at the dawn of the nineties. There was a couple in the garden holding hands. It had been paused, and now someone must have pressed play again, because suddenly Marge wasn't just watching it, she was the woman in the film. It was her who was sitting in the garden... The little patch of grass at the back of the cottage flat she'd lived in then... It was a sunny day. Ian was holding her hand. As a tear began to run down her cheek, she opened her mouth to speak. 'Ian, I need to tell you something. I'm pregnant.'

It was his confused expression that broke her heart first. He worked with numbers. He had a mathematician's brain. The answer to the calculation was right in front of him and yet he couldn't accept it.

'But how...?'

It wasn't that they hadn't slept together, because after barely a month of dating, they had crossed that barrier a couple of weeks ago and it had been wonderful. Truly. The kind of experience that Marge read about in her favourite Danielle Steel books, where the physical side felt sexy, but every beat of her heart was with him too. Afterwards, they'd both squeezed into her bath, filled it with grapefruit bubble bath she'd bought from the Body Shop with some Christmas vouchers, and drank Asti Spumante from a bottle, passing it between them after each sip. It was so unlike her. So out of character. For a start, she had perfectly good wine glasses in the cupboard. Yet, this was the way Ian made her feel. Like herself, but much more fun. Carefree. That was what he brought out in her.

'So I have a question for you,' he'd begun on that heady day as he handed the bottle back to her.

'Oh, I like questions,' she'd replied. 'I never miss an episode of Mastermind *and I'm a star when I watch* University Challenge.'

That had made him laugh and she loved to see it. She'd never thought of herself as funny. Sensible. Smart. Organised. Strong. Determined. Prim. Those were all the labels that people had given her over the years, and she hadn't disagreed with those assessments. But funny? This was new and she had a hunch that it was because he was the first person she'd truly connected with. And listening to herself when she was with him, there were a few more adjectives to add to the list. Teasing. Provocative. And – oh the absolute shame – giggly. When, in the name of the holy embarrassment, had she ever, in her whole damn life, been giggly?

'Congratulations,' he'd teased her. 'University Challenge *is a pretty impressive level of achievement.'*

'That's what I thought,' she'd quipped, before taking another decadent swig from the bottle. 'So ask me anything. Science. Maths. History. Fire away.'

'What would you say if I told you I was falling in love with you?'

The shock had silenced her for at least a few seconds before she'd found her voice again. 'I'd say they've never asked that on University Challenge.' *A pause. And then – mortified – a giggle. 'And I'd say I liked that very much. Because perhaps I'm falling in love with you too.' It was mad. Crazy. Spontaneous. All the things she wasn't. Yet, she knew it was absolutely true.*

When the water was cold, when the Asti was done, when their skin was like prunes, when they'd both laughed until their cheeks hurt, they had gone back to bed and stayed there until nightfall, eating cheese and fruit off a breadboard when they could no longer ignore the hunger pangs.

That's when she'd realised why the sex had been so wonderful. This wasn't just a meaningless fling, it was a love affair. And now, just two weeks later, she'd crushed him by giving him news that she could see he was still struggling to comprehend. Eventually, the logical side of his brain was forced to assert its authority and spell out the reality.

'You were already pregnant when we met.' His words were steeped in such sadness she couldn't bear it.

'I was. Although I didn't know it, I swear. I only found out today.' A few weeks

before, on the day she'd met him, she'd felt queasy, and put it down to too much champagne the previous night. But over the weeks since then, the nausea had continued to turn her stomach in the mornings, and had then been joined by tender breasts and uncharacteristic weariness, until it had all become impossible to ignore. This morning, she'd done the test alone in the same bathroom they'd drunk wine in on that giddy first day, and it had confirmed her fears. Two blue lines. It had broken her heart. And now she was breaking his.

If he'd got up and walked away, she would have completely understood, but he didn't. Not yet.

'Are you still seeing him? The father?' His question surprised her because she hadn't even considered that he would think she was seeing two men at once. Until now, she hadn't even had a serious relationship, and she'd slept with exactly three men in her whole life: her college boyfriend, the father of the baby and Ian. Hardly the kind of person who could juggle her men.

'No. It was... just one night. A mistake. And obviously before we met. I thought we used a condom. I mean, we did use a condom, but I guess...' Going into more detail wasn't going to exactly cover her in glory, so she stopped. The truth was, she'd been a little too tipsy at a fundraiser for a national hospice organisation. There was a charity auction, then a sumptuous ball, that was attended by what seemed to be the entire medical community. Marge had wondered why they didn't just save the cost of the lavish food and drinks and donate it straight to the charity instead, but she didn't vocalise the thought. Instead, she'd decided to enjoy the glamour of it all. The white wine on the table had flowed and her glass always seemed to be filled to the top, even though she was taking sips all throughout the dinner. By the time the dancing started, she was merry. When it got to the end of the night, it had all been a bit of a blur, but someone she trusted implicitly had taken her home, said lovely things to her and before she knew it he was kissing her and... and... she let him. Maybe even encouraged him. Then he was pulling a condom from his pocket and they were having sex, on her sofa, with the wooden arms digging into her back. She couldn't quite remember what happened next. She'd woken up the next morning, in an awful shroud of fear and loathing, mortified and sore and fully aware that she had been a willing participant, so it was all her fault. The terror and dread had stayed in her gut, consumed her, until the next time she saw him. She'd expected an uncomfortable exchange. Conversations about regret. Embarrassment. Perhaps even disdain. But to her shock and, yes, relief too, he had been perfectly polite and acted like nothing had happened, to the point

where she almost doubted that it had. Unfortunately, this morning, she'd learned otherwise.

'And how do you think he's going to feel about this?'

Marge realised that in the emotional maelstrom of the last few hours, she hadn't given the father's feeling a second thought, too busy processing her own. What she did know was that he'd be appalled. Horrified. This kind of news would cause a scandal that could destroy his reputation, wreck his family and even damage his career. There was no world in which it would be welcome news. This poor baby. What chance did it have with a start like this?

'I don't know, but it's... complicated. He's... he's...' Marge couldn't bear to say the word, but eventually she spat it out. 'Married.'

'Oh, Marge.'

She put her hand up. 'I know. You don't have to say a thing. It was a mistake. One night. Stupid. I'm so sorry, Ian. I truly, truly am. And I already hate myself so if you're going to hate me too, then please leave and do that elsewhere because I'm already heartbroken that I've spoiled what I honestly feel could have been a wonderful future with you.'

Just as she'd asked, he got up and she closed her eyes, unable to watch him walk away from her. She heard his footsteps fade and waited, inhaled, exhaled, before she opened her eyes again. He was still there. He hadn't left. He'd was standing at the end of the garden. Leaning against the oak tree that she sat under when she was reading on a sunny day.

He stayed there for five minutes. Maybe ten. And she didn't move, too scared to break whatever train of thought was going through his mind.

A breeze had picked up by the time he walked back and stood in front of her again. She shielded her eyes from the sun with her hand, as she looked up at him.

'Are you going to keep the baby?'

Marge had given this much thought but she hadn't entirely made up her mind. It was all too new. Too shocking. But she went with her first instinct because it was the truthful one. 'I think so.'

'Okay.'

He walked to the end of the garden again and stood there, staring at the tree as if waiting for inspiration. She'd already learned that he was a man of process. Logic. He liked to amass all relevant information on any subject. He thought things through and analysed them from every angle. Just as she'd never been giggly, he swore that he'd never been the type to act on impulse. He'd already admitted – as had she – that declaring their love for each other so swiftly had been the only spontaneous thing either of them had done in their time on this earth. He saw his need for lengthy deliberations as his biggest flaw, but Marge saw it as his biggest strength.

When he came walking back a few minutes later, she noticed the set of his jaw, the determination in his stride and another wave of nervousness swirled her stomach. It wouldn't have been a surprise if he'd stomped right past her and out of the garden, out of the house, and out of her life.

But he stopped. 'Another question.'

'Yes?'

'Do you think you could... could you... Marge, would you marry me?'

She was shocked into silence once again.

'But the baby?' she managed eventually.

'It's a bit soon to ask it, but I think it'll go along with whatever you decide.' His unexpected humour shattered the wall of fear that had been guarding her heart, bracing it for rejection.

'You see,' he went on. 'What I feel for you has been the most unexpected and incredible thing and I don't even want to consider letting that go. You're the first person I've ever felt this way about and I'd very much like you to be the last. I love you, Marge, and I truly believe I will love your child too. I'm sorry I don't have all the romantic words...'

'Yes...' she blurted.

'I'll definitely work on that...' he said, misunderstanding her agreement.

'No, I mean yes!' It seemed so right, so gloriously apt that this conversation was following the same muddled path as their exchange when he'd asked her out on their first date. Communication on matters of the heart clearly didn't come easily to either of them. But apparently, they were going to have a whole lifetime to work on that. 'Yes, I'll marry you, Ian Drummond. If you'll definitely have me? Have us?'

She had to check that she wasn't imagining or misunderstanding or suffering from some kind of stress-induced delusion.

He answered her by kneeling down beside her and taking her hand. 'I will. For as long as you'll both have me too.'

Marge did the one thing that was as new to her as their love – she giggled. And nodded. And cried. And then giggled again as he kissed her. That morning she'd thought she'd made the biggest mistake of her life, but somehow it had turned into the best day ever. Ian had made that happen. When they went to bed that night, he held her close and...

Marge felt the weight of a head on her shoulder and clenched her eyes to stop the sunlight piercing through again. No, it wasn't the sun. It was the overhead lights again, the ones in the hospital room, and the head on her shoulder belonged to Estelle, who was lying next to her on the bed. She did that sometimes. If there were rules against it, then the nurses were turning a blind eye, because they hadn't complained. Besides, Estelle was here all day, almost every day now, so she'd do herself an injury sitting in that chair for such long periods of time.

Estelle must have felt Marge stirring because she sat up, stretched and then stroked Marge's hair. 'I love you, Mum,' she murmured.

It was such an unexpected gesture that Marge's eyes welled up as she smiled.

Marge's throat barely released her words. 'I love you too, darling.'

'I know,' Estelle said, before shaking off the moment and sliding off the bed. They'd both resolved to have no sadness in this room and her daughter was strong enough to keep to that, switching to a jokey, 'Better move before Jeanie comes back and chases me for crushing her blankets.'

Estelle went to the bedside cabinet and poured them both some water from the jug on the top. That's when Marge noticed the phone and her memory was jogged.

'Did Bernadette call back?'

Estelle handed over the water, then checked the screen. 'No, Mum. No missed calls.' Estelle took a sip, then her brow dipped the way it always did when she was contemplating something. 'Mum, doesn't Bernadette work in this hospital?'

Marge tried to think, but sometimes the memories and details got confused. Yes, Bernadette was a nurse here. At least, when she'd seen her on this date last year, Bernadette was still working here. Although, she could have moved by now, perhaps gone off to live with her new chap. An Irish man, if Marge remembered correctly. Marge hoped he was treating her well, because if there was one thing that Bernadette deserved, it was kindness.

'Mum?' She saw that Estelle was waiting for an answer and realised that her mind had drifted away again.

'Yes, darling?'

Estelle's voice was gentle as she repeated herself. 'Bernadette. That's Kenneth Manson's ex-wife, isn't it? So doesn't she work here? I'm sure I remember you telling me that years ago.'

Marge realised she'd already asked that question. Sometimes it felt like her mind was in fog and didn't know where it had been or where it was supposed to be heading.

'Yes. Or at least, I think so.'

'What department does she work in?'

For a moment, the fog thickened, then cleared again.

'Intensive care.'

No, that wasn't right. Bernadette had mentioned something last year. She'd moved from intensive care back to the Emergency Department.

'No, it's the Emergency Department. That's right.'

Estelle put her water down on the table. 'Why don't I nip down there and see if I can leave a message for her?'

'Yes. Yes, that's a good idea.'

Marge watched her gorgeous Estelle go, thinking that her daughter had no idea that the woman they were trying to track down was a keeper of a secret that could change Estelle's life.

And then she closed her eyes.

15

AMBER

Amber stared at Murray, lying under a thin sheet on the hospital bed. She didn't even think of him as Ray anymore. Ray was the attractive, smart, sexy man she'd been getting to know for the last two months. This guy – Murray fricking Atkins – was an obnoxious, entitled, rude, bad tempered arse that she'd have run a mile from. 'Ray' was dead to her – and staring at Murray now, lying there with his eyes closed, she wondered if he was also deceased, or sleeping, or just feigning a coma to avoid having to talk to her.

If she was being honest, she was fine with at least two out of the three options, because since he'd been wheeled back from the X-ray department, he'd been even more irritable and irritating than before he went. She was seriously questioning why she'd ever seen anything attractive in this man. What was wrong with her? Was her judgement completely skewed after all those years of marriage? Or maybe it had always been that way. She used to think she'd picked a good one with Ewan, but look how that had turned out. Maybe it was time to face it – her decent-bloke radar was in need of some recalibration.

And she still had a very slight concern that her internal lie detector might have been unplugged at the wall too. She thought back to her question earlier.

'Are you married?' When she'd said it, his face had twisted into something resembling disgust.

'How could you ask me that? Is that the kind of man you think I am?'

She tried to remember the lessons she'd learned in a Basic Psychology course she'd taken as an additional module in sixth year at high school, swayed by the fact that the boy she'd had a crush on back then was doing it too. He'd ended up dating someone else and she'd dropped the course to join the gardening club instead. Clearly her man-radar was off then too. But back to the point. When someone answers a question with another question of their own, does that mean they're appalled, deflecting or guilty? She really wished she'd paid more attention to the study material than the cute guy back then.

'No, I'm not married,' he'd answered with such categoric firmness and obvious offence that she felt terrible for asking. He did back-pedal slightly though. 'We've been separated for two years.'

Separated? Something didn't seem right about that, and Amber had flipped back through their conversations, before replying, 'You told me you were divorced.'

'I am. That's what I mean. We split up years ago. We're divorced.'

Amber had wanted to believe him. And, actually, she had to give him the benefit of the doubt, because he did have a suspected concussion and was probably still traumatised after his near-death altercation with SpongeBob. Of course he couldn't be married. That would be ridiculous. Before their first date, she'd briefly googled him, but the information online was sketchy and there had been nothing new for a couple of years. He'd told her that, as a doctor, he kept his personal life off social media to protect his privacy and that had made sense to her. Although, now she was beginning to question everything.

Before she'd been able to delve any deeper, the porter had arrived to sweep him round to X-ray, leaving her alone.

When he'd been wheeled out, she'd leaned her head back against the white wall of the room and closed her eyes. What. A. Shitshow. If this was single life, you could keep it.

She'd felt a familiar mini-wave of fury tighten her chest. Damn Ewan for doing this to them. Damn him for wrecking what she thought was a perfectly happy marriage, just for the sake of a quick shag. And yes, for many months now she'd prided herself on her belief that she was over it, moved on, searched for the positives, found them and made the best of the situation –

but now she just wanted to punch him in the willy and berate him for breaking their family again. And she also wanted to cry. Today seemed to have opened the tap on a whole keg of emotions that she'd been allowing to quietly ferment in the background for months. And yet... all she wanted to do right now was speak to the people who mattered.

She'd pulled her phone out of her pocket and dialled Ewan's number. When he answered, it had taken every ounce of effort she had left to make her voice sound normal and not like she was stressed, upset, on the verge of a full-scale meltdown and more than a little pissed off with her ex-husband, the man she'd slept with this morning and herself.

'Hey, just checking in. All good?'

'Yup,' he'd confirmed, and either he was having a medical episode or his mouth was full because he sounded altered. She'd crossed her fingers for the food, because she'd had enough hospitals for the day. 'Me and the kids are on the couch eating popcorn and watching *Monsters, Inc.* Don't judge me. The old ones are the best.'

She hadn't disagreed. 'Can I say hi to the kids?'

'Of course. Alfie, Sid – that's your mum on the phone.'

They usually checked in with the kids at least once a day when they were with the other parent, so she'd known he wouldn't think there was anything odd in that.

'Mum, we're having a popcorn party. Can you come?'

That came from Sid, and the cracking sound was a chisel taking a piece off her heart.

'Oh honey, you know I'd love to, but this is Daddy's special day when he gets you guys all to himself.'

'S'pose,' Sid had replied, and Amber could picture his face and the disappointed slump of his shoulders. The chisel cracked another piece right off.

She'd chatted to both boys for a couple of minutes before they'd given the phone back to Ewan.

'I'll send some popcorn back over with the boys so you don't feel left out.'

She'd wanted to reply that no amount of popcorn was going to solve that. She felt so left out she could barely breathe. And once again that threw up a whole mix of emotions: love, sadness, regret and fury at him for causing this.

Still she'd managed to keep her voice calm and normal. 'Thank you.'

'Anyway, you having a good day? Are you doing something amazing? I mean, obviously nothing can top *Monsters, Inc.* and popcorn.'

Amber's gaze had scanned the white walls of the room, the space where the bed had been before the porter had wheeled it out, the bag of Murray's clothes that were still lying in the corner because she was afraid if she gave them back to him, he'd flee the scene before he'd been declared fit and healthy...

'Nope, nothing can top *Monsters, Inc.* and popcorn. But yes, I'm having a lovely day, thanks.'

'Well, if you change your mind, Sid's offer still stands. We've got *Cars* lined up next and a space on the couch.'

A space on the couch. As she'd hung up, her only thought had been that she'd have given anything to be there instead of in the middle of this messed-up episode of *Scrubs*.

A while later, when the porter had brought Murray back in, his mood had escalated from irritated to blazing fury because, apparently, they'd kept him waiting for an unacceptable period of time and now he was being asked to wait even longer for the results. Clearly he wasn't used to living in the real world, where things didn't just happen at the snap of his fingers.

That's when he'd checked out of the conversation, closed his eyes, and ignored her.

Glad of the peace, Amber had let the silence stretch until now, when the worry over whether he was actually dead or slipping into a coma over-ruled the worry that she could cause a premature, potentially life threatening bolt for freedom. If someone came through that curtain now with good results and agreed to discharge him, then she was going to be the one making an immediate bolt for freedom, so it was time for full disclosure.

'Murray...' If he thought it strange that she used his full name, he didn't comment, although he did open his eyes, thereby ruling out death and a coma. It was only a mild relief.

'I just want to let you know that the Lidl bag in the corner over there contains your clothes and everything else you left at my house.'

Instant anger. 'Why didn't you tell me that before?'

She went with a more diplomatic answer than the truth that she hadn't trusted him not to flee the scene. 'I'm sorry. I thought I had.'

His look of absolute scorn made it clear how he felt about that reply, and it had two effects. It wiped out the last shred of compassion she had for him, and it nullified the guilt over her untidy shower's part in the fiasco. Something snapped.

'You know what, *Murray*...' Emphasis on his name, because as she'd already decided, the time for cutesy, friendly nicknames was long gone. 'I think we both know that this isn't going to work out. I'm extremely sorry that you slipped in my shower...' She'd watched enough of those corny legal adverts to know that she shouldn't admit any culpability without a lawyer present. '...But I think it's probably best if we say goodbye and I go now.'

Just when he thought she couldn't be more surprised by this man, he blurted, 'But I need you to go and get my car and bring it here.'

Not, 'I'm so sorry, I've acted like a dick.'

Or even, 'Thanks for the quick shag this morning – I hope we can do it again.'

No. Just a barked order, as if she was at his beck and call. Or a valet.

Given that his head injury did qualify him as having an even crappier day than her, she decided to let that one go and choose a calm, classy, dignified exit.

'Unfortunately, my car retrieval service isn't operating today. However, I'll leave you the number of a taxi and your car keys are in that bag. I'm sure you'll work it out.'

Sod the wait for his results. She was done. There was nothing else to say, so she lifted her handbag off the back of the chair, stood up, and was about to duck out of the curtain and make a bid for freedom, when her path was blocked by someone coming in the opposite direction.

Okay, possibly a change of plan. Bernadette, the lovely nurse from earlier was giving off an urgent energy, as if she was here to deliver important news. And she didn't look happy about it. In fact, her expression definitely bordered on concern. Amber's heart sank. Had they found something on the X-ray? Was it worse than they thought? Would surgery be required? Was it terminal? That's it. It must be terminal, because why else would she be looking so worried?

'Murray, can I, erm, have a quick word with you alone?' she said, and Amber felt sick. This wasn't just her usual catastrophising. She was right this time. This was bad. He was going to have long-term injuries, and then he'd remember standing on SpongeBob, and he'd sue her, and she'd have to sell the house to pay the legal bills and settlement, and then her and the kids would have to live in a tent... and the sex hadn't even been that fricking good.

Murray was obviously getting similarly disturbing vibes from the nurse because his eyes widened and there was an unmistakable flinch of concern before he turned to Amber.

'I think you were leaving anyway?'

She wasn't sure if it was an escape route or a challenge, but either way she was taking it. 'Thank you for everything,' she told Bernadette – politeness cost nothing – and was about to walk past her when the curtain flew open and a lady with white-blonde hair, bright red lips, a snatched jaw and possibly the most impressive cheekbones Amber had ever seen, stepped inside what was now way too small a space to be accommodating so many people.

'Murray. Hello, my darling,' she chirped. Amber's catastrophe senses began to tingle again because it wasn't said in the manner of a friendly greeting – more the way a cartoon snake would greet its next victim before it unhinged its jaw and swallowed it whole. And judging by the way that Murray's complexion had drained to the colour of the white/grey bedsheets, he was having the same feeling of impending doom.

The new arrival's gaze then went to Bernadette, and the woman groaned – actually groaned – before rolling her eyes and drawling, 'You have got to be fucking kidding me. You, of all people.' Amber got a definite hunch that there was a dynamic going on here that she knew nothing about and she'd never wished more that she was on a couch watching *Monsters, Inc.*

The nurse didn't reply, but her shoulders moved an inch or so back and her chin raised slightly in what Amber could only describe as a gesture of defiance.

That's when the woman's gaze shifted again and landed squarely on Amber. She felt her toes curl inside the Ugg boots she'd hastily pulled on when she was leaving the house.

The woman's gaze went up and down, taking in Amber's clothes, her hair, and then there was some kind of realisation, followed by a knowing smile.

'Well, isn't this cosy.' The jaw was unhinged again, and Amber felt the fear as the stranger went on. 'And who would you be?'

There was such scorn, such dismissiveness, such lofty entitlement, that she reminded Amber of exactly how Murray had been behaving all afternoon. Who did these people think they were, talking to other human beings like this? Sod that. She wasn't bowing down to this. She wasn't going to crumble. This woman might be standing there looking like she'd just walked off the cover of a magazine, but Amber had two boys under six, so she was well equipped for confrontations and emotional power plays.

'I'm Amber. And who would you be?' She managed to mask her feeling of impending doom and wrap her words in a carefree, friendly tone. Do not show fear. Do not be intimidated.

The woman's lip curled as she spoke.

'Ah. I would be Lila Atkins. And I'm this idiot's wife.'

16

MARGE – SUNDAY 21 FEBRUARY 2021

'Marge, are you sure that you don't mind me leaving? I've been out since 5 a.m. this morning and my boobs are about ready to burst.'

Marge watched as Amber turned her back on the other mourners and tried to discreetly adjust her top. She remembered both the wonders and the aches of breastfeeding, even though it had been decades since she experienced them. Amber's gorgeous little boy, Alfie, was only six months old and she brought him over to the house often, usually with Estelle too. Sometimes, Marge would babysit him to let Estelle and Amber have a couple of hours of adult-only time, but only for as long as Alfie's breastfeeding schedule would allow.

'Of course I don't mind,' Marge assured her. 'I'm so grateful that you came with me. I'm just going to stay for a little while longer anyway and then I'll get off home too.'

In truth, Marge hadn't anticipated being at Kenneth's wake all day, but as one of the people who'd helped Nina and Stuart organise today, she felt a responsibility to wait until the very end and make sure there were no unforeseen issues or problems. As Kenneth's secretary for the last thirty years, it was no less than he would expect. And if she were being honest, now that the bar had been liberally frequented by many of the mourners, she was beginning to fear that a couple of potentially dangerous situations were brewing.

'Okay, well, I'll get off then. If you need anything, just call and I'll come racing back – just as long as you give me time to pump these boobs.'

Marge gave her a distanced hug, so as not to put any more pressure on Amber's chest. 'Thanks again, Amber. And I'll see you next weekend with the little one.'

'Are you sure you're happy to watch him, Marge? He's a handful.'

'Och, I love it. Especially now. Gives me something to look forward to now that everything is up in the air.' Marge knew that Amber understood what she was referring to because they'd spoken about it a couple of times since Kenneth's sudden death just over two weeks ago. Did she really want to keep working or was it time to retire? Her pension had matured a couple of months ago when she turned sixty, and she still had Ian's pension too. The mortgage was long paid off and she lived a fairly frugal life. Did she have the energy or the inclination to start all over again and work for someone new? Right now, she didn't think so, but she was taking time to mull it over. No rash decisions, especially in times of turmoil. That had been Ian's motto and it had never served them wrong. In fact, the only rash decision he'd ever made was the one when he'd asked her to marry him. And that hadn't worked out too badly for them.

But the decision to stop working would mean a complete life shift. Estelle and her boyfriend, Craig, worked hard and had busy lives, so Marge only saw her daughter a couple of times a week at most. And yes, she had friends, but still... What would she do with her time if she retired? She already struggled to fill her weekends. That was why she loved to babysit – it made her feel useful again.

Marge walked Amber over to the door, then hugged her goodbye. Estelle was so lucky to have this friendship in her life. And Amber was too. Sometimes Marge wished she had that kind of bond with another woman, but she'd always worked such long hours that the person she'd most wanted to spend her free time with was Ian. In hindsight, she should probably have made more of an effort to cultivate close friendships, but the casual ones she'd had – occasional lunches, her book club, or dinner parties with other couples – had been enough for her. Or so it had once seemed, but how had that worked out for her? Basically, alone now, with not even her work to keep her fulfilled.

Maybe it was time to grow her circle, step out of her comfort zone and take a new approach to the next chapter of her life. That would be something to think about in the coming weeks and months, but right now, she was still focusing on her final responsibilities as Kenneth Manson's secretary.

As soon as Amber got into the lift, to descend down to hotel reception and exit, Marge went back into the bar area of the function suite, where the wake was still surprisingly busy. The cynic in her head told her that was what happened when there was a free bar, even when the assembled attendees were the great and the good of the city.

Marge took a cup of coffee from the table that was serving hot beverages and carried it over to a free table in the corner of a raised floor area, giving her the perfect vantage point to the rest of the room. If this were a different event, in a different time, for a different occasion, she wondered where Kenneth Manson would be sitting now.

Would he be over at Lord Connolly's table holding court? She doubted it. Kenneth would have chatted to him, affirmed their friendship in front of everyone, taken the plaudits for saving Lord Connolly's grandson's life with his surgical brilliance, but then he'd have moved on, because there was nothing – other than social clout – to be gained there.

Her gaze went to another corner of the room. Maybe he'd be at that table, where her former boss, Sir Lester Kelaney, President of the Scottish Society of Surgeons, was sitting with his wife and an assortment of other influential people in the medical circles. Of course, when Marge had worked for him, he'd just been Professor Kelaney. The knighthood had come later, for services to medicine and, according to Kenneth, had been well deserved. Marge had met his wife a couple of times over the years, and she seemed like a very nice lady. Quiet. Refined. Reserved. From what she could see now, that hadn't changed. Sir Lester appeared to be deep in conversation, while she sat quietly by his side. No, Kenneth probably wouldn't sit there for too long either.

Marge's gaze swiftly moved on to a table near the bar that Kenneth would definitely be avoiding at all costs. Danielle Strang, a former model, was having what could only be described as a very animated conversation with Annabel Stevenson, Member of Scottish Parliament. Marge had spotted them together right before Amber left, and it was one of the situations that was definitely causing her concern. These women were not friends, and they were both the type of ladies who were used to getting what they wanted and altogether unpredictable when they felt scorned or rejected. And the reason that Marge knew that was because Kenneth had once had affairs with them both. Not at the same time, of course. His twisted moral values and social snobbery would have considered that uncouth.

Marge took a sip of her coffee, as her almost computer-like memory identified the correct files. The Danielle Strang affair had been about ten years ago, and it had, at one point, been so intense, Marge had wondered if it would break Kenneth's marriage. She should have known better. Kenneth had never shared details with her – again, that would have been uncouth in his book – but from what she'd pieced together, he'd ended it when Danielle discovered he was still very married. Apparently, it was a small detail he'd omitted. Outraged, she'd given him an ultimatum and there had been no contest. Nothing would have made Kenneth give up the perception of a perfect marriage and a happy family because both were judicious for his career and provided the ideal cover for his dalliances.

The end of his relationship with Annabel had been every bit as contentious and had broken down for the same reason. Marge only knew that because she'd stormed into his office and thrown a pair of thousand-pound Tiffany earrings at him. Kenneth had asked Marge to return them for a refund the next day.

There were a couple of other ladies in the room who'd been on her radar at one point or another. Ones who'd called the office. Left messages. Asked him to return calls. Or he'd blocked evenings off in his diary and asked her to make reservations and then send flowers to their addresses the next morning. If Amber's shop had been open in those days, she'd have made a fortune.

Marge's stare flicked back to Danielle and Annabel's table, when the potential for escalation rose exponentially with a new arrival to join the other two ladies. Diana Atkins. Murray Atkins' former wife. Marge had already noticed that Diana and Murray had avoided each other all day, not unusual for a divorced couple, especially when the split had been notoriously acrimonious. There had been many gossipy tales in the medical offices across the city, citing slashed tyres, shredded suits and threats of litigation.

What the gossipers never knew was the biggest story of all, one that would have kept them talking for months. And the reason they never found out was that Marge was the only other person working late on a Monday night, when Murray Atkins had stormed into Kenneth's office, berated him for sleeping with his wife, and then proceeded to punch him in the face, causing his nose to burst all over the pile of patient records that she'd just left on his desk. Yes, the same Murray Atkins that had just delivered his eulogy. Marge didn't know when or how the two men had later made up – she suspected they'd both realised it was more career-enhancing and socially beneficial to them to be friends as opposed to enemies, but a few months later, she had witnessed them at a gala dinner acting as if absolutely nothing had happened.

The three women at the table suddenly turned their heads in synchronicity, expressions conveying nothing but scorn, and Marge followed their gazes to what had to be the most unlikely, yet strangely unsurprising pair in the room. Murray, of course. But he was standing at a tall table, very obviously leaning in to a conversation with... Marge could barely even allow herself to think that woman's name, let alone say it. She forced it to speed along the ticker tape of her mind. Lila Anderson. Without a doubt the most abhorrent creature Marge had ever had the misfortune to deal with. She was the one that – more than any of the others – had made Marge mistrust Kenneth's judgement and wonder if he'd actually lost his mind. And she'd lasted the longest too. At least seven years. Possibly eight. But she was different from the others in one other very significant way – she one hundred per cent, absolutely, without a doubt, knew that Kenneth was married right from the start of their affair. In fact, Marge was utterly sure that the young woman thrived on that as a challenge. The shocking gall of her to show her face here. The audacity. The shamelessness. Marge would have had her tossed out on her ear the minute she'd spotted her, but she'd been too fearful that it would cause a scene that would distress Kenneth's family and leave everyone here with a scandal to gossip about forevermore. Marge had kept a beady eye on her, ready to intervene if it looked like she was going to pull any kind of attention-seeking stunt, but so far Lila's efforts were concentrated on the man in front of her. There she was, Marge decided, reeling in her next conquest. Marge almost felt sorry for Murray Atkins. Almost. Not quite.

The chair beside her made a noise on the marble floor as it was pulled out, and Marge turned to see that Bernadette was joining her, and her gaze was going in exactly the same direction that Marge's had been focused just a few seconds before.

'Wow. If ever there were two people who deserved each other...' Bernadette sighed. There was no need to add anything further, because they both knew the full story. Kenneth had never facilitated any kind of relationship between Marge and Bernadette – in fact, he'd insisted that Marge only communicate with his wife on logistical matters and only when he asked her to. But there was no way she could operate as his secretary for as long as she did and not strike up an amicable, courteous, mutually respectful relationship with Mrs Kenneth Manson.

'I couldn't agree more,' Marge said, with conviction, noticing that Bernadette had a very slight slur to her words, as if she'd already had a couple of glasses of wine, before the one she was currently holding. If anyone in this room deserved a tipple, Marge knew, it was Bernadette. Marge had no idea whether Bernadette was aware of all the other affairs, but given the way she was now eyeing Murray and Lila, she was clearly familiar with her late-ex-husband's relationship with that particular woman.

'I know we shouldn't speak ill of the dead, but I don't know how you managed

to work with him for so long, Marge.' The wine also seemed to be lowering Bernadette's inhibitions when it came to topics for discussion. Marge had never heard her be derogatory about Kenneth, even during or after their divorce.

Marge really hoped that Bernadette wasn't expecting Marge to explain her reasons, because the answer was too complicated, and definitely not one that she wanted to give to his ex-wife at his wake. Bernadette had already been through enough.

'I know you had respect for him, Marge, but the truth is – and I'm only saying this to you, because you knew him inside and out and I can't keep up another single second of pretence today – he was a terrible person.'

Marge thought about pointing out that he had had his positive attributes too, or maybe that her experience of him was very different from the way he'd treated his wife, but she refrained, because Bernadette was clearly processing what must be incredibly complicated emotions today. Ergo, the wine and the unexpectedly personal chat. And also, Marge knew that Bernadette wasn't entirely wrong. Two things could be true. He was both a great doctor and an awful husband.

'Isn't it staggering to look around this room. It's like a history of his life. A chequered, very revealing one that shows exactly who he was. I mean... How many women in here do you think Kenneth slept with while he was married to me, Marge?'

This time, Marge was so astonished by the question she almost literally bit her tongue as she clamped her mouth shut.

But, of course, the computer side of her brain was already up and running with the calculations as it scanned through the list of women she'd just been perusing and a couple more that she hadn't got to yet.

However, once again, she'd never share that information with Bernadette. Because the truth – the real truth – would break her heart.

4 P.M.–6 P.M.

17

BERNADETTE

Bernadette put two cups of tea on the table, slid one of them over to the young woman in front of her, then pulled out a chair and joined her.

'I think I need something a bit stronger than this,' the other woman said with a sigh.

Bernadette eyed her mug, smiled. 'I think I do too. It's been quite a day.' She realised something. 'I didn't even introduce myself properly, I'm Bernadette.'

The young woman gave her a rueful smile. 'As you heard back there, when I was introducing myself to Murray's wife, I'm Amber. And thank you, Bernadette. For this' – Amber held up her mug – 'and for saving me. You must think I'm a complete tit. Or a terrible person.'

'Definitely neither of those things. But I do think you've had quite the day too.' Bernadette thought that might be the understatement of the year.

When Lila Atkins had pulled that curtain back, she wasn't sure who was more shocked in that room. If Murray Atkins had been in there with heart issues, she'd have been concerned she'd need to wheel in a crash cart.

'Well, isn't this cosy.' Lila had spat, as she'd clapped eyes on Amber. 'And who would you be?'

'I'm Amber. And who would you be?'

'I would be Lila Atkins. And I'm this idiot's wife.'

And then, from what could already have been considered a stunning low point, things had deteriorated even further, when Amber had countered with, 'You mean *ex*-wife?' Her head had then swivelled to Murray. 'You told me you were divorced. So this must be your *ex-wife*?'

That question had clarified exactly what had happened for all of them. As had Murray's shamefaced confusion, his refusal to answer the question, and the deflection that came with his next furious outburst. 'How did you find me? Did you do this, Bernadette? Did you call her? How dare you do that!'

Bernadette had recognised the reaction as one she'd seen countless times throughout her marriage – when backed into a corner, go on the attack.

She'd immediately set him straight with rightful indignation 'Indeed I did not. We take patient confidentiality very seriously in this hospital, Murray.'

He had already turned his aim elsewhere. 'Then what the hell, Lila? Are you having me followed? How could you possibly know I was here?'

Lila had smirked, completely unflustered, almost amused. 'Honey, this isn't my first infidelity rodeo. There's an AirTag in your pocket. It told me you were at some address in Glasgow – which clearly wasn't the private clinic you said you were consulting at today – but by the time I got close, your location had moved to this hospital. It just took me a while to work out what department you were in. I think I've been in every room in the building. I was thrown because I was looking for a doctor, however, you appear to be a patient.'

'I banged my head,' Murray had explained wearily.

Lila hadn't seemed too concerned about the injury, focussing on another aspect of the situation. 'And that made your clothes fall off?'

'They're in the bag in the corner there,' Amber had conceded, nodding to a Lidl bag on the floor. 'I brought them in the ambulance with us.'

To Bernadette's surprise, Lila had laughed. Laughed! Albeit there was an edge of menace in her tone as she'd turned back to what they'd now ascertained was her very current husband, and said, 'Oh honey, you'd better be dying, because if not, there's an exceptionally high chance that I'll kill you.'

'If I don't kill you first,' Amber had added, glaring in his direction.

That had been the point at which Bernadette had felt it necessary to intervene, realising that no good could possibly come of having these three people in a confined space. Besides, she only had one particularly pernicious, debilitating allergy in life, and it was to Lila Atkins.

'Why don't you come with me?' Bernadette had suggested to Amber. 'Murray, your results will be here shortly. I suggest that you wait here until that happens, although you are welcome to get dressed. Mrs Atkins, you can stay with him, but if you'd refrain from killing him, that would be excellent. We're already overloaded and I don't want to add another emergency to the workload.'

With that, she'd opened the curtain, held it for Amber to pass and then led her over to the nursing station, slightly concerned that the woman's face had rapidly paled, and she was now trembling.

'Are you okay?' It was one of those questions that had been caring but unnecessary, because the answer was already clear to see and to hear in the shakiness of Amber's voice.

'I just... I just... No.'

Bernadette had quickly glanced at the clock on the wall and made a split-second decision. It was just after four o'clock. Her shift had finished ten minutes ago. The staff had everything as under control as it ever was on a Saturday and, right now, the person who needed urgent care was the woman who was standing beside her.

Caleb had been over at the whiteboard, but she knew one eye and ear had undoubtedly been on the unfolding drama surrounding Murray Atkins. 'Caleb, I'm finished for the day, so I'm just going to nip over to the cafe, and then I'll be back for my things and to give you a complete... update. Can you take over Mr Atkin's care and the patient in bay 16? That one is just waiting to go to the fracture clinic.'

A rugby player. Three dislocated fingers and a broken wrist. Apparently, a player from the other team was in bay 24 and threatening to charge him with assault.

'No problem, Nurse O'Brien, I'll see to that straight away,' Caleb had responded, with complete professionalism and only Bernadette would have detected the undertone of intrigue in his voice. He'd totally be demanding a full rundown of events later.

'Why don't you come with me and we'll get a cuppa,' she'd said to the trembling woman next to her. 'I bet you've had nothing to eat or drink all day.'

'No, I'd better...' Then a change of heart. 'Actually, yes. Thank you.'

Now that Bernadette had delivered the promised beverage, she could see that a little colour had come back to Amber's cheeks, and she'd stopped shaking.

'I'm so embarrassed. How did I not see that he was married? What gets me,' Amber was saying now, 'is that I had no idea. I just accepted everything he said and walked right into that. How stupid am I? It should have been patently obvious.'

Bernadette tried desperately to take some of the sting out of the whole mess. 'Not stupid. I don't think there's anything wrong with trusting someone until you have a reason not to. And from experience, I can tell you that when someone is having an affair, they can cover their tracks and be very plausible.'

'I think I've just learned that lesson. Actually, I knew that already. My husband had an affair. We're divorced now. Even more reason that I should have been so much more fricking suspicious than I was. You know, I think the fact that Murray is a doctor had something to do with it. Just added an element of trustworthiness somehow.'

Bernadette deliberated how much to say. Since she'd divorced Kenneth, she'd found real power in sharing her experiences with other woman, especially ones she suspected were struggling with their relationships. The support group she'd set up for women leaving destructive or abusive relationships had a constant stream of new attendees, many of them patients she'd met in the ED. She'd never crossed a line by asking them directly about their situation, but she'd carefully left information where they'd have access to it and mentioned that there was available support. Some of them she never saw again. But some would walk through the doors of her support group a week later, a month later, sometimes a year. But that all came from her ability to demonstrate understanding and empathy from shared experiences, so...

'I understand. My ex-husband was a doctor. And a terrible human being. He and Murray were very good friends and the reason I know that woman in there – Murray's wife – is because she was also my ex-husband's mistress. Before she married Murray, obviously. Actually, not "obviously" – nothing would surprise me about Murray or my ex.'

Amber's eyes widened with astonishment. 'Oh. My. God. I'm so sorry. I didn't realise your husband was like that. Murray told me who he was, and I know this is one of those weird twists of fate, but I actually did the flowers for Dr Manson's funeral. When I saw you this morning, I had such a feeling that I knew you and when he told me who you were, it all made sense. Or as much sense as any of this makes.'

Bernadette cast her mind back. 'That's strange because I had exactly the same feeling of recognition, but I couldn't place you.' Bernadette still couldn't make the connection. Five years ago, she hadn't organised the funeral flowers – Nina had taken care of all the arrangements – and there were so many people at the service, the chances of her remembering one face in the crowd was slim, so how would she recognise this lady? 'Did we speak at the funeral?'

'No. Actually, yes. The reason I got the job was through Marge Drummond. I'm a friend... I *was* a friend of her daughter, Estelle. And then... it's a long story, but I ended up coming to the service with Marge, to support her. I saw you there.'

Bernadette was flummoxed. Stunned by the coincidence. 'That's so bizarre. I'm actually meeting Marge tonight. We meet up, with some other friends, on the anniversary of Kenneth's funeral every year. Sorry, I know that sounds very odd.'

Saying that triggered a memory, a missed call from Marge earlier. Bernadette hadn't had a chance to call her back. She'd do it as soon as she made sure Amber was fine and on her way home. Or maybe Amber might want to stick around and come meet up with Marge too? She still looked like she could do with a friendly face and some company.

Amber seemed equally surprised by this. 'So that means today is the anniversary of his funeral? Oh wow. That means it's also the anniversary of the first time I saw Murray bloody Atkins. He gave the eulogy...'

'He did.'

'If I wasn't so utterly mortified over what has happened to me today, I'd definitely be repeating this story at dinner parties. How completely freaky that I've met you again today in this way. It's like that documentary where twins who'd been adopted at birth sat next to each other on a train forty years later. My mum always says that coincidences are just the universe pointing you in the right direction or telling you to pay attention to something. I think I just got the message loud and clear. Don't be a tit when it comes to men. Although, at least the universe also sent you to make me feel better.'

'That's kind of you to say. Crazy thing is, I wasn't even supposed to be on shift today. I'm glad I was, though.'

'I am too.' Amber put her half-empty mug back down on the table. 'Well, I'd better be going – I've taken up enough of your time. Thank you, Bernadette. I can't tell you how grateful I am to have talked to you. I don't feel quite so high up the idiotic scale now. Maybe somewhere between "clueless" and "stupidly naïve".'

'Glad to hear it. Listen, I wondered...' Bernadette was about to follow through on her thought of inviting Amber to meet up with Marge later when she noticed that Amber's attention had gone elsewhere, her gaze lifting over Bernadette's head towards the door, her eyes widening in what looked like shock. Maybe horror. Bernadette spun her head round, ready to tackle Lila Atkins to the ground if necessary. Or maybe it was Murray, back to berate Amber a bit more. She mentally strapped on her bulletproof bra for the second time today and got ready to intervene. But no. It wasn't Lila. Or Murray. It was a tall, very pretty young woman, who was walking towards them, staring at Amber and mirroring her shocked expression.

Bernadette had no idea what the hell was going on. And Amber's next words didn't help.

'Oh bugger, Bernadette. I think the universe just sent me another message.'

18

MARGE

'How are you doing there, Marge?'

The voice woke her again, and as soon as she saw who it was, she smiled.

Keli was the other charge nurse on the ward. Nurse Yvie had already popped in before Marge fell asleep and said she'd soon be clocking off and would see her tomorrow morning. If Keli had come on shift now, that must mean it was around four o'clock.

'I'm doing great, Keli,' Marge replied, her words a shallow croak again. This blasted throat – every time she woke up it was just as dry as before.

'Let me get you a drink, Marge. Do you need anything else?'

Her health. If she could have one thing right now, one wish, it would be to have her health back. Or maybe just to rewind the days and do them over again, this time not wasting a single moment, especially on things that didn't matter. How much time had she spent worrying about things that didn't happen? Or fretting over something that she couldn't even remember a week or a month later? How much time had she spent at work, making sure someone else's life was as smooth and organised as it could possibly be, at the expense of her own? Not that she'd grudged the time she spent on her career. It had been fulfilling. She'd taken pride in it and she hoped that she'd made a difference, in the background somewhere, whether it was rearranging Kenneth's schedule to fit in an extra surgery that could save someone's life, or going above and beyond to help a patient's family deal with the trauma of a sick loved one. That had mattered to her and she'd been privileged to do it. She saw that same vocation in Yvie, Jeanie, Keli and the rest of the staff here too.

'No, nothing else. Just juice, please.'

There was a familiar clicking sound as Keli went round to the other side of the bed, thanks to the tiny beads at the ends of the braids she wore pulled back into a ponytail. Marge had actually met Keli's brother once or twice over the years too. Noah Clark was a consultant paediatrician down on the children's ward, and he'd consulted with Kenneth on a couple of children's cases on Kenneth's very occasional NHS service too. When Marge had first started working for Kenneth, he'd focused almost exclusively on private patients, but over the years, he'd taken on a few specific NHS cases that interested him, either because they were particularly challenging or because the patient had a high profile or a well-connected relative who called in a favour. Selective lifesaving. How could that kind of power not affect a person?

There were two jugs on Marge's bedside chest – one with water and one with orange squash. Keli poured some juice into plastic tumbler and handed it over to her, then waited, ready to help, as Marge managed to raise it her mouth to take a few sips.

'Thank you.' Marge said, giving the tumbler back.

'You're very welcome. Do you need anything else? Are you in any pain?'

Marge shook her head and Keli gently patted her hand. 'Okay, that's good. Let me just have a quick check of everything else then.'

It was a familiar routine – the blood oxygen monitor on the finger, and the temperature check first. Then the blood pressure cuff on her arm and the squeezing sensation, then the beep that seemed to take longer to reach as her arms got thinner. Or maybe it was just that time was passing slower.

After every task, Keli wrote on her chart, until everything was complete and she hung it back on the end of the bed. 'Right then, Marge, that's you for another four hours of blissful peace until I come and do that all over again.'

'Thank you.' Marge meant it. She was so grateful for their care.

She expected Keli to leave, but instead, the nurse sat down next to her bed. 'I just got word that a bed has opened up down in palliative care, Marge, so we can move you down there tomorrow. It's a bright, sunny room, and Liv, the ward manager down there, is a wonderful nurse. She'll take such good care of you, I promise.'

As she nodded, Marge tried to take calming breaths, desperate to stay strong and not put this lovely nurse in the stressful position of having to console a sick patient who was fighting against her fate. There was no point in weeping and even silent tears had caused her throat to ache more since the intubation. Besides, she'd known this was coming, so it wasn't a surprise. They'd discussed it many times over the last couple of weeks and the plan had always been to move her there when a bed became available.

'They'll give you the very best quality of life and Estelle will get the proper support down there too, Marge. They might even be able to get you home, if that's what you want.'

Marge managed a very gentle shake of her head. No. She didn't want to go home. She'd lived alone since Ian died, and if she were to go back there now, it would put all of the pressure on Estelle. That wasn't what she wanted. She had no desire to burden her daughter with that kind of responsibility. At least here, Estelle had a professional support system outside the door twenty-four hours a day. Palliative care was Marge's choice, and maybe a hospice when the time came.

'Okay, Marge, I understand,' Keli said softly, and Marge felt the gentle rub of the nurse's thumb against the back of her hand and gave a silent thanks once again for her kindness. 'Dinner will be here shortly and then I'll check back in on you, but if you need me, you know to just buzz.'

'Thank you.' An audible one this time, as Keli left to the sound of hair bead clicks and soft shoes on the floor.

Alone. It was so rare, that Marge felt such a peace from the silence, but it didn't last for long. Maybe seconds later, maybe minutes, the calm was shattered with the sound of screams. Her screams.

'Marge, I'm right here. Just tell me what to do. Tell me how I can help.' But, of course, he couldn't.

'Just you stay exactly where you are and keep rubbing her shoulders,' Marge heard the nurse say, just as another contraction gripped her.

They'd been at home, sound asleep when the contractions had started, a week earlier than expected. Of course, though, her hospital bag was ready, as it had been for the last two months, fully stocked, checked and double-checked, according to the list that had been provided by their prenatal nurse at one of the classes that they'd attended religiously. 'This is going to be the most organised baby that ever entered this world,' Marge would joke, as Ian would come home with yet another baby book from the library, or she would speak to a medical professional in that field, and take down copious notes to be compiled and studied later.

The subject of the child's father had been something they'd deliberated in the first days of their engagement, when they'd analysed different courses of action and settled on the one they felt to be the most morally sound. They'd contemplated the options for a couple more days, sat with their decision, and concluded that their chosen course of action was the best for all concerned. The child's father had to be told. It was the only way, because how could they ever admit later that they had deprived the child of the chance to be loved just because it was an uncomfortable situation? No, there should be no secrets.

Over the next few days, they'd sat at the kitchen table and written draft after draft of a letter, until they were both satisfied that it conveyed everything that needed to be said.

The finished missive read...

I need to inform you that I am pregnant – something that will become very clear over the next few months. I've thought about many ways to broach this with you, but I'm afraid there was no way to do it that wouldn't involve distressing exchanges and possibly words said that couldn't later be retracted. Therefore, I wanted to put everything down on paper, to ensure that it is clear and there can be no misunderstandings.

The child is yours and will be born in October, all being well. I have decided to keep it, and I am not open to discussion on this point. However, I do recognise that this is my decision alone, and you must also have free choice in this matter.

I shall leave it up to you to decide if you wish to be a part of this child's life, and if so, what role you would like to play. I would welcome your participation in the baby's life, but I want to be clear that I will honour your decision either way. Furthermore, should you choose not to be a part of the child's life, I will neither expect nor demand any contribution from you, financially or in any other capacity. In short, you can choose to parent this child, or never acknowledge that this child is yours.

If the latter is your choice, then I will fully accept it. All I ask is that we never discuss it again, and that you destroy this letter. Since the night of the child's conception, we have moved on, never discussing it, and acting in a professional and cordial manner. I request that same courtesy is extended in the future.

She'd thought of a couple of ways to deliver it but discounted them both. Posting it carried risks that it could go missing or be opened by someone else. If she had it delivered by courier, and got no response, she'd never be positive that he'd received it and there might always be an element of doubt. In the end, she'd put the message in the letter to the test, by delivering it to him personally, putting it in his hands so that she would always know that he was fully aware of her situation.

'What's this?' he'd asked, nothing but curiosity in his expression.

'A choice,' Marge had answered. 'And please take the words on board, as I mean every one of them.'

That was how she'd left it. Ball in his court.

Another scream and this time the midwife reacted with a hint of calm, professional urgency. 'Okay, Marge, this is it. On the next contraction, I want you to push, okay? A deep breath, then press down as hard as you can.'

Always someone who followed the rules to the letter, that was exactly what Marge did. And then, at the instruction of the midwife, she repeated it on the next contraction too. And that was when the sensation changed, as did her world, because Estelle came quietly, with only a gentle cry to alert them to her arrival.

Marge's first feeling was an overwhelming, gushing sensation of love.

Her second was sadness that the baby's father would never feel that same adoration for his child. Because from the moment she'd given him the letter, he'd acted like it had never existed. No conversation. No reply. No acknowledgement of any kind. Instead, he'd carried on as if, like their encounter, it had never happened. She supposed she should take heart in the fact that he'd abided by at least one of her requests. It was the least he could do. The very least.

And perhaps it was for the best, because she watched, as the midwife handed her swaddled child over to the man that she had married just six months before, in a simple ceremony at the registry office, witnessed by strangers, but sealed by the kind of love and commitment that Marge knew would last their lifetimes. A man who was twice the person that Estelle's biological father would ever be.

'Oh, Marge, she's perfect.' Ian whispered, before handing her over. 'Here you go, my darling. Here's our daughter.'

19

AMBER

Amber was still pretty sure that her heart rate hadn't returned to normal since she'd looked up from her mug of mistress-discovery-consolation-tea and seen Estelle Drummond standing there.

I mean... There was probably more chance of winning the lottery than being in the same place at the same time as the one person in this city that she made it her life's mission to avoid. Actually, Murray Atkins and his wife were definitely on that list now too, but that wasn't the point.

At first, she'd hoped that Estelle hadn't spotted her, but that optimism had been kicked out of the cafe when Estelle had walked straight towards her.

'Amber?'

'Hey, Estelle.' A completely inadequate and inappropriate response to seeing your former best friend for the first time in two years, after you'd stopped speaking to her, blocked her and completely cut her out of your life.

Which, now that Amber heard herself pondering that, did sound a smidgeon extreme. In her defence, what Estelle had done had hurt her almost as much as Ewan's betrayal. If Amber were honest, maybe more. Back in college they had matching mugs that said, 'A boyfriend is for high shelves and luggage – a best friend is for life.' Amber had believed at least the second part.

There had then followed a pause so pregnant it could have shot out triplets, before Estelle shocked her again, by turning her attention to Amber's tea companion.

'Hi. Are you Bernadette? I'm so sorry to bother you, but I'm Marge Drummond's daughter.'

'I guessed that. I always loved your name. And Amber here was just telling me how she and you were friends. It's such a small world,' Bernadette had said, with a warm smile that Amber thought must come naturally to her. She'd make a great therapist, because she had the kind of aura that made you want to talk to her, to tell her your problems, and a reassuring way that could make you believe that everything was fixable and it would all work out fine. Although, Amber wasn't entirely convinced that was true at that moment.

'Yes, I suppose it is,' Estelle had replied, in a tone that suggested this wasn't a good thing, before going on, 'One of your colleagues told me I'd find you here when I explained why I was looking for you. It's just, my mum...'

Despite her disappointment and her pent-up resentment towards her former friend, Amber had felt a massive jolt of compassion when Estelle's eyes had suddenly welled with tears. Estelle wasn't a crier. She was calm. Stoic. They'd always joked that by the time she'd spent ages thinking things through, she'd already got over it.

'My mum is upstairs on the elderly ward. She's not been well. And she asked me to find you.' Two tears had begun falling down Estelle's face and Bernadette had immediately jumped up and hugged her, beating Amber to it by a split second.

When Bernadette had finally released her, she'd beckoned Estelle to sit with them, but Estelle had immediately looked to Amber questioningly, as if checking that would be ok.

'Please. Join us,' Amber had reiterated.

Estelle had pulled out a chair and sat down. 'I'm sorry. I don't usually make a habit of crying in cafes.'

Therapist Bernadette had immediately put her at ease. 'That's okay. This cafe has seen more tears than you could ever imagine. Tell me what's happened to Marge.'

Amber's heart was thudding out of her chest at that point. She'd always adored Estelle's mum, and it had weighed heavy on her conscience that when they'd fallen out, her relationship with Marge had been a victim of that. Now she wished more than anything that it hadn't, but she'd been in such a dark place, losing Ewan, losing Estelle, dealing with two small children and running a business while being so heartbroken that she could barely remind herself how to breathe when she woke up in the mornings.

'Mum has lung cancer. Stage four. They're moving her to palliative care as soon as a bed becomes free.'

Bernadette's words had oozed sympathy. 'Oh, love, I had no idea. I'm so sorry.'

Amber couldn't get words out past the boulder in her throat, but she'd stretched over and taken Estelle's hand. Fuck their fallout. She could go back to being mad about that later.

'She's been up on the ward for the last month...'

Bernadette had gasped. 'Oh my goodness, I wish I'd known. I could have come up to see her...'

'I don't think she told many people. Mum always liked to keep things private. Close to her chest. It's just the way she's always been, and even more so since my dad died. They pretty much just lived for each other and me.'

Amber had remembered a conversation at the funeral – Marge saying how she looked forward to seeing Alfie. And after Sid had been born the year after that, Marge had been delighted. The memory had made Amber feel even worse as it had sunk in that she'd deprived that poor woman of joy in what, from what Estelle was saying, were the last years of her life. She'd thought nothing could make her feel smaller than the events of this afternoon, but she'd realised she was wrong – this was as small as it got.

'I always wondered about that,' Bernadette had said. 'Your mum was my husband's secretary, as you know, and he kept his professional and personal life very separate, so even though I've known your mum for decades, I didn't really get to have any kind of relationship with her until after he died. I'm sorry I haven't been there for you both through this.'

'Please don't apologise. I know you weren't close friends, but today, for some reason, she became very agitated and insistent about speaking to you.'

'Because we were supposed to meet tonight. That's probably why.'

'Ah, that makes sense. She hadn't told me that. The cancer has spread now, and it makes her confused. Sometimes I think she isn't with us anymore, and then other times she's just as she always was. It's heartbreaking to watch, because she was always so strong.'

Amber had stayed silent through the whole exchange, taking it all in, careful not to get in the way of what Estelle needed to say to Bernadette.

'I'm so sorry, Estelle,' she'd said, squeezing her hand. Inadequate, but heartfelt.

'Listen, now that I know where Marge is,' Bernadette had said, 'why don't I go up and see her, and leave you here to have a break and a cup of tea. My shift is finished for the day and I wasn't doing anything until I met up with your mum and our other friends later anyway. I'd love to go up and sit with her for a while.'

Amber had already realised that in Bernadette's world, tea and conversation were medicinal and used liberally.

Estelle's eyes had met Amber's, as if asking a question for the second time, and Amber had nodded again, before Estelle agreed with Bernadette's suggestion.

'That would be kind of you, thank you.'

Bernadette didn't need to be told twice. As she got up, she'd said, 'Amber, it was lovely to meet you – even considering…' They both knew what she meant. 'I hope we'll meet again. I'm always here with a cuppa if you need anything.'

'Thank you. I'll take you up on that. The cuppa, that is.'

That was all Bernadette had needed to hear before she went rushing off to provide chat and sympathy to someone else who needed her. Amber didn't think she'd ever met anyone like her.

'I want to take her home with me,' she'd said to Estelle, who had apparently reached the same conclusion.

'Me too.'

And that was as far as they'd got before the awkwardness had descended. Amber had broken it by going up to the counter and buying two coffees, but now that she was back at the table, it returned with a vengeance.

Estelle was the first to break the silence. 'I just realised I didn't ask why you're here? Are you okay? Are the boys okay?'

Amber nodded. 'Yes, yes, we're all fine. I came with… a friend who had a fall, but it's all ok. I was actually just about to go home.'

Another silence.

'I'm sorry about Marge,' she said again, in another desperate measure to break the ice. She'd never been great with silence. 'And I'm sorry I didn't know.'

'Why would you? It's been two years,' Estelle said, and there was just enough of a challenge in her voice for Amber to realise that the only way through the strain of the conversation was to face it head on. Still, she wasn't going to confront someone who was already having a terrible time, so said nothing. It was Estelle who picked the scab first. 'Amber, I don't know how many times I need to apologise to you about what I did before you'll accept it.'

Amber shrugged sadly. She didn't have an answer to that either.

'All I can say,' Estelle pushed on, 'is that I truly thought I was doing the right thing.'

'And that's what I'll never understand. How could you think that? How could you possibly think that hiding my husband's affair from me was a great move for a pal?'

'Because it was over,' Estelle argued.

'And what difference does that make?' Amber said, so loudly that two elderly ladies at the only other occupied table in the cafe both visibly leaned in their direction to try to hear what was going on. This would give them something to talk about over their strawberry tarts.

Amber took a breath, trying to get her heart rate down again. This was the crux of the issue – one that they would never agree on. Scenes from that awful time played on fast forward in her mind. Sid was still a toddler, Alfie was in nursery, so Amber hadn't yet glimpsed the light of normality or free time at the end of the long tunnel of all-consuming pre-school motherhood. And yes, if she were honest, her marriage had slipped to the bottom of the priority pile, below the boys, and running her business, and paying bills, and snatched hours of sleep. Ewan had his own challenges too. He'd gone into partnership with Estelle's boyfriend, Craig, only a couple of years before that, and they'd built a joinery business that now had several projects on the go, a growing customer base and the wages of twelve full-time staff to cover. Maybe she should have checked on him more, understood the pressure he was under too, but that said, she was never going to allow herself to take the blame for Ewan's choices.

It was the distance she'd noticed first. His preoccupation over a few weeks in December, that felt out of sorts, but that she'd put down to the Christmas chaos, her longer than usual hours in the shop, his long shifts at work too, and the strain to cover the cost of that year's visit from the festive fairies. And yet, even when they managed it, when it got to Christmas Day, he was still off. Still acting strange. Nothing she could put her finger on, just a feeling. But she'd been too exhausted, too worn out, too busy playing the thirty-fifth game of Buckaroo, so she'd ignored it. Until she couldn't.

The way she'd found out was such a cliché. A text. On Christmas night. From *her*. He'd left the phone on the arm of the sofa while he carried a sleeping Alfie up to bed and it had buzzed. She didn't even need to open it because the message was right there, on the screen.

> I miss you. Our night was incredible. Please change your mind. Can you come over?

No, he fucking couldn't come over because he was with his wife and his sleeping children. By the time he came downstairs, she'd opened the phone and read it all. He hadn't been clever enough to change his password and the messages were still in the deleted folder. And then it had all come out. Yet another cliché, really. The joiner sleeps with the attractive, rich, bored housewife who'd employed him to instal a beauty room in her basement. The thought of it still made Amber want to retch.

The flirtation had lasted all of November and December, until he'd finally slept with her a couple of weeks before, on the night of their company Christmas party. The one that Amber had missed because Sid was running a temperature, and she didn't want to leave him. Ewan swore that he'd ended it the next day. Realised what he'd done. Hated himself. But not as much as Amber hated him at that moment.

The next thing Amber remembered was running. Then Estelle opening the door. She didn't even step inside. She'd blurted it out right there, on the step, in the rain, hair sticking to her and wearing slippers shaped like Christmas puddings.

'Ewan is having an affair.'

If she had expected shock and horror, she didn't get it. Instead, in her best friend's face, there was nothing but sadness.

And that's when Amber had realised... 'You knew.' It wasn't a question.

'Craig told me. I'm so sorry, Amber. Come in and—'

Amber hadn't moved. 'When did you know?'

'Please, Amber...' Estelle had dodged the question.

'WHEN DID YOU KNOW?'

'A couple of weeks ago. When it happened. But Craig said it was over. It was a mistake, Amber...'

'YOU FUCKING THINK??????' Amber had yelled, but the wind and rain had taken most of the volume from her words. 'How could you hide this from me? How could you take his side?'

Estelle was upset now too. 'Amber, I didn't. Please, come in. Please. Let's talk...'

Amber had already taken a step backwards, horrified, devastated, the heart that had been broken by her husband, now ripped out by her best friend. 'No. Not ever.'

That's when she'd turned around and walked home. Through the rain. Ignoring the wind. The Christmas puddings sodden and falling off her feet by the time she got there.

And she'd never spoken to her best friend again.

Until now.

She was still waiting for Estelle to answer her question. *'And what difference does that make?'* Even if Ewan's affair was over, her best friend should have told her about it. Amber couldn't understand why Estelle didn't see that.

Eventually Estelle spoke. 'I thought it could just be like it never happened. I didn't want you to hurt. I didn't want it to wreck your family. And I knew if you did find out, then that's what would happen.'

Neither of them had to point out that she was right, at least on that count. But Amber would never apologise for leaving him. This wasn't on her. It was on her husband.

'Tell me something – would you do the same thing again?' Amber asked her now.

Estelle thought about that for a few moments, before slowly nodding. 'I don't want to lie to you, Amber. But I would.'

There it was. The reason they could never be friends again. Because how could she trust the person who was always supposed to be on her side when that was her answer?

'Okay. Then at least I know.' Amber felt nothing but sorrow as she stood up. 'I'm so sorry about your mum, Estelle. Please tell her I send my love. And if it's okay with you I'll come by and see her tomorrow.'

'Of course. She'd like that very much, but, Amber, don't go. Please. Let me explain.'

That was the last thing Amber heard as she walked away.

20

BERNADETTE – SUNDAY 21 FEBRUARY 2021

Bernadette took a sip of water and reflected that stopping drinking an hour ago had been an extremely smart, but possibly a tad overdue, decision. What had she been thinking saying such a thing to Marge? It was one of those comments that was fuelled by the combination of an empty stomach and a glass too much of the white wine that had been circling the room all day.

'Isn't it staggering to look around this room?' she'd wittered. 'It's like a history of his life. A chequered, very revealing one that shows exactly who he was. I mean... How many women in here do you think Kenneth slept with while he was married to me, Marge?'

Holy mother of God, the poor woman had turned bright pink and almost combusted from the shock of it.

And Marge, of all people. Bernadette doubted that Marge had ever had a discussion about sex with another human being. She was utterly wonderful, and Bernadette had no doubt she didn't suffer fools, but she was also very formal and extremely reserved and proper. There was no way Marge would pop over to Val's on a Thursday night to lie on the couch, kick off their shoes, eat sausage rolls dipped in tomato sauce and make borderline inappropriate comments about what they would do if they were ever stuck in a lift with Ollie Chiles, that bloke on The Clansman.

Or, if she did, Bernadette had a hunch that Marge's answer would involve something like discussing the history of Scottish rebellions in the sixteenth century.

Bernadette wanted to put her head in her hands when she replayed Marge's response to her inappropriate question about her former husband's infidelities. Marge had spluttered, then grasped for an answer, instead of just killing the question with denials. She was too honest for that, God love her.

She'd finally settled on, 'He was a complicated man, Bernadette,' and both the truth and the sadness in her words had pierced a hole in Bernadette's alcohol-sodden heart. But not enough to make her stop talking, apparently.

'I always wondered if you knew what he was like. I wonder if all the people here knew what he was really like. Actually, I don't think they'd care. What mattered to them was his brilliance, his charm, the way the sun shone directly from his arse.'

There must have been one tiny modicum of sense that hadn't yet taken a dive into her pool of Chablis, because something in her mind had demanded, Stop fecking talking, Bernie. Just stop. Finito. Done. Enough. And put that wine glass down while you're at it.

However, the rest of her inhibitions were apparently still doing the backstroke in the vino.

'He was brilliant, yes,' she'd gone on. 'But he was also cold. Cruel. A terrible husband. An awful father to Stuart. He even managed to piss off Nina, and I think she was possibly the only person in the world that he truly loved. You know, I deliberately stopped at two because I didn't want to bring another child into his world. I don't know if I've ever told anyone that.'

Poor Marge had looked as if she were about to keel over. But then, shouldn't two grown women be able to have honest, frank, even controversial discussions? Bernadette had them every day at work and she had yet to have an open dialogue that didn't at least give insight into a difficult situation. And watching the great and good of Scotland celebrate Kenneth was definitely, for Bernadette, a difficult situation.

'Did you love him, Marge?'

Her internal voice had piped back up. Oh, feck stop! Quit the open dialogue nonsense. The poor woman is now choking on her tea.

'I mean platonically, of course. Only, I always thought you must, because you stayed with him for all those years. There must have been other jobs. Better bosses. Promotions. And yet you stuck with Kenneth.'

Bernadette was desperately trying to soften the outrageously personal question, and that's when she had taken the decision to lay off the wine and switch to water. Isla, the lovely waitress who'd been serving them, passed at that point and she'd asked for a glass of tap water, while Marge had requested another tea.

Marge had taken advantage of the interruption to recover from choking, and had come back with a calm, reasoned reply.

'I'm someone who values security and stability. I'm not a risk taker. To answer your question, no, I didn't love him. I respected his work. Admired his intelligence. I'm so sorry to say that I was very aware of his faults, and perhaps that should have been enough to make me leave, but he was always unfailingly professional with me and treated me well. He had a temper, and could be demanding, but I think, in many ways, I had that "better the devil you know" mentality.'

'I can understand that. And for what it's worth, I know how much he valued you. I think you were the most constant person in his life in the end. By that time, I was gone. Nina barely saw him because he'd never approved of Gerry. He had no time for Stuart. All that was left was you, Marge. Oh, and Lila over there, but she soon got bumped off too. I never saw that coming. I thought she'd have been the trophy wife he always felt he deserved.'

Marge had followed Bernadette's eyeline, to the other side of the room, where Lila Anderson was apparently reeling Murray Atkins into her Venus flytrap. Or perhaps it was the other way round. Bernadette wouldn't trust either of them as far as she could kick them. Although, she had to admire Lila's gall in showing up here today. That took a special level of entitlement and audacity that Bernadette couldn't even imagine possessing. Nor did she want to. She wondered if she should feel resentment, anger, disgust at Lila's presence, but actually she felt nothing at all. Complete indifference. If anything, Lila had done her a favour that day she'd turned up on the doorstep and revealed the affair, because it had booted Kenneth right off any arrogant high ground that his narcissistic brain could have manufactured to stop Bernadette leaving him.

When the two women had turned back to face each other, Bernadette could tell that Marge had known exactly who Lila was and what she'd been to Kenneth. Their affair had lasted longer than some marriages. Marge's next words had confirmed it.

'Yes, I've had the displeasure of meeting Miss Anderson and I won't lie to you by minimising their relationship, but to my mind, Kenneth was never serious about any of his dalliances. He certainly gave no indication that he wanted to make any of them permanent. I know you might not believe this, Bernadette, and I don't want

to say anything that will upset you, but he was never the same after you left him. It was like a form of grief.'

That wasn't a surprise to her. 'I do know that. It was a shock to me, but from the time I left him, right up until he died, he was trying to get me to go back to him. At first, I thought it was some kind of game for him, because, God knows, he had no true understanding of love. Then I studied more, started up a support group where I saw similar stories, spoke to many people far smarter than me, and I learned what I still believe to be the explanation. It was his narcissism. He couldn't bear that I had left him. His ego couldn't bear it. And I think he misinterpreted that as love and loss. Jesus, Marge, this might be the deepest conversation I've ever had at a funeral. I'm sorry. I've been talking your ear off. I think a dam broke after I'd been forced to be polite, and listen to how wonderful he was all day.'

'I understand, Bernadette. And this might be the longest conversation that I've had in a long time. I've always been somewhat of a loner, especially since Ian died...'

'Oh, Marge, I'm sorry. I've been so busy talking about myself that I didn't even ask how you were. It's the wine, I swear.'

Marge had protested instantly. 'No, no, please don't apologise. It's been nine years now and I've become quite used to it. And I have Estelle...'

'I've loved that name since the day Kenneth told me that's what your daughter was called. I think she was born just a few years after Nina...'

Marge had nodded. 'Yes, that's right...' Then went back to her original point. 'But what I meant to say was that I've enjoyed speaking to you, Bernadette, and I hope we can stay in touch. I think perhaps we have more to talk about. More we could share. I would welcome that.'

Bernadette prided herself on her perception, even after several glasses of wine, and she'd recognised Marge's body language and tiny steps towards her. She saw it on people in the ED who badly needed someone to talk to, but didn't have the strength to speak up. People who were lonely and craved connection, yet didn't know how to reach out.

'I would like that, Marge.'

'Mum!' A stage whisper from Nina, who was standing just a few feet away clutching her phone to her ear, had interrupted them and Bernadette saw Nina beckoning her over.

'I'll be right back, Marge.' Something had occurred to her. 'You know, you never answered my question earlier. About the other women.'

'No, I didn't. Bernadette, I'm so sorry...'

That was as far as Marge had got, because at that moment, over at a table near the bar, Sir Lester Kelaney's wife dropped a wine glass, which smashed, scattering shards and Chablis across the marble floor.

The sound of it had chilled Bernadette to the core. How many times had Kenneth smashed something – a whisky tumbler, a photo frame, a plate – to make a point while he was in a rage?

Marge had jumped out of her seat, and immediately headed over to implement a crisis-management protocol, leaving Bernadette frozen to the spot.

If she'd dropped a glass at a function, in front of his peers, Kenneth would have been insane with fury, but he would keep a lid on it while they were in public, and then verbally torture her the minute they were alone. The abuse would last for days, sometimes weeks, until Bernadette was almost broken with the exhaustion of it. And still she'd stayed. It struck her that she probably had no right to question Marge's choice to work for Kenneth for all those years, when Bernadette had stayed for decades too.

While Marge had gone to organise the clear-up, Bernadette had made her way over to Nina, who'd got off her phone just as Bernadette reached her and immediately rushed into an explanation of why she'd summoned her.

'Mum, that was the babysitter – Milo just threw up everywhere and she thinks he might have a slight fever.'

If Bernadette's switch to water hadn't already cleared her head, that would have done the trick.

'You go on home, love.'

'But I can't! How can I leave my dad's wake before it's over? I'm supposed to be the one in charge here. What if something goes wrong?'

'Don't worry, Stuart is here...' As she'd said it, she'd spotted that Stuart was making his way to them, with Connor by his side. Those two were so lucky to have found each other. Bernadette had never seen her son as happy as he'd been since they had realised they were meant to be together. Although, as she'd watched him approach, she could see the strain on his face and knew how much this must have taken out of him. He was someone else who would find a day of people praising Kenneth Manson to be a form of psychological torture.

'Sis, we're just about to head off.'

Nina's panic had escalated. 'But, Stu, the babysitter has just phoned and Mum said—'

Bernadette had immediately cut her off. 'Sweetheart, it's fine,' she'd assured her daughter. 'You and Gerry go on home and take care of the wee one. And Stuart' – she'd turned to her son – 'you get off now too.'

'But, Mum, if something goes wrong...?' Nina had said again.

'Then I'll be here to fix it. I'll stay. It'll be fine. And Marge is here too – she knows all the details. Between us, we'll take care of everything.'

Nina's groan had come from gratitude, relief, and the understanding of what Bernadette was doing. 'Urgh, Mum, I'm sorry. After everything, you're still the one that ends up making sure everything is okay for Dad. I swear you deserve a medal. Or a blooming trophy. If I win the lottery, you can have it all – how about that?'

Bernadette had laughed. 'I'll settle for enough to have a cleaner, a chef and four holidays a year. Phone me later and let me know how the wee one is doing.'

She'd hugged her daughter, then waved her off, before switching back to Stuart.

'Okay, what am I getting from you, if Nina is pitching up with the cleaning staff and the holidays?'

She'd always been able to get round Stuart by making him laugh. He'd been a shy kid and that had made him a target for someone like Kenneth, who'd perceived Stuart's shyness as weakness. In the couple of years before he died, Kenneth had made an effort to build some kind of relationship with his son – mainly, they all suspected, as a way to show Bernadette that he'd changed – but it had been too late.

'Unlimited Saturday bottomless brunches and we'll come on those holidays with you.'

'Deal. I couldn't possibly say no.'

'Anyway, don't worry – we'll stay and keep you company. I'm not leaving you alone with this this lot,' he'd said, scanning the room. 'If the company you keep shapes your personality, no wonder Dad was a dick.'

Bernadette had to supress a chuckle. She wasn't sure she could have summed it up any better than that.

'No, honestly, it's fine. You two go while you can. Save yourselves. If I don't make it out, you can have my china and my overdraft.'

That had made Stuart smile again. 'You're sure?'

'Positive. Honestly. Besides, I know that Marge will want to stay until everyone's gone too, so I'll stay and keep her company.'

'Are you absolutely sure or just saying this so we don't feel bad?'

'Absolutely sure.'

As she'd given her son and his boyfriend a hug, Bernadette had realised that she meant what she was saying. She did want to stay with Marge.

And now, as she took another sip of her water and replayed the important points of their conversation in her mind, Bernadette decided that they still had more to discuss.

Because she couldn't shake off the feeling that the woman who'd been loyal to Kenneth for the last three decades had something on her mind that she wanted to talk about.

6 P.M.–8 P.M.

21

BERNADETTE

The lift pinged as Bernadette reached the floor of the elderly ward, but as the doors opened, she took in the quiet calm – so different from the Emergency Department she worked in every day.

Over the years, Bernadette had worked on many of the wards in this hospital, including a one-month stint to cover shortages on this one, so she knew exactly where she was going. First stop, the nursing station, and as she approached, she saw a familiar face.

'Bernadette! You don't usually come up this high. You'll be getting a nosebleed.'

As soon as Bernadette saw who was taking care of Marge, she felt a wave of relief. Keli Clark was one of the most exemplary nurses she'd ever worked with, and a close friend of Caleb and Stevie, her faves down in the Emergency Department. Bernadette often joined the trio of pals in the cafe when they were all having lunch together.

'I'm starting to feel dizzy already,' Bernadette quipped. 'But it's worth it to see you, ma love.'

'Stop! I'm trying to train myself to be immune to all kind words and flattery. It's part of my training to help me stop picking terrible men.'

Bernadette's laughter filled the corridor. 'Good luck with that. I wish I'd taken that training course when I was your age. Would have saved me a whole lot of trouble.'

'I hear you,' Keli chuckled, and Bernadette wished she was just here for a blether, instead of a visit that was making her heart ache. Marge. The news about her health had been such a devastating shock.

'Anyway, love, I'm risking the nosebleeds because I just met Estelle Drummond in the cafe and she let me know her mum was here and asking for me. Marge is an old friend. God, I feel awful. If I'd known she was here, I'd have been up to see her long before now.'

Keli nodded sympathetically. 'Yes, she's in room 4. I had no idea you knew her. She's such a lovely lady. We're really fond of her. And I'm sure she'll be glad to see you. She doesn't get a lot of visitors. Estelle, mainly.'

There was no one else within earshot, but still, Bernadette leaned forward, lowering her voice, 'Estelle told me about her illness. How bad is it?'

Keli's expression told her everything. 'We're moving her to palliative care tomorrow. I'm sorry, Bernie.'

Bernadette felt the punch of that in her stomach. Madge was someone she'd known for half her life. Someone she cared about. Someone who – over the last five years – she'd had a unique connection with. They were part of each other's story, and they didn't need to see each other every week or month to know they cared about each other.

'Thanks, Keli. Is it okay if I pop in now?'

'Of course it is. If you need anything, just call for me.'

As Bernadette walked towards the door, she took a breath, prepared herself to react with nothing but a friendly smile, no matter how unwell Marge looked, but it wasn't necessary because when she opened the door, she saw that Marge was fast asleep.

Sitting down beside her, Bernadette took in her friend's appearance. Marge's soft grey hair was, as always, pulled back in a ballerina bun at the nape of her neck, but the lips that were always impeccably outlined in a pale pink lipstick were now bare, her cheeks sunken. Still beautiful, though. Still Marge.

As if she sensed her presence, Marge opened her eyes, and Bernadette reached for her hand, flashing her very best grin. 'I believe you ordered a nurse, Marge?'

Marge immediately went with the joke. 'I believe I did.'

Bernadette didn't miss the hoarseness of her voice. Marge had always been someone who could – when necessary – assert her authority with firmness, conviction and occasional terror. Now that gusto was gone and Bernadette ached for her. But she knew that sympathy and tears weren't what Marge needed right now.

'Och, Marge, you'll go to some extremes to get out of our big annual meet-up. And it was your turn to buy the first round tonight.'

'Ah, I'll get it next year.' As Marge managed a weak chuckle, Bernie saw a single droplet of water run down one cheek, before her smile turned to sadness and Marge whispered, 'I should have called you sooner. Should have told you about the cancer. I'm sorry.'

Bernadette squeezed her hand gently. 'Don't apologise, Marge. I just wish I'd known so I could be here for you.'

'I thought I'd be okay. Thought I'd beat it. I didn't know how bad it was going to get until we got here.'

'I understand,' Bernadette said softly. 'How's Estelle holding up? I met her downstairs. She's lovely, Marge. You must be so proud of her.'

'I am. But, you know, I think it's time to tell her, Bernadette. We've held on to this for long enough.'

Marge didn't need to explain what she was talking about because Bernadette knew it could only be one thing – the story Marge had entrusted her with back at Kenneth's funeral five years ago. The story of Estelle's birth. Of the man who had fathered Marge's gorgeous girl. Down in the canteen, Bernadette had seen the resemblance. Now Marge was telling her that it was time to release the secret her friend had kept for thirty-five years, and the one she'd found the strength to share with Bernadette that day, surrounded by people pretending to mourn her late husband.

For the next few slow, pained moments, she listened as Marge found her voice for long enough to tell her what she wanted her to do. When she was done, Bernadette leaned towards her, still holding on to her friend's hand, her heart breaking for her, for Estelle, for the inevitable devastation that was about to come.

'Marge, I'll do anything you ask of me. But are you sure?'

Marge nodded slowly. 'I am.'

Bernadette nodded. She had no idea if this was the right decision, but her feelings weren't important here – all that mattered were Marge's wishes. 'Okay, my love. Leave it with me – I'll work it out and come back tomorrow.

The nurse, Keli, told me you're moving downstairs, so I'll come find you. And don't worry, Marge, we'll be here for you. For you both.'

A second drop of water ran down Marge's cheek and Bernadette gently wiped it away. Before she could say any more, the door opened behind her and Estelle came in, so Bernadette immediately shifted her energy back to cheeriness.

'Well, Marge, I need to get off. I have a meeting I need to go to and, apparently, I'm now buying the first round.'

As Marge smiled, Bernadette shifted the conversation to Estelle.

'Now that I've found your mum here, you won't get rid of me. I've promised I'll be back tomorrow. Will you be here, Estelle? It would be lovely to get to know you. You're not far off the age of my daughter, Nina. I think she'd like to meet you too.'

As Estelle smiled, Bernadette thought how much she looked like Marge too. The lass was a definite mix of both her parents. 'Yes, I'll be here. And I'd like that very much.'

As she hugged both of them, Bernadette knew she didn't have to repeat the words she'd said earlier, because Marge would feel it.

Don't worry, Marge. We've got you.

All the way down in the lift, Bernadette's eyes were closed, thinking through Marge's request, realising that this was going to be one of those pivotal moments where a life would change. Bernadette just hoped Estelle had her mother's strength.

By the time she got back to the ED, Bernadette saw that the normal Saturday night madness was beginning to ramp up, the whiteboard was filling up, and the noise was a few decibels louder than when she'd left. She quickly dipped into the nursing bay and opened the staff drawer to retrieve her phone. The screen was stacked with notifications. The first two were from a couple of the other women who were meant to be meeting them tonight – Danielle Strang and Annabel Stevens. Bernadette opened Danielle's first.

> Just realised the date! So sorry – in Turks and Caicos with new man. Bliss! You ladies have a drink for me. Kisses! Xxx

Much as she'd miss her presence tonight, that made Bernadette grin.

Danielle used to be a globe-trotting model in her bygone days, and she was always up for both romance and travel. It seemed she'd found both. Good for her.

The second one, from Annabel Stevenson, the esteemed Member of the Scottish Parliament, had slightly less joy.

> Late vote in the house tonight. Incompetent eejits. Raincheck.

Last year there had been six of them at their meeting. Tonight, there would be three. But that was enough for what Bernadette needed to do.

The next text was from Stuart and Bernadette felt a twinge of happiness that her son had finally got back to her.

> Sorry I missed your call this morning. All good here. See you tomorrow. Love you! xx

Her shoulders rose just a little higher. She had no doubt that, in years to come, he and Nina could be in their sixties, and eighty-odd-year-old Bernadette would still feel a tingle of relief every time she got a happy text from them.

And finally, *finally*, a text from Jack. The Hallelujah Chorus struck up in her head.

> Sorry Bernie. Slammed today. See you tomorrow love.

He wasn't a man for xxxx's or emojis. Still, at least he'd finally answered. But was this enough? Could she really carry on conducting most of their relationship by text? No. She wanted more. But the thing that had been her most important thought this morning, the question of her future, of building a more permanent life with Jack, was now only the second most crucial thing on her mind because she had a more pressing situation to worry about right now. Marge. Estelle. She supposed she'd always known this day would come but…

The thought was interrupted by a nudge on the shoulder from Caleb. 'Hey, I thought you'd gone?'

'Came back for my phone,' she said, waving it as proof. 'I just saw Keli up in Elderly – had to pop up to visit an old pal who's been admitted.'

Caleb must have caught something in her voice. 'Are you okay?'

'I am.' Was she? She was devastated about Marge's illness and worried for the challenges Estelle was going to have to face. She had doubts over what her future held with Jack. And she was dreading the news she was going to have to share at tonight's gathering. 'I think I just got a reminder that life's too short.' No, she wasn't okay. There was a surge of anxiety spreading from her core to her finger tips and toes, but she shook it off. This wasn't the time or place to indulge her own feelings. 'Anyway, before I go...' Her gaze went to the whiteboard. 'Murray Atkins?'

'Consultant is being super-cautious and has just told him that he has a serious concussion and we want to keep him in overnight for observation. At which point, today's favourite patient, and I say that with as much sarcasm as my soul possesses, lost his shit and is currently discharging himself. Says we've wasted his day. Another highlight of job satisfaction in the ED. Luckily, I get my joy from food, sleep and being gorgeous.'

Bernadette chuckled. 'Well, remember I'm off tomorrow and, much as I love you, don't dare call me.'

'Not a chance – I'm off tomorrow too. Right, I've got an enema in bay 13, then I'm gone.'

Bernadette also took the moment to flee, all too aware that if she stood still, there was every chance she'd get roped into helping with some new emergency or drama. And all too aware that she could never say no.

Moving quickly, she nipped into the changing rooms and threw her clothes back on. The black trousers and polo-neck sweater weren't what she'd planned to wear tonight, but there was no time to go home now, so they would have to do. She fluffed in a bit of dry shampoo, sprayed some deodorant, popped a mint, applied some lippy and was ready in ten minutes.

The cold air slammed into her as she walked outside. It was already dark, and she was about to put her head down and speed to the car when she saw a tiny orange light, a cigarette, someone holding it, standing in the shadow to the left of her.

Bernadette could see just enough to recognise the face, so she stopped. Approached. Listened as the other woman spoke first.

'I bet you're loving this,' Lila Atkins drawled, with the bitterness Bernadette had come to expect from her.

Bernadette shook her head. 'Not at all.' She took a step to walk on, knowing that she was the last person that her ex-husband's former mistress wanted to speak to, but then kindness and experience got the best of her and she stopped. 'You know, Lila, I'm sorry this happened to you. Truly. No one deserves it.'

Lila shrugged it off. 'I knew what I was getting into.'

Bernadette wasn't ready to let go. 'Look, I need to go. But if you ever want to grab a coffee and talk about this or anything else...'

Lila's head whipped around as if she'd been slapped. 'So you can pity me? Nah, I'm fine, thanks. Do you know how pathetic that is? You think you of all people get to feel sorry for me? No. No, you don't.'

Jesus, this woman would try the patience of a saint.

'I don't feel sorry for you, but I think what happened with Murray this morning couldn't have been easy.'

Lila was well and truly on the defensive now. 'That's the thing you don't understand. I'm not the victim here. I have the house I want. The car I want. The life I want. If infidelity was a deal breaker, I'd have married a priest. Murray and I knew what we got when we married each other.'

Actually, maybe Bernadette did feel a twinge of sympathy. And perhaps empathy too. Hadn't she also been in a marriage that was missing the most important things in a relationship?

'And what about love? Happiness? What about waking up and feeling like you've got the best life?'

'Didn't you hear me? I do have the best life. And I'd rather have what I've got, than a hellish existence stuck in there all day,' she gestured to the hospital doors.

There were many things that Bernadette had learned in life. That no one is perfect. That people make mistakes. That the worst could happen when it was least expected. And the best too. And also, that some people were just complete knobs and lost causes. Bernadette could give Lila a full spiel on how material things didn't buy happiness, but what was the point? There was no helping someone who had no soul, no conscience and no moral compass.

'You do you, Lila. Good luck with that.'

And off she went to meet good women who weren't perfect. Who had made those mistakes. But who remembered what it was to have a heart.

22

MARGE

Marge surveyed the scene, checking that every single detail was perfect. 'In case you're under any illusion, I would hate this,' Marge shuddered. 'If you ever decide to do anything like this for me, I'll divorce you.'

Ian's laugh caused her to immediately shush him. Estelle would be here any second and Marge didn't want anything to spoil the surprise that her daughter would have when she walked through the door and saw all her friends in the little Italian restaurant they'd been coming to for Sunday dinners for years now. It was Estelle's favourite place on earth, and the owner, Gino, had worked with Marge to make sure her girl's twenty-first birthday would be perfect. All Estelle's favourite dishes, the colourful décor, the music, the big pile of gifts on the table, brought by twenty or so of her chums. Estelle's best friend, Amber, had helped them with the guest list, and it included Estelle's wide group of mates from college, which was just as well, because neither she nor Ian had much in the way of extended family. Not that they minded in the least. Marge, Ian, Estelle: the three of them had always been enough. They'd never had more children – not because they didn't want to, because it just hadn't happened. Unexplained infertility had been the medical verdict. For a while, they'd considered other options – adoption, IVF – but in the end, it was Ian who'd made the decision. 'We're just fine the way we are, Marge. If you want to try for more, or look at other options, I'll be right with you, but I don't need that – what we have, the three of us, is all I need to be happy.' That had ended the deliberations and quelled the angst for Marge, because the three of them were more than enough for her too. Ian's love and the utter joy of being Estelle's mother were all she'd ever needed.

When Amber and Estelle came through the door, the whole restaurant erupted in cheers and the sound of hooters and streamers being popped, and Marge watched as Estelle threw her head back and laughed. Their daughter had always been such a naturally happy child and if she were being honest – truly, brutally honest – Marge was a little jealous of that. Estelle didn't care if everything was organised perfectly. The thought of a surprise didn't fill her with horror. She wasn't always wrapped up in plans and details. Her artistic, creative girl thought things through and was unfailingly organised, she made measured, mature decisions, but she was also happy to go with the flow, see how things worked out. That definitely wasn't in her genes. Marge needed to be one step ahead of everything, and as for Estelle's biological father... Marge was fairly sure he'd never had a carefree day in his life. Marge could only think that Estelle's calm, strong energy was learned behaviour that came from Ian, and she was grateful every day, for him and for their family.

The rest of the night passed in a joyous celebration of Estelle, full of laughter and dancing until Estelle spun over to them, threw her arms around her dad's neck and kissed him on the cheek. 'I've had the best time, Dad.' She moved on to Marge. Another kiss. 'And, Mum – I can't believe you organised all this and I didn't even suspect a thing. Actually, I can believe it. Thank you. I love you both so fricking much!' With that, she shimmied back over to rejoin Amber and the rest of her friends on the makeshift dance floor.

Another delightful attribute her daughter possessed – the ability to be free and open with her emotions in every situation. Marge and Ian's love was just as strong, but it was quieter. Peaceful. Assured. Just the way they both liked it.

At the end of the night, Marge and Ian managed to resist Estelle's requests to join her gang as they went on to a nightclub. 'Come on, Mum, live a little,' she teased them.

At which point Ian spun his daughter around, laughing. 'You go enjoy yourself, darling. We'll clear up here and see you tomorrow.'

Estelle went off into the night, as giddy as someone who had her whole wonderful life in front of her should be.

'Were we ever like that?' Marge asked Ian later, as they walked home. They'd decided against a taxi, because the October night was chilly but not too cold and they enjoyed the walk. They'd promised Gino they'd be back the next day to collect the gifts and what was left of the cake.

'I don't think so. I spent my twenty-first in a library studying for my finals. The only wild thing I've ever done is fall in love with you the minute I met you.'

'Same! How did we not know that before now? Isn't it a joy to be both boring and compatible?' Their laughter made a dog walker further along the street turn around and smile. The truth was, she'd never been bored a day in their marriage. Happy, yes. Thankful too. But never bored.

They strolled a while longer in peaceful silence, content as always, just to be together. Words weren't always needed. In fact, Marge cherished the quiet moments most. It was Ian who broke the peace first.

'So you know what this means now, Marge, don't you?'

Marge didn't even have to ask what he was referring to, because she knew. But she listened, her mouth going dry, as he went on.

'We said we'd tell her the truth when she was sixteen. Then eighteen. And then we said twenty-one. We can't keep putting it off, Marge – she deserves to know.'

'She does,' Marge agreed, with a sad sigh.

Even as she said it, Marge knew that she still wasn't ready. It was the one thing that had sat in the corner of their happiness during their lives together, just waiting there, ready to come out. The truth was they should have told Estelle about her biological father long ago, but somehow, the longer they left it, the more she found reasons not to. If it were up to Marge, maybe she'd never tell her, and yes, she knew, deep in her heart, that came from a place of cowardice. Or maybe shame that she'd slept with a married man. Or perhaps she just couldn't bear to leave even one shadow on her carefree, happy daughter's heart. But it had to be done because it was part of Estelle's story. She had half-siblings out there. Genetic connections she wasn't aware of. She deserved to be given the full information about her origins. Even though her biological father had chosen to be absent from her life, she deserved the right to challenge that.

It was an impossible situation: tell her and tear apart the fabric of her life, or keep it from her and deprive her of the truth about who she was. They'd struggled over this dilemma for ever, but their inherent sense of what was right had overruled their fears. Telling Estelle was the right thing to do – Marge just didn't know how to do it. The woman who had a plan for everything, had no plan for this.

They stopped at the pedestrian crossing, pressed the button, waited for the green man to tell them to go.

'We'll tell her tomorrow,' Ian said, softly, as they began to cross the road. 'I'm dreading it as much as you, and God knows, I wish it were different, but...'

The lights were all that Marge remembered after that. No screams. No crash. No sickening sound of the man she adored being hit by a car that had jumped the lights and come around the corner to carry away the love of her life.

Just the lights.

The blinding lights.

'Mum, are you okay?' Estelle's voice. Marge squeezed her eyes together, then opened them and squinted as her pupils reacted to the lights above her bed again. 'You gasped in your sleep, as if something was wrong.'

Marge saw the concerned face of her daughter, and immediately tried to make her feel better. 'I'm fine, darling, I promise. Just a dream.'

Only it wasn't. Marge had replayed that night in her mind a million times and the ending was always the same. Ian was taken from them. And after that, she could never bring herself to tell their daughter the truth, because how could she break her heart all over again?

Estelle sat back down in her chair and pulled the blanket she'd left there over her knees again. 'It was lovely to meet Bernadette. She wasn't what I expected at all. From everything you told me about Dr Manson, I expected her to be more… I don't know… stuck-up?'

Marge felt her cheeks rise in a grin. 'No. Definitely not stuck-up. I'd like you to know her better, Estelle. I should have introduced you long before now.'

'That's okay, Mum. Plenty of time.'

The way she said it jarred with Marge, but she didn't correct her. Once upon a time, she'd thought there was plenty of time for everything in life too. The night she'd lost Ian had proved to her that there wasn't. And now…

'Anyway, she must have tired you out because you fell asleep before she was out the door.' Estelle's words were full of warmth and chattiness, as if that was just another normal moment on a normal day. 'And I didn't get to tell you who I met downstairs… Amber was there.'

Marge's eyes widened, the lights no longer bothering her.

'Amber? In the hospital?' Marge couldn't quite work this out. 'Is she sick? Are the boys okay?'

'Yes, they're fine. She said she came into the Emergency Department with a friend who'd had a fall but it's all okay.'

'Did you speak to her?' Marge felt her hopes rising. Amber had been someone important to her too, and she'd been so upset when the girls had fallen out. Many times over the last year, she'd thought about calling Amber, telling her about the cancer, hoping it would bring her back to mend things with Estelle so that one good thing could come of this bastard disease, but she'd never been sure enough that it was the right thing to do. She'd never been one to meddle, and she hadn't wanted to risk making things worse. Instead, she'd chosen to keep quiet. It was a familiar theme in her life.

Still, she missed the boys and she worried for Estelle. Her boyfriend, Craig, was a sweet man, but Amber had been her closest friend, like a sister, and Marge wasn't sure her daughter would ever come to terms with losing that relationship from her life.

She listened as Estelle replayed the conversation, sadness in every word.

'I couldn't lie to her, Mum, but perhaps I should have. Maybe that would have been the best thing to do, but you know I really did think I was doing the right thing, and I couldn't promise I'd do anything different if it happened again.'

Marge felt partly responsible for Estelle's decision back then too, because the truth was, she'd been party to her daughter's actions. When Estelle had found out about Ewan's affair, she'd come straight to Marge's house, burst in, harassed and upset. Marge had got the fright of her life, seeing her like that, and sat her down, plied her with tea as she told her the story.

'I heard Ewan and Craig arguing in the kitchen. They didn't know I was home. Ewan's been seeing one of their clients, Mum. An affair.'

Marge had felt her blood run cold. Poor Amber. 'And Craig was telling him to end it? Is that why they were arguing?'

'No. Ewan was telling him it was already over, and Craig was saying it had better be because he'd risked the reputation of the company as well as his marriage and his family. Urgh, it was a whole big mess of a fight.'

'And what did you say to Ewan?'

'Nothing. I left before they even knew I was there. I know I should have gone in and punched him in the face. That's what Amber would have done.'

She probably wasn't wrong, but... 'We don't all handle things the same way,' Marge had consoled her. 'That might have made it worse.' Was she trying to make Estelle feel better or herself, because that's how she would have handled it? She would have turned a blind eye. Walked away. Ignored it. Just as she had with Kenneth Manson all those years. Just as she had with her promise to Ian that they'd tell Estelle the truth. Walk away. Say nothing.

'What do you think I should do, Mum? I made Craig tell me the whole story afterwards and he says I need to stay out of it. But how can I?'

'If it were the other way round, would you want Amber to tell you?'

She'd thought about that. 'Yes. But it's different. There are kids... What if me telling Amber wrecks their family? How could I live with that?'

'Then I think you have to trust yourself. Sometimes saying nothing is the right thing to do.'

Now, seeing Estelle wrestle with her decision all this time later, Marge wondered again if she'd been thinking about herself when she'd said that. Had she skewed Estelle's decision to salve her own conscience? It was a tough one. She completely understood Amber being upset at Estelle, but at the same time, she empathised with her daughter's actions because she'd have done the same – she'd have avoided the confrontation and hoped it would all work out in the end. But then, hadn't she already realised that wasn't the best way to handle secrets?

'Did I say the wrong thing, Mum? What do you think?'

Marge thought about that for a moment, as she felt herself drifting off again.

'I think it's never too late to fix a mistake, darling.'

The lights above her dimmed again.

It's never too late to fix a mistake. Is it, Ian? And, darling, I'm about to fix mine.

23

AMBER

'Someone has to take action, hen, and by God if those clowns at the council won't do something about the potholes, then I will. Me and my pal have got a tar bucket that we've customised...'

By the time the taxi driver had taken Amber from Glasgow Central Hospital to her street twenty minutes away, he'd sorted out the spending budgets of Glasgow City Council, the entire political future of Great Britain, climate change, at least two wars and he was now on to his patent-pending solution to the scourge of potholes. But still, she didn't want to test his vast capabilities by asking him to sort the absolute crapstorm that was her life.

How had it come to this? How? Just over two years ago, she'd been blissfully happy, with her gorgeous little family and her perfect husband, a fantastic best friend and a whole lifetime of happiness in front of her, and now... Now she was the kind of chick that hooked up with married men and created health hazards that resulted in a strain on the already stretched resources of the NHS.

And seeing Estelle there tonight... As if the Gods of Colossal Humiliations hadn't had enough fun with her, there was Estelle, reminding her that even in the pothole of life that she'd somehow fallen into, none of that mattered next to what poor Marge was going through.

If the driver heard her loud sniff as she fought back the great, heaving sob that was rising in her throat, he just stared straight ahead and moved on to his theory that UFOs were landing at Prestwick Airport.

She couldn't get Marge out of her mind. All those years that woman had been so kind to her and Amber had cut her dead. And true, Marge hadn't got in touch with her either, but did that really matter now? Did Amber really care who did what to whom? The only thing that was important was that someone she loved was dying and Amber was consumed with guilt and regret. Why had she been so bloody stubborn? In fact, wasn't that the story of the last two years of her life? She'd cut Ewan and Estelle off too, and yes, in her mind she'd had good reason, but what did it all really boil down to? They'd made a mistake. One mistake.

Hadn't she done the same today? Okay, so her mistake was slightly less life-changing, at least for her. But accidentally sleeping with a married man was a colossal fuck up nonetheless, and Amber could quite feasibly have been sitting here right now listening to a theory that we were about to be replaced by robots, having unwittingly wrecked Murray's wife's life. Maybe his wife was preparing to divorce him right now and Amber had played a part in that. It was a mistake. A really stupid mistake that she would take back in a heartbeat.

There was another loud sniff as her mind went back to Marge, and she wondered if there was anything in Marge's life that she would take back. Did she have regrets? Things that made her sad now? Decisions that she would change? And what if there were, and it was too late?

The taxi turned into her street as her train of thought took her in another direction. If she were in Marge's position, ill and close to the end of her life, what would she change? What regrets could she not live – or die – with? What would she want to rewind?

Everything. Every damn thing for the last two years. She'd want her marriage back, her family intact, her world to be whole again. Sometimes she wondered if she should have given Ewan a second chance, for the sake of the kids, if nothing else, but she hadn't been able to bear the thought of him touching her after he'd been with someone else. And it hadn't mattered to her that it was only once. It was the lies, the deceit, the broken trust and the knowledge that he was capable of destroying their family for the sake of a quick shag. How could she ever get over that? He'd begged her to change her mind so many times, but the pain had been too real, too raw. His actions had distorted the way she felt about him, shredded her love for him, so that all that was left was resentment and a grudging desire to be cordial for the kids. But now... Her thoughts circled back. One mistake. Could she really punish him forever?

'Because the thing is, those new robo-taxis over in America, the ones with no drivers, are missing the point. We're a public service. We don't just drive people around, we share their problems and provide a valuable social outlet...'

'Excuse me,' she blurted, just as they pulled to a stop outside her house. 'Sorry to interrupt, and you're right – a valuable social service. And as for what you're saying about solving problems – any chance you could wait here for five minutes while I run in there and then take me somewhere else?'

'Och, I'd love to, but I'm due a tea break...'

Her chin dropped. 'What happened to being a valuable social service? How about if I bring you a ham sandwich, a bun and a can of Irn-Bru?'

Amber wasn't sure what did the trick, but he grudgingly agreed. 'Aye, fine then – but I'm leaving the meter running.'

'Problem solving doesn't come cheap,' Amber joked as she dashed out of the car and into the house, deliberately averting her gaze from the red sports car parked at the end of her path. A red flag on four bloody wheels and she still hadn't spotted it.

She'd asked the taxi driver to wait because, after the champagne she'd had earlier with that tosser, she didn't want to risk getting behind the wheel and she couldn't rule out needing a stiff glass of wine at some point in the next few hours. Besides, the way her day was going, any disaster could befall her. Was it really only this morning that she'd come downstairs with two paramedics and a married shagger on a stretcher? Her face began to burn, and it wasn't because she was galloping up the stairs. In her bedroom, she put her hand up to the side of her face so that she couldn't look at the messy bed as she passed it, and went straight into the carnage of the bathroom.

'SpongeBob, I actually think I owe you a thanks...' she muttered, as she picked him out of the shower tray and turned on the jets. She meant what she said. If Murray hadn't slipped this morning, and everything else hadn't unfolded today, how long would it have been until she discovered he was married? And when would she have found out that Marge was ill? After she was gone and it was too late? And when would Amber have realised that she herself was stubborn, and uncompromising, and judgemental, and unforgiving? Actually, she'd always known all of those things, but she'd just chosen to ignore them because, well, she was stubborn and uncompromising and judgemental.

As soon as the shower was warm enough, she jumped in, gave herself a thirty-second clean, then out, towel dried and pulled on the jeans she'd stuffed in the wardrobe when she was tidying her room prior to daytime sex this morning, then added a cream jumper and a pair of boots. She brushed her hair back into a messy ponytail – not deliberately, but she didn't have time to make it neat – and then shot back down the stairs. After a quick pitstop in the kitchen to make the sandwich and grab the bun and the Irn-Bru, then a pause to pick up her handbag and jacket from the rack at the door, she was back in the taxi fourteen minutes later.

'There you go,' she said, handing the lot over to him, before giving him the next destination. By the time they got there, she was wondering if it was possible to patent the ability to eat a ham sandwich and drink a can of Irn-Bru while driving and waxing lyrical on the history of solar panels. It was like hanging out with a talking Wikipedia.

'Can you wait again, please?' There was every chance this could go very wrong and she'd be back out on her arse in the rain. 'For five minutes. Maybe ten. I might need to go back where I came from.'

'I tell you what,' Wiki Driver said, 'pay for what you've used so far, and I'm going to stay here and eat my bun and have a wee break. I need to catch up on the latest in international affairs. My passengers like to know these things. I'll stick around for ten minutes and if you don't come back, I'll shoot off.'

'Deal. Thank you so much,' she said, tapping her credit card against the little machine on the back of the front seat, not even looking to see what the fare on the meter said. She'd probably just spent the equivalent of a one-way ticket to Alicante, but she would worry about it when the credit card bill came in. She could always remortgage the house.

She jumped out, ignoring the cold, the drizzle and the fact that one boot went straight into a puddle, and ran up the path, then up the four steps to the door of the townhouse and rang the bell.

When the guy answered, his first reaction was very obvious surprise, followed by an immediate leap to concern.

'Hey. Is everything okay? Is something wrong?'

'No. Yes. I mean, can I talk to you?'

That's when her ex-husband stepped back and let her in the door.

'The boys are asleep – they both crashed out on the couch, and I was just about to lift them up to bed, but I can wake them...' he offered, still clearly confused as he led her through to what she saw was an open-plan kitchen and living room. And yes, there were her babes, Sid in his favourite Spiderman pyjamas, and Alfie, arm slung over his brother, was wearing a Buzz Lightyear spacesuit. Obviously no one had told him there are no dinosaurs in space.

She kept her tone low so as not to disturb them. 'No, no – you don't need to wake them, it's you I've come to speak to.'

Amber resisted her curiosity to look around. She'd never been in the house he'd moved in to after they split, but from what she could see, it looked spotlessly clean and well cared for – although there did appear to be a basketball hoop in the middle of the kitchen, but she let that go.

'Sounds ominous. Do you want a coffee, or do I need beer for this?'

He leaned against the worktop, and this was perhaps the first time in two years the Amber could look straight at him without immediately averting her eyes because rage, or hurt, or some other negative emotion would start twisting round her gut.

'No, I'm fine, thanks.' She was already way too amped up for more caffeine. 'I just need to ask you something. What you did... do you wish you could go back and undo it?'

He held her eye contact, not even flinching. 'Every single day. You know that. It was the biggest mistake of my life.'

'And if I could find a way to forgive you...?' It was a question, but she couldn't get the rest of the words out, because they were stuck somewhere in her chest, right next to her heart.

'Then I'd beg you to come back to me. I don't want to do life with anyone else but you.'

He wasn't usually one to go into deep conversations about his emotions or their relationship, but this was the first opportunity she'd given him to speak calmly, without reproach or condemnation, since the night she'd found out about the affair. Back then, he'd argued that it was a one-night stand, but to her it was an affair because the emotional exchange, the foreplay, the deceit, had started weeks before. She wasn't interested in hearing his defence or his explanations, so she'd blocked all conversation. Refused to bend. So now, hard as it was, she wanted to listen to what he had to say.

'I know I've got no right to say it,' he went on, 'but this is what I want. You, me, the kids, Saturday night on the couch watching movies. I love you and it kills me that I blew it. I'll never stop being sorry. To all of you.'

She nodded slowly, fear and relief and love and so many other feelings bubbling inside her, so she didn't know which one was going to rise to the top. It was as if today had mopped up all her emotions, tossed them in a tumble drier, and somehow, at the end of the cycle, she was left with a steaming hot towel of self-reflection, doubt and regret wrapped around her heart.

Was she crazy to even consider this? Was this all just an extreme knee-jerk response to the shitshow of a day? Or was it real? Could this really be their lives again?

Her gaze went from the man she'd loved for a decade – actually, the only man she'd ever loved – over to her sleeping boys.

'And how long will the offer of a place on the couch be available?'

'Until you take it.'

Until you take it.

Was that what she wanted? She wasn't sure so she wasn't going to give him an answer now. Not today, when she could barely think straight and her decision-making skills had already landed her in an emergency situation. She wasn't going to confuse the kids by getting them all back together and then having to let it go because the resentment or anger was still there.

'Okay. I need to go somewhere. But I'll think about it and get back to you.'

He stayed exactly where he was, leaning against the worktop, letting her call every shot. 'I'll be here.'

Before she did anything she would regret, she backed out of the kitchen, turned and then went out of the front door, where her valuable social service was still waiting.

'That bun was the best thing I've ever tasted, hen. Right, where to next?'

Home. Yes, she should go home. But...

'Can you take me back to Glasgow Central Hospital?'

24

MARGE – SUNDAY 21 FEBRUARY 2021

'Ladies, we're about to close the bar now, and I just wanted to check if I can get anything else for you?' This was the fourth trip to the table that Isla, the very lovely waitress who was down here from Skye, studying at Glasgow University, and working in the hotel at weekends to pay her rent, had made to their table. Marge and Bernadette had chatted to her every time she'd come over and were close to knowing the name of her first pet and her star sign. That was how long they'd been here.

Marge had been surprised when the rest of Kenneth's family had left, but totally understood that Nina had to get back to the wee ones. What shouldn't have surprised her was that Bernadette had stepped in to help by staying behind and overseeing the rest of the wake. She was the kind of strong, decent woman that would do anything to help her family, even to the detriment of herself. Her marriage to Kenneth Manson had proven that.

'Isla, I think I'll have another one of these,' Bernadette said, picking up the empty wine glass from the table in front of her. When Bernadette had sat down with her again a couple of hours before, she'd confessed that she'd switched to water because she'd been feeling a little tipsy. After her second glass, she'd cracked.

'Sod it, Marge – I'm going back on the wine. I think this day calls for it.'

Inspired by their conversation and enjoying the chat, Marge had been about to order another cup of tea when she'd been momentarily possessed by the spirit of her Aunt Agnes at every family party since the beginning of time.

'I think I'll have to join you then. I'll have a small sherry please, Isla.'

That had been four small sherries ago – which added up to a couple of blooming large sherries – and now Bernadette and Isla were waiting for her final order.

'And another sherry for you, Marge?' Bernadette was asking now.

Marge knew she really should go back to coffee – the sherry was making her decidedly light-headed.

She picked up her empty glass, about to request that it be swapped for a latte, but apparently the spirit of her old Aunt Agnes was still in charge. 'I'll have another small sherry please.'

As the waitress went off to fulfil their order, Bernadette giggled. 'Oh my goodness, I just had the most delicious thought. If Kenneth could see us now, he'd be utterly outraged. You, his perfect secretary, and me, his downtrodden wife, swapping stories and getting tipsy at his funeral. If there's an afterlife, he's up there raging in the corridors and kicking the door, I promise you. He'll have had at least four written complaints into the afterlife management by now, demanding to be reincarnated and sent back here so he can reprimand us.'

Marge shook her head. 'I don't think there will be official complaints, Bernadette...' she said with a woeful sigh. 'Because I'm not up there to type them.'

The shriek of laughter Bernadette let out caused everyone in the room to turn around and stare, before she clamped her hand over her mouth, shoulders shaking.

'Oh Marge,' she said, when her fingers moved from her mouth to wipe her eyes, 'that might be the funniest line I've ever heard.'

Bernadette's words gave Marge such a warm glow. Or that might have been the sherry, but she was sure it was the words, too. There had only ever been one other person who had found Marge funny, and that had been her darling Ian. Unlike Kenneth, he'd have thought it lovely that she was having such a bonding moment with Bernadette. He'd be happy for her, and thoroughly amused that two women who were minimal drinkers at most, had chosen this occasion to overindulge and have a very revealing heart-to-heart. In fact, for the last two hours, they'd somehow ended up having a conversation so candid and eye-opening that Marge was sure she'd be replaying it in her mind for days. She'd shared things with Bernadette that she'd never spoken of before, and she hadn't had a single doubt that her confidences would be kept.

As Isla came back with their refills and placed them on the table, Marge did a quick scan of the room. Almost everyone had gone now, except a few medical students that Kenneth had been mentoring. Marge was fairly sure they were sticking around for the free bar and canapés. The table of ladies, who'd caused a minor ruffle with the smashed glass earlier were still there too. Marge had rushed over and organised a swift clean-up, a new glass of wine for Lady Clara Kelaney, and it had all been resolved in minutes. After that, the afternoon had passed without further incident, although Marge did fear that Kenneth's estate would be bankrupted by the bar bill at the end of the night.

She picked up her sherry, just as Bernadette put her wine glass back on the table and resumed their conversation. It was still absolutely astonishing to Marge that this was the first open, personal exchange they'd had in almost thirty years. They'd been in the same room many times, at formal functions or ceremonies, but Kenneth had always been there and the formality of their relationship had always been maintained. Today had been a revelation in more ways than she could count.

'Did you ever get totally pissed off with it all, Marge, all the secrets and lies?' Bernadette asked, sitting back in her chair. 'We gave Kenneth so much power because everything was in the dark. His abuse. His affairs. Do you ever wonder what would have happened if we had just called out his shitty behaviour and made it clear he couldn't get away with it?'

Marge shook her head and answered honestly. 'No. The truth is, I did get miffed and disappointed with his actions on many occasions, but I've never considered changing how I dealt with it. I think I just took it all at face value and accepted it for what it was. For who he was. I compartmentalised his personal antics, told myself they were none of my business, and focused on my work. And when the two worlds overlapped, I turned a blind eye to it. Or covered for him, when I had to.'

'I don't know how you did it, Marge.' There was no judgement in Bernadette's voice, only curiosity. 'If my boss was constantly up to no good and I was forced to lie for him, I don't think I'd have been able to work for him for as long as you did.'

Marge couldn't find the words to make sense of it either. 'I'm ashamed to say I never contemplated leaving. I'm not proud of that. I should have taken a stand against the way he treated others. And now that we're actually speaking properly, Bernadette, I want to apologise for that.'

Bernadette immediately objected. 'No, no, no – don't do that, Marge. Do not apologise for things that he did or positions he put you in. I made a whole lifetime out of doing that and I won't hear of it. That's my point exactly. It's a culture – of secrets and entitlement. And it's not just him. I know of a dozen other men who were here today who have had affairs. And probably the same number of women.'

That almost made Marge splutter her sherry, although Bernadette wasn't wrong. Marge had overheard enough chats between Kenneth and his friends, been privy to endless gossip in the hospital staffrooms, to know that infidelity was more commonplace than she would ever have imagined.

'You know, Marge,' Bernadette went on, 'since I left Kenneth, I haven't avoided getting into a relationship because I no longer trust men. I've avoided it because I don't trust myself. Well, that and I can't work those bloody dating apps for the life of me. Nina set me up on the Tinders nonsense and I'm fairly sure I'm now engaged to a bloke from Newcastle.' Bernadette's chuckle reassured Marge that she was kidding. 'Anyway, I wonder how that would be different if I'd stood up to him, if I'd shared my truth. If I'd acted on it, challenged him every time I knew he was lying. Maybe I'd have more faith in myself now.'

'I understand that. But I also think there's strength in silence. Bernadette, I need to tell you something.' A voice in her mind heard the words coming out of her mouth, and began screaming, No. Don't do it. *But apparently, whether it was the sherry, or the occasion, or the dam bursting on thirty-odd years of guilt, she couldn't stop the words from tumbling out. 'I'll understand if you're disgusted, or if it makes you look at me in a horrified light, but I'm no better than the women that Kenneth betrayed you with. You see...'*

For the next ten minutes, Bernadette listened in shocked silence as Marge bared her soul, sharing the story of Estelle's conception and paternity for the first time since she'd broken the news of her pregnancy to her darling Ian all those years ago.

And just like Ian, Bernadette listened, stunned, until she finished.

'I understand if you want to get up and walk away, Bernadette. You must be disgusted.' Marge's heart was beating out of her chest, her head was ready to explode, but weirdly there was a tiny sapling of relief that she'd finally told the truth.

Before Bernadette could respond, they were interrupted again, not by the lovely waitress, but by the very formal restaurant manager, who was looking more than a little uncomfortable.

'Miss Drummond, the bar is closed now, and we've arranged for the flowers and the table centrepieces to be donated to the local nursing homes as you requested.'

Marge somehow managed to find her voice and act with a semblance of normality. 'Thank you, Finlay. I really appreciate your excellent service today. And I know Mr Manson's family do too.'

'We do,' Bernadette added, and Marge noticed that she was slurring, just a little. Marge couldn't tell if that was the alcohol or the shock of what she'd just told her.

Finlay wasn't making any effort to leave them. 'I'm so pleased. Which brings me to a slight conundrum. Unfortunately, we have to get this room set up for another function this evening, but we still have a few guests here.' Marge saw that the medical students had now left, and Finlay was nodding to the one other occupied table in the room. 'But I don't want to offend anyone, so I was just wondering what you would like to do about the ladies at the table over there?'

Marge and Bernadette both turned like synchronised swimmers, but without the bathing caps and the noseguards. Marge took in the attendees at the table. Diana Atkins, Murray Atkins' ex-wife. Annabel Stevenson MSP. Danielle Strang, model and the face of the new Scottish Tourism campaign. And, weirdly, Lady Clara Kelaney, wife of Sir Lester Kelaney, was still sitting with them too, despite Sir Lester having apparently vacated the building.

Marge felt her pulse begin to race at the prospect of dealing with this situation, but evidently, Bernadette had no such qualms. Marge wasn't sure if she was relieved or horrified when Bernadette stood up, glass in hand, and said, 'Don't worry, Finlay, I'll deal with this.'

Relieved. Yes, she was definitely relieved.

Right up until Bernadette added, 'Come on, Marge. Let's get rid of all these bullshit secrets that have made fools of us for far too long.'

Marge wasn't prone to indecisiveness or fear, but her legs felt slightly weak as she followed Bernadette across the room. And it wasn't from the sherry.

As Bernadette approached the table, Marge saw her adopt a convivial smile. 'Ladies, I'm afraid the hotel manager is about to close the function suite and he's asked us to clear the area.'

'Oh.' That came from Annabel Stevenson, MSP, who was now glancing around her, as if realising for the first time that they were the last people in the room. 'I'm so sorry. We'll leave straight away. Thank you very much for your hospitality and my condolences. Kenneth was a—'

'Please don't say "wonderful man",' Bernadette countered, and Marge wondered if she might faint. In fact, yes. If ever she were going to faint, it should be now.

There was a perfectly understandable frozen silence, before a smile began to play on Annabel Stevenson's lips. 'Then I won't,' she said, in a way that felt like there was a whole chapter and verse going unspoken.

'He was a terrible man,' Bernadette said, perfectly calmly. 'And I think you ladies around this table knew that. In fact, I think that was probably what you've been discussing for the last four hours.'

Oh jings. Marge sent a silent prayer to Kenneth to stop raging about his former wife and secretary's antics and arrange for an immediate fire alarm in this room.

It didn't come. And Bernadette was still speaking.

'Annabel, if I remember correctly, you learned what a scoundrel he was sometime around 2006 – in Venice, if I remember correctly. And, Danielle, you became familiar with his complete lack of scruples around 2011.'

Marge had never seen such a rapt audience of so many chins drop at the same time. And the only reason her own hadn't fallen was because her lips were pursed in absolute terror as to what Bernadette might blurt out next.

'Diana, I'm not sure when you succumbed to his charms, but I do know that it caused a temporary rift between Kenneth and your former husband.' Bernadette glanced around. 'Who, if I'm not mistaken, left here today with Kenneth's former mistress. Well, isn't it a small, incestuous world when it comes to all those arrogant, duplicitous arses.'

No response. Just frozen faces and not because there was a generous amount of Botox on display.

'Lady Kelaney... Clara, since we're all friends here... I wasn't aware that you had a connection to my ex-husband, other than the fact that he was utterly sycophantic to Sir Lester and viewed him as the perfect ladder for social climbing.'

Marge gasped, now positive that the shock of this might kill her.

Lady Kelaney was the first one to come back with a response. 'I can assure you, I had no intimate knowledge of Kenneth's... habits. But I don't disagree with your assessment. In fact, I find it quite wonderfully refreshing.'

The fact that it was said with a cut-glass accent made it all the more shocking. This was Charles, Diana and Camilla level antics.

'Glad to hear it. I'd hate to think I missed one. So, ladies, where does that leave us all then?'

Annabel Stevenson, probably aware that this situation had the potential for a public scandal that could seriously damage her political career, was the next one to find her voice.

'Without confirming or denying, given that you have approached us with these allegations, perhaps we should ask you that question – where do you think that leaves us?'

Bernadette turned to Marge. She was definitely going to faint. Was Bernadette about to expose what Marge had just told her?

'Where do you think, Marge? Where does that leave us?'

Even if Marge had a megaphone, she wouldn't have been able to make a sound.

Thankfully, it was apparently a hypothetical question, because Bernadette turned her attention back to the ladies.

'As Marge and I were just discussing, I think where that leaves us is...' There was a long pause before Bernadette found her words. '...Sick of all the bullshit secrets. And in need of somewhere to continue this conversation, because I'm enjoying it and I'm famished. What do you say, ladies – fancy joining Marge and I for dinner downstairs and we can lay a few ghosts to rest? That wasn't a pun. Sorry. It just came out like that. It's the wine.'

Annabel Stevenson was the first to stand up. 'I think I'm a tad peckish too,' she said, in a tone of wry amusement that Marge doubted had ever been used in Parliament.

Clara was next. 'I'm feeling rather hungry too.'

'Starving,' Diana said, getting to her feet.

Danielle was last, unfurling her long model legs. 'I'm in. I hope they've got chips. Today's my cheat day.'

'In more ways than one,' Bernadette quipped, causing a stunned pause, before every woman at the table creased into laughter.

When they regained their composure, they all went downstairs, where they spent the rest of a very unexpected night sharing stories that didn't flatter Kenneth Manson.

It was almost ten o'clock when Marge excused herself and went to the ladies'.

She was washing her hands in one of the beautiful marble sinks, when Clara Kelaney came in and stood beside her, reaching over for soap and turning on the tap as she spoke to Marge in the mirror.

'It's good to finally meet you, Marge. I feel like I've known you for a lifetime, even though we've never been properly introduced.'

Marge felt her hands begin to shake under the water. 'Likewise. I've had a lovely evening. Surreal, but lovely.' Marge wasn't lying. It had been a night of shared stories and so much laughter that they'd attracted glances from other tables. What must they have looked like? All dressed in black, yet not a mournful demeanour between them.

'It's been interesting talking about Kenneth. It did make me wonder if I'll one day have the same conversations about my husband. I'm afraid Lester has many of the same predilections and weaknesses.'

Marge could feel sweat patches forming under her arms. This woman was so beautiful, so cool, so composed. Over the years, as Sir Lester's assistant and then Kenneth's secretary, she'd dealt with politicians, and famous athletes, and millionaires and even a not-so-minor royal, and she had never felt more intimidated than she did now.

'But then, I'm sure you know that. You used to work with my husband, many years ago. In fact, it must have been about thirty years ago? Am I right?'

'Yes, you are.' This was like a car crash unfolding in slow motion right in front of her and Marge couldn't find the brake pedal.

Still, Clara Kelaney was cool and composed. 'I saw you come in earlier with a young woman? Is that your daughter?'

Marge shook her head. 'No. That's my daughter's friend. Estelle isn't here today.'

Estelle. Her thirty-year-old daughter.

'Estelle,' Clara repeated softly.

'Yes.'

There was a pause, before Clara said, 'If it's all right with you, I think I'd very much like to speak to you about Estelle. Do you have time to talk now?'

8 P.M.–10 P.M.

25

BERNADETTE

Bernadette rushed along the icy road, the wind biting her ears as she went. There had been no point bringing the car, because the cafe they met in every year on this date was just along the road from the hospital and it was just as quick to walk. Although, she hadn't factored in the possibility of hypothermia, which was getting more likely by the second.

When she burst into Carlo's Cafe, she spotted Lady Clara Kelaney and Diana Atkins, already at a table for six in the corner, the same one they reserved every year, although this year their number was sorely diminished.

The twenty-first of February. Inspired by her ex-husband's infidelities and Danielle's throwaway comment about the one day a week that she ate chips, it had been solemnly nicknamed Cheat Day on that first night they met in the St Kentigern Hotel, and commemorated every year until now. It had been a wonderful adventure, a true feat of forgiveness and sisterhood and Bernadette had been grateful for the love, the mutual support and the laughs. It was also a strictly no-judgement zone because they were well aware that there had been nuggets of fault in them all. Danielle had no idea he was married at first but had continued to see him after she discovered the truth because she'd stupidly fallen for the "we lead separate lives" lie. Annabel should have known but had been too swept away to do her due diligence – especially as she'd shagged him in a hotel room at Gleneagles two hours after meeting him at a gala ball. Diana had of course known that

Kenneth was married, yet she'd fallen for his persuasive charms. In fact, she'd also been married to Murray at the time, and her interlude with Kenneth had been a revenge fling because she'd found out Murray was shagging his mixed doubles partner at their tennis club. Meanwhile, Bernadette had been aware of them all and done nothing to warn them. And as for Clara Kelaney and Marge – given their connection, they more than qualified to have a seat at the Cheat Day table too.

'Bernadette!' Diana was the first to jump up and greet her with a tight squeeze. She'd never married again after her divorce from Murray, and his subsequent remarriage to Lila had devastated her. Every year, she'd regaled them with rumours that Murray and Lila were on the rocks, and Bernadette had realised somewhere along the line that it was wishful thinking. Perhaps today's antics, however, would suggest that she was right. Not that Bernadette could share a single word about that – much as she adored Diana, she was far too professional to break patient confidentiality.

'Hello, my love,' Bernadette gushed as she returned the hug, truly delighted to see her.

When she released her, Clara was already on her feet and next in line for a hug.

Bernadette wrapped her arms around Clara's cashmere-clad shoulders. 'Hello, lovely. Ah, it's great to see you. Although, I'm going to stop hanging out with you if you continue to age backwards.'

'Facelift,' Clara whispered. 'A marvellous French doctor. It was a treat to myself.'

That made Bernadette chuckle. 'My last treat to myself was a pack of three white chocolate Magnums from Asda. I think we have different worlds and different definitions of a treat, Clara.'

They were still laughing when Bernadette shrugged off her coat and pulled out a chair. Before they could get chatting, the waiter arrived to take their order.

'I'll have a coffee, please,' Bernadette said, noticing the other two had already chosen wine. Usually she'd be on the vino bus too, but tonight wasn't a night for drinking. Tonight was for carrying out the wishes of an old friend.

'Where is everyone else?' Clara asked. 'Are they all running late? That weather out there is terrible. I saw on the news that there had been loads of accidents on the roads. Have they been delayed?'

'Ah, the problem wasn't the roads, but we have had some call-offs.' Bernadette sat back to let the waiter slide a mug of coffee onto the table, and she folded her hands around it to help them defrost. 'I've had texts from both Annabel and Danielle to say they wouldn't make it. Annabel has been held up at work and Danielle has been held up by a gorgeous man in Turks and Caicos, apparently. She says it's bliss.'

'Urgh, that cow always gets swept away on fancy holidays.' Diana rolled her eyes. 'It's those legs of hers. A man just sees them and immediately books a first-class trip to the Caribbean. It's like some kind of hypnosis. Or witchcraft.'

Bernadette had quickly learned that Diana's dry, wry bitchiness was all part of her endearing charm. If Danielle were here, she'd take no offence whatsoever and find it hilarious.

Bernadette nodded solemnly. 'Blackpool. That's the last place Jack took me. What does that say about my legs?'

'Could probably do with a razor,' Diana fired back, making Bernadette crease.

'You're not wrong.'

Clara was still smiling, but not too widely due to the recent facelift, when she said, 'And what about Marge? Is she on her way?'

Bernadette had to summon all her acting skills, garnered over decades of putting people at ease, delivering reassurance and masking worst-case scenarios, to deliver a half-truth. Marge had been very clear that she didn't want the full reality of her situation to be shared, because she didn't want visitors. Except one. But that was for later.

'Ladies, I'm sorry to say Marge won't be joining us. She had surgery a few weeks ago and is still in hospital. But she sends her love, and she says she'll see you all next year.'

'Oh no! Can we ask what her surgery is for? Is it serious?' Clara asked.

'Lung cancer,' Bernadette conceded, to gasps from them both. 'But she's hopeful that the treatment has worked, so we just have to stay positive.'

Fudging the truth didn't come easy to her. God knows, this group had suffered enough lies and duplicity, but she had to respect Marge's wishes.

'Please give her our love. Oh, poor Estelle, she must be devastated about her mum. I'll get the details of Marge's ward off you so that I can send flowers or visit if she's up to it.'

Bernadette saw that Clara's brow was knitted with concern, and she understood. Since that first night, Marge and Clara had formed a particularly special bond.

'Yes, me too!' Diana chirped in, before her phone buzzed and distracted her. She checked the screen and then made a 'one minute' gesture and got up from the table.

Bernadette took the moment to speak to Clara.

'Clara, can we have a quick chat later, just the two of us? Marge asked me to pass on a message...'

There were some things that both women knew didn't need an explanation.

'Of course. Maybe you could walk with me to my car when we're leaving?'

'Good idea,' Bernadette agreed gratefully.

'Oh bugger, bugger, bugger...' Diana blurted, all wide-eyed and amped up as she came back to the table. 'You're never going to believe this – that was Murray on the phone.'

Bernadette felt a sudden desire to put her head on the table. Of course it was Murray. That bloody man had been the bane of her life today. She never wanted to hear his name again.

'You'll never guess where he is.'

Bernadette could definitely guess, but she didn't. Bloody Hippocratic Oath.

'Jail?' was Clara's first suggestion.

Diana clearly shared Bernadette's surprise. 'Clara!' Diana chided. 'The man is an eminent surgeon and a highly regarded pillar of the community. Why would you say that?'

The most regal lady of them all had the perfect answer. 'Because I've met him.'

Diana couldn't even feign outrage. 'You know, for a posh bird, you're pretty funny.'

'I've heard that said,' Clara shrugged, a twinkle in her eye.

If Diana noticed that Bernadette hadn't joined the game, she didn't say, as she motored on. 'He's along in Glasgow Central. Apparently he slipped in the shower this morning...'

Bernadette noticed the sketchy details didn't specify whose shower it was.

'And banged his head. They've run lots of tests and he has a suspected concussion. They want him to stay in overnight, but he's discharged himself...'

Bernadette had a horrible feeling she knew what was about to come.

'And him and that tart he married have had a huge fight. Apparently, she wasn't sympathetic at all. I mean, what kind of woman is that?'

Yep, it was definitely coming.

'And she's buggered off and left him there. How could she walk away and leave a sick man? That's barbaric. She never loved him, you know. Not like I did.'

Still coming.

'Anyway, I'm so sorry, ladies, but when I told him I was nearby, he begged me to go and collect him and I can't say no.'

And there it was. Murray bloody Atkins. Narcissist. Liar. Cheat. Manipulative twat. And so menacingly good at playing the game, that he could still get his ex-wife back on the hook with just one phone call. The familiarity of it triggered something deep in Bernadette's soul and made her shudder. She'd only left Kenneth once, and she'd never gone back, but she'd given in to him time and time and time again, trusted his promises, believed his denials, gone running when he snapped his fingers – at least at first. Bernadette desperately wanted to warn her, to tell her exactly what had happened to him, but again, bit her tongue because Murray would have her nursing registration cancelled before she could say 'cheating git' if he ever found out that she'd shared his personal information. Besides, Diana knew exactly what he was like, and yet she was still going – Bernadette doubted that there was anything she could say that would stop her.

Diana picked up her jacket and her bag, then leaned over and hugged them both in turn. 'Let's get together again when we're all free. Maybe next month?'

'Maybe,' Bernadette agreed, knowing that it wouldn't happen. There wasn't going to be another time when the whole group could meet again, because Marge couldn't be there again. The thought caught her off guard and she had to make a real effort to keep the emotion out of her voice as she said goodbye to Diana. 'You take care, lovely. And remember you know where to find me if you need me.'

'I have a feeling that'll be sooner rather than later,' Clara said under her breath, as they both waved Diana farewell.

'She'll learn,' Bernadette said simply. 'It took me over thirty years to snap and escape Kenneth's hold. She's still got time.'

'I hope so.' Clara lifted her wine glass and they were both immediately aware of a shift in energy. 'So this makes it easier for us to chat. Tell me about Marge.'

'She's being moved to palliative care tomorrow, Clara.'

Bernadette watched Clara's eyes widen as she whispered, 'Oh no. Poor Marge.'

'And she asked me to speak to you, because she is going to tell Estelle the truth about her father. I'm sorry, Clara. She feels it's the right thing to do. As do I.'

Clara barely hesitated. 'Of course it is. I completely understand. If this were my girls...' She let the words drift off. Clara and Sir Lester had three daughters, all of a very similar age to Estelle, so Bernadette knew she understood Marge's angst.

'And I know it's a big ask, Clara, but Marge would like you to come to the hospital and be there when she tells her. She said she completely understands if you don't feel you can. And she said not to feel pressure at all, but—'

'I'll do it.'

'You will?'

'Yes.'

Bernadette felt an urgent sense of panic that she'd somehow forced Clara to do something that could have huge consequences for her life. 'Look, take your time and think about it.'

'I don't need to, Bernadette.'

'And you don't want to speak to Sir Lester?'

That suggestion got a reaction, but it wasn't the one Bernadette had expected. Clara was a quiet, thoughtful woman. Someone who thought things through and made measured decisions. All part of being in the public eye, Bernadette supposed.

'No, I do not. At least, not beforehand. I think it would be best for me to speak to Marge first, possibly Estelle too. I'll not have him forbid me to do it. All those years ago, he made decisions regarding our family without consulting me. I absolutely have the right to do the same.'

As quiet and thoughtful as she was, Bernadette suspected Clara had a core of steel.

'Okay, that's settled then. Marge will be so relieved. Thank you, Clara. When do you think you'll be able to make it up to see her? Would tomorrow be too soon?'

Clara thought about that for a moment, before, 'Can I go speak to Marge tonight? I'm already out, and the hospital is five minutes away. And, to be honest, if I don't do it now, I don't know that I'll still have the courage tomorrow.'

It took Bernadette a moment to process that idea. She checked her watch: 8.45 p.m. Visiting finished at 9 p.m., but Marge was in a private room, and at this stage in her illness, the staff were as flexible as possible. Many times, Bernadette had allowed family members to stay overnight on chairs or roll-up beds because they didn't want to miss a single moment with the person they loved. Besides, it was Keli Clark who was on duty tonight, and she had a heart of gold.

'I think we can. Grab your jacket and let's go, Clara. Cheat Day is officially adjourned.'

26

MARGE

Marge could feel the water, warm on her hands as she stood in the ladies' washroom with Clara Kelaney. Sir Lester's wife was so poised. So serene. Yet Marge had never been more terrified in her life than when Clara said, 'If it's all right with you, I think I'd very much like to speak to you about Estelle. Do you have time to talk now?'

For all the fear though, there was also a strong sensation of the kind of relief that can only come when an imagined scenario that has haunted you for years finally materialises and there's no other option than to face it.

The time had come for the truth to be told. For her to face what she'd done. And she could confront it or walk away.

Marge raised her chin and forced a calm, receptive smile that bore no connection to the pounding of her heart. 'Yes. Shall we take a seat outside?'

Over the years, Marge had played out this conversation in the darkest corners of her imagination, and never had she thought that it would actually happen, or that when it did, it would be on a luxuriously over-stuffed, purple sofa in the sumptuous lobby of the St Kentigern Hotel.

The butterflies swooped in to accompany her racing heart as she watched Clara, her hands crossed neatly on her lap, contemplate her words. When she eventually spoke, in a soft, but firm voice, it confirmed that this was indeed a moment she'd always feared.

'Your daughter, Estelle, is my husband's daughter too.'

No accusation. No berating. No fury. Just facts. And if nothing else, Marge was a woman whose logical brain did well with facts.

'Yes, she is.' There it was. Done. 'Can I ask how you know that?'

Marge's eyes briefly flickered to the door, checking that Sir Lester Kelaney wasn't rushing in there right at that moment looking murderous. No. Just an Italian tour group chatting loudly about dinner plans.

'Many years ago, I read the letter that you sent him.'

'Ah. He showed you.'

Marge had always wondered if he'd told his wife.

'No. It was in his desk, but only for a day or two and then it disappeared. I'm guessing he destroyed the evidence. I didn't confront him, and I still haven't told him to this day that I read it. That might seem odd to you.'

'Strangely, no. It doesn't at all. Because if you read the letter, then you'll have seen that I said I'd never mention it again, that I'd ignore its existence and that's what I did too.'

Clara took that in. 'I was never sure if he'd spoken to you. If he'd made some effort to help. To acknowledge his part or his responsibilities.'

Marge shook her head. 'He didn't. I continued working for him for some time after that and it was never mentioned, not even once, by either of us.' Marge knew how incredible that would probably sound to every other person on earth, except the woman sitting across from her, who had, in effect, done the very same thing.

'I met and married my husband very shortly after I found out I was pregnant, and at first, Ian wanted me to leave and find work elsewhere, but I loved my job, it was well-paid, and I was pregnant. And, as you can imagine, Lester had no hesitation in giving me extended time off for maternity leave and then flexible hours when I returned. I know that many people wouldn't understand that, but I used it to my advantage. I only left when Kenneth set up his own practice a few months later and offered me a position that had all the same perks, but without the daily reminder of what had happened.'

Clara's eyes dipped. 'Lester was a coward. No, Lester is a coward. He always has been. I'm so sorry.'

When Marge had imagined this moment, she'd expected fury, rage, condemnation, but she had never, ever expected an apology. She thought back to what Bernadette had said earlier and saw the wisdom in it, so she repeated it now.

'No, please don't. Do not apologise for things that he did or positions he put you in. This is his responsibility. And mine. I'm so sorry that I...' Her toes curled and she

felt her whole body cringe as she found the words, '...Had an illicit encounter with your husband. I was equally at fault, and I won't use the excuses that I was young, or drunk, or horribly naïve, although all of those things are true. I put myself in that position, but it was once, and as you read in the letter, we never spoke of it again and it was never repeated. In some ways, it was, of course, the biggest mistake of my life, but it gave me Estelle. And for that, I'll always be grateful. Especially as my husband and I unfortunately didn't go on to have any more children. But to you, I apologise from the bottom of my heart.'

'Thank you.' Clara accepted that with more grace than Marge could ever have hoped for. 'But much as it pains me to say it, I can assure you that you were not the first or the last encounter my husband has had over the years, so I think the bulk of the responsibility lies with him. And, as you said, let's not apologise for the positions he put you in.'

'I'm sorry,' Marge replied, instinctively, then realised what she'd said and felt the need to clarify. 'Not for him. For you. I'm sorry you've had to deal with that.'

She'd never witnessed anything suspicious when she worked for him, but in the years since then, Marge had heard many rumours about Lester Kelaney, so she'd known that their encounter wasn't an isolated incident. She'd just always assumed that his wife was in the dark. Now that she knew different, she felt awful for her. What a life. Like Bernadette's marriage to Kenneth. And yet both women had stayed for decades. Bernadette had eventually found the strength to leave, but Clara?

'Can I ask – and please tell me to mind my own business – but why do you stay with him?'

Clara's answer came with a sad smile. 'That's a very complicated question, with a complicated answer. But perhaps you'll understand when I say there are similarities to the reasons that you continued to work for him after you had your child. At that time, I had three children under three.'

That made Marge feel even worse, but she didn't have time to drown in self-reproach, because Clara was still speaking.

'And I wasn't prepared to uproot their lives, to put them in the middle of a tug-of-war situation that would tear their worlds apart. Staying with Lester would give them a wonderful start in life and I could never bear to disrupt that. I knew that he would never leave – image is everything to someone like Lester. The man is spineless, he's weak and he is deeply flawed, but for the entirety of our marriage, and for

the moment, it suits me to stay. There may be a time when that is no longer the case, and when that comes, I'll leave.'

Oh, this one was a dark horse. Marge could sense that there was so much more going on here, but she wasn't going to probe deeper. Clara owed her nothing. She was just going to have to be satisfied with knowing that Clara was in control of the situation, and clearly, from her words, her tone, and her spirit, wasn't there because she had no other option. She had a choice. She just hadn't used it yet.

Clara's body language changed, and Marge saw that she was getting ready to stand up, but she still had one more question.

'So, Clara, what now? Do you intend to tell Lester about our meeting?' Marge's fears had come thundering back. Would this change everything? Would he want to meet Estelle. Would this force Marge to tell her daughter the truth? On that night Ian was ripped from their lives, she'd promised him that they'd tell her, but she'd never had the courage to do it. How could she take away her father when he was already gone?

'I'd very much like to know where you stand and where we go from here. Estelle...' Marge was cringing again, dreading saying aloud the truth that was never far from her conscience. 'Estelle doesn't know. She has always believed that my husband was her father. It's something that plays very heavy on my mind. I haven't found the strength to be honest with her and I don't know if I ever will.'

The silence stretched for a few moments, before Clara said, 'I think, if it's agreeable to you, then we'll keep this just between us for now. But please know that if you ever decide to tell Estelle or make public your connection to Lester, then I'll understand and, more than that, I'll support both you and Estelle. It's the least I can do as she's the half-sister of my daughters. Lester has had ample opportunity to step up and he has failed you both – I won't do the same.'

Marge didn't think she could be more grateful or more stunned. At least until Clara stood up and reached out her hand.

'So, shall we go back and join the ladies?'

As Marge accepted her hand, she felt the warm touch... the gentle stroke... heard her voice...

'Marge? Marge, it's Clara. I hate to wake you, but I just wanted you to know I was here.'

Marge opened her eyes and saw the lovely face of the woman she'd first spoken to five years ago. True to their agreement, they'd never discussed their connection again. It was almost like it had never happened. Until...

Panic gripped her chest as the rest of the room came into focus. Bernadette was there, standing just behind Clara. And on the other side of the bed...

'Your friends popped in to visit you, Mum.'

Estelle. *Oh God, Estelle.*

The picture continued to clear, the details falling into place in her mind. She'd asked Bernadette to speak to Clara. To tell her she was ready to share the whole story with her daughter. But she'd thought Clara would come tomorrow. Maybe the next day. Because now that her friend was here, Marge knew she wasn't ready at all.

She couldn't do it.

Couldn't break her daughter's heart.

Couldn't tell her that her whole life had been a lie.

Couldn't admit her shame and her weakness.

But yet...

She thought back to this morning, to Wilma, with her new kidney, to her family, to the realisation that once Marge was gone, Estelle would be alone.

And somewhere in that came the strength to do what she had to do. She had to give Estelle the chance to have a tether, to have a connection, a family – even if it was only one of DNA. She had to give her the truth.

'Estelle...' Marge whispered, holding out her free hand to her daughter, who leaned forward in her chair and took it.

'Right here, Mum.'

'I need to tell you...'

The words got stuck. Jammed. They wouldn't come out. She prayed that Bernadette or Clara would step in, but they didn't, because they both understood that this had to be Marge's conversation. She had to decide what to say, how much to reveal. And if she changed her mind, couldn't find the courage, she had absolutely no doubt that they would cover for her and her secret would go with her to her grave.

But wasn't that the problem? It was cruel to let some secrets die.

'Estelle, I wanted you to meet Clara.' Her voice was hoarse again, still barely a whisper, and Bernadette immediately jumped up, lifted her water glass and held it to Marge's lips.

She took a sip, the liquid cooling her throat enough to continue.

'Estelle, I... Clara... I...' Damn, the words. She couldn't find the order she should place them in. She took a breath, went back to the start, summoned the kind of strength of voice she'd been unable to find all day. Estelle's future depended on it. 'I need to tell you something I should have shared with you long before now. And I'm so sorry. I need you to know that before I tell you. I'm so, so sorry. And please forgive me.' Marge felt water slide from the corners of her eyes.

Bernadette helped her drink a little more.

'When I got married to your dad, I was already expecting you.'

An almost visceral sob wracked her body. She'd said it. She'd done it. *Did you hear that, Ian?*

'And Clara...' A cough rose and Marge gave into it, grateful when Bernadette raised the glass to her lips yet again.

When she could speak again, she turned to Clara...

'Clara? Please...' she whispered, giving unspoken permission.

'I'm so sorry to meet under these circumstances,' Clara said, in that gentle voice that Marge knew so well. 'And I'm sorry too – I know this must all be such a shock. As your mum said, when she got married, she was already pregnant with you. And the reason I'm here is because your father is my husband, Lester.'

Marge saw Clara's gaze return to her, and she mouthed a silent, 'Thank you,' before turning back to her daughter, ready to face the consequences of her secrets and her decisions.

She was ready for anger. For disbelief. She wouldn't blame Estelle if she walked out right now and didn't return. What she'd done was treacherous. Unforgivable. But when her gaze met Estelle's...

...all she saw...

...was understanding.

'Mum, it's okay, I promise. There's nothing to forgive. Because I've known that for a long time.'

27

AMBER

'Do you want me to wait again, hen? I tell you, I could get used to this personal chauffeur business. If you ever win the lottery, me and my Skoda are at your service. In fact, do you know that Skodas...'

Wiki Taxi Driver launched into a diatribe about the history of the Skoda, which was mercifully cut short by their arrival at the main door of Glasgow Central Hospital. As they slid to a halt, Amber answered his earlier question. 'No, it's fine, thank you. I don't need you to wait.' She had no idea how long it would take for her to find Marge's room, and going by the people streaming out of the doors, visiting time was already over, so they might not let her in, and if they did, Estelle may not even be there.

This might be a completely wasted trip, but she had to try, because if she didn't, she wasn't sure she wouldn't wake up tomorrow and change her mind about the whole bloody thing.

Seeing Ewan tonight was like throwing her brain into a bubbling vat of Sid's favourite slime, and then watching it explode and paste the walls. Actually, that was a bit too graphic an image and it was now making her feel queasy. But the point was, she was confused. Mixed up. Had no idea what she wanted or why. If anyone had told her yesterday that she would be knocking on Ewan's door today, or trying desperately to track down Estelle, she'd have given them Calpol and told them to have a lie-down.

Yet here she was.

'Right, here you go...' she said to Wiki Taxi Driver, tapping her credit card against the machine, and this time giving a generous tip. He deserved it. He'd single-handedly facilitated her crusade to sort out her life tonight. Or to wreck it. It was yet to be decided. 'Thanks again,' she said, hand on door. 'You've been an education. And I'll definitely remember you if I win the lottery.'

'Do you know that the lottery...' he began, but she was out of the door before he got any further.

Dodging the visitors who were coming out of the doors in the opposite direction to where she was headed, she walked swiftly into the foyer and searched for the information board. There it was. She marched over, consulted the list. Elderly ward. Fourth Floor. Right then. Lifts?

Another scan of the lobby. Other than her prolonged visit to the Emergency Department today, she'd only been in this hospital a few times – twice to give birth in the maternity unit, once due to the unfortunate incident with the pruning shears, and an overnight stay in paediatrics, where she slept on a roll-up bed next to Sid, who'd been admitted with suspected appendicitis – so she wasn't familiar with the layout.

There was a huge interactive map in the middle of the room, so she headed for that and tried to work it out. Okay, she was there... She pointed to the large red cross on the board, and the cafe was there... Her gaze went from the map to her left, and yes, there was the cafe she'd sat in earlier with Bernadette... so that must mean that the lifts were... Hang on.

Her focus went back to the cafe and she peered intently, really wishing she'd worn her specs – she'd left them in her bedside drawer prior to the misguided sexy time with that lying twat this morning, and had forgotten to pick them up when she popped home.

But was that...?

She peered harder. Yes. It was. Maybe. Possibly. Estelle?

Leaving the map behind, she strode over, pressed her face against the glass, and saw to her relief that she was right. Estelle. But she was sitting at a table with a woman Amber didn't recognise: a petite, slim, striking lady, her white hair pulled back in a very elegant chignon at the nape of her neck, perhaps in her sixties or seventies, it was hard to tell.

Aw bollocks, a new quandary. Interrupt them, or wait until they were finished, or go home and forget all about this, put it down to a mental aberration and go to bed with a bucket of chocolate chip ice cream.

Bugger it. She hadn't come this far...

Neither of the women glanced up when she pushed the door open, so she was all the way to their table before Estelle noticed she was there. 'Amber!'

Amber went to speak, but... nothing. This was as far as her plan, such as it was, had got her. Go to hospital. Find Estelle. She should have asked Wiki Taxi Driver what she should say next.

'Em, hi.'

Okay, not exactly profound, but a start.

'I'm sorry to interrupt, but I just wanted to have a quick chat. I can wait over by the cakes until you're done though.'

A sudden, violent gnawing pain in her stomach, combined with the sight of the cake display, reminded her that she'd had nothing to eat all day and she was famished.

'No, please, don't.' The white-haired lady was saying now, in a voice that made it very obvious she probably came from the posh side of the city. 'I was just leaving.' She then put her hand on top of Estelle's and said, 'Perhaps we can speak again in a day or two? Please give me a call and let me know when is best for you.'

'I'll do that. And, Clara, thank you so much. You've no idea what this means to me.'

The woman Estelle had called Clara then smiled and said softly, 'I think I do, and that makes me very happy. Take good care of your lovely mum for me. She's a very special lady.'

'I will,' Estelle replied, nodding, and Amber saw that, for the second time today, her former best pal of a decade, who hadn't even cried when they'd got to the sad bit in *Mamma Mia*, had tears in her eyes.

Amber stayed standing until Clara had passed her, with mutual smiles, and then sat down in the seat Clara had just vacated, suddenly bursting with something to say.

'Okay, I know it's none of my business, but who was that?'

Estelle wiped her eyes with the palm of her hand. 'Erm, her name is Clara Kelaney.'

The name vaguely rang a bell, but it took Amber a couple of seconds to put it together. 'Oh. Is she married to Sir Lester Kelaney? He was one of the speakers at that funeral I went to with your mum years ago. The doctor guy. And it's so crazy, because it was his ex-wife I was sitting here with when I met you in here earlier. How random is that?'

'Actually, not so random. Turns out they all know each other. My mum. Bernadette. Clara. A few others. They're all in some sort of friend group that meets up every year on the anniversary of that funeral. Clara just told me all about it. All these years, I thought my mum was the most straightforward, uncomplicated, strait-laced woman there ever was, and it turns out she had a whole other side to her. My mind is blown.'

'Must be the day for it,' Amber said, empathising with every bit of Estelle's weariness. 'I've been thinking I'm having an out-of-body experience all day.'

It gave Amber a tiny twinge of joy to see that made Estelle smile. Putting everything that had happened between them to one side, she was devastated for what Estelle was going through.

'Me too,' Estelle nodded. It was a brief but much-needed moment of lightness, but it took a step back into awkwardness when they both fell silent.

Amber realised that she was the one who'd come here, so she was going to have to be the one who took the lead. Besides, Estelle looked utterly exhausted, and right now all Amber wanted to do was hug her.

'Look, I know this is a terrible time for you, but I couldn't stop thinking about you, and your mum. If I'm being completely honest, I feel beyond crap that I cut Marge off too after we fell out. I was just so... Urgh, I don't want to make excuses, but I was just so hurt. And devastated. And truly, I've had absolutely no fricking idea what I've been doing for the last two years because I was just trying to get my heartbroken arse through every day and take care of my boys and hold it together. I'm so sorry. I just needed to tell you that. If you hate me, I understand.' She paused, and wondered if it was too soon for half-jokes and half-truths. 'I mean, it's fine if you do. I kinda hate you too.'

The twinge of joy was back when that made Estelle smile again as she said, 'Completely understandable. I'd hate me too. I'm sorry, Amber. I really am. When you asked me earlier if I'd do it again and I said I would... I'm sorry about that too. I have my reasons. I don't expect you to get it.'

'Then tell me. Explain it to me. You might need to tie me to the chair, but I promise this time I'll listen. It's a new me.'

Estelle began to shake her head and for a second Amber thought she was going to refuse, tell Amber she was a cow, and leave, so there was more relief when she didn't. Instead, she said, 'I had the happiest childhood ever. And amazing parents. I think you know that.'

Amber nodded. 'I do. I was always a bit jealous. My lot are a chaotic study in dysfunction, and you had Mary Poppins and George Clooney. I know those two don't go together, but you get the point.'

'I do,' Estelle conceded. 'When I look back on growing up with them, I can't think of a single thing that I worried about, or that caused me pain or scarred me for life.'

'I've got a list the length of a toilet roll, but go on.' They both knew she wasn't joking. Her parents had seven marriages between them, and it didn't take a psychologist to work out that Amber found it difficult to trust – or that she'd run for the hills when her trust was broken. That was why she'd put a mountain between her and Ewan and Estelle for the last two years. Maybe listening to Estelle now was the first steps of her descent.

'Exactly. It was all happiness. Other than the normal kid stuff and the Spice Girls breaking up, there was nothing to be sad about. But what I didn't know then...' She took a breath before going on, 'Was that my dad wasn't actually my dad.'

'What? No. How? No way. I don't...' Amber ran out of words, then offered a contrite, 'Sorry. Please go on.'

'My mum had a one-night stand before she met my dad and by the time she found out she was pregnant, they'd already fallen in love. They decided to keep me, and Dad raised me as his, and I didn't find out until he died.'

Amber was still desperately trying to put the pieces in place. 'But wait, I was with you when your dad died, and for all the years after.'

'I know.'

'And you didn't tell me?'

'I didn't tell anyone that I knew. Not even my mum. I suppose that's difficult for you to understand, but that's just the way we were. The way we are, actually. We keep things to ourselves. It's that whole, "Lest said, soonest mended," thing. My mum and I are just experts at putting problems in boxes.'

Amber realised she was missing a bit of vital information. 'And your... dad? The biological one?'

'Clara Kelaney's husband.'

'Fuck. Off.' It was out before Amber could stop herself.

'Nope. My mum worked for him when she fell pregnant. They had one night together. He was already married, and, from what I've learned tonight, he's a serial shagger.'

'Oh, poor Marge. And poor Clara.' Amber did wonder if her reaction might have been different had she not also slept with a married guy this morning, albeit inadvertently. 'But also, wow Marge. I'd never have believed it. How did you find out?'

'My mum wrote a note to Lester Kelaney and my dad – the one I grew up with – kept a copy of it. I found it in his things when he died.'

'Oh Estelle, I'm sorry. I wish you'd told me.'

'But that's the thing. It worked out for the best that I told no one, because my mum didn't need to have all that dredged up when she was already mourning my dad. And I honestly feel grateful that my parents didn't tell me when I was younger, because then, maybe my life would have been different. Maybe I'd have been different. Apparently my biological dad wanted nothing to do with me anyway, so I'd have had to navigate rejection and maybe disappointment and confusion too – that's why I'm thankful that they kept it from me and gave me the gift of growing up knowing nothing but love and care. Other people might disagree, but I think that sometimes loving someone can mean protecting them from the truth.'

Amber had a sinking feeling they were about to get to the connection in this story and she was about to feel like crap.

'And that's my point,' Estelle continued. 'Rightly or wrongly, that's what I was trying to do. I didn't tell you about the affair because it was over and I didn't want you to feel that pain. And more than that, I didn't want to be responsible for breaking up the parents of Sid and Alfie. I thought you could just carry on with life and be happy.'

'Yeah, newsflash...' Amber said, weakly.

'I know. Didn't quite work out as I thought. But I hope, maybe, you can understand at least a bit... even if you don't agree and still think I'm a cow. I did what I thought was right, based on my own experiences. But I'm sorry, Amber. And I miss you.'

Amber wasn't sure how to respond to that. She'd had her heart torn out. Run over by a bus. Which then reversed. Ran over it again. And drove off, leaving her broken. Could she really move past any of this? Find a way to understand and forgive? She still didn't know if she could with Ewan, but Estelle?

'I miss you too. But I can't be friends again.'

Estelle looked crushed. 'But why?'

Amber inhaled. Shrugged. 'Because I've just found out your dad is a "Sir". You're now way too posh to be my pal.'

For the third time today, Amber watched as Estelle Drummond burst into tears. And so did she.

And it was only after using six napkins from the table dispenser to dry their eyes that Amber said, 'So now we've got that sorted... I know visiting is over, but any chance you can sneak me up to see Marge?'

28

BERNADETTE – SUNDAY 21 FEBRUARY 2021

'I was just about to send out a search party for you two,' Bernadette said, as Marge and Clara came back to the table. She searched their faces for a glimpse of discord or hostility and was relieved to see that, other than Marge looking a little flustered and red in the face, all seemed to be fine.

In the unexpectedly honest, frank discussion she'd had with Marge earlier, right before the manager had interrupted them at the end of the wake, Bernadette had been stunned when Marge had revealed the truth of Estelle's paternity. It had almost seemed like a relief to Marge to get it off her chest.

'Did Kenneth know that she wasn't your husband's baby?' Bernadette had asked, curious as to her former husband's part in this.

'He did. We'd been friends – or perhaps acquaintances would be a better word – for a while at that point. In fact, I was with him, and a group of other doctors, at a party on the night Estelle was conceived. Kenneth saw me leave with Lester and later he did the maths. I've always thought that was one of the reasons Kenneth offered me the job,' she'd said, with what Bernadette thought was incredibly perceptive honesty. 'It was his way of subtly keeping Sir Lester on the hook for anything Kenneth might want. Lester would never know whether I'd told Kenneth or not and therefore he'd do anything to keep him onside – including making sure they were seen together at all the right places.'

Bernadette had felt a shiver go right down her spine. 'I'd love to say that was a surprise, but I knew him too well. He was a master of that kind of manipulation and a relentless social climber, so that makes so much sense.'

'I don't even feel that I can judge or criticise anyone after what I did, though. The guilt of it made me so ashamed. It still does. I understand if you want to get up and walk away, Bernadette. You must be disgusted.'

Of course, Bernadette had done no such thing. In fact, her heart ached for Marge, for Clara, for all of these women.

Earlier, she had seen how hard it had been for Marge to confide in her, and now, as she watched them return to the table, Bernadette wondered if Marge and Clara had just had a similar discussion. Bernadette hoped so. They'd decided earlier that if there had been a theme of this dinner tonight, it was that the truth, no matter how unpalatable, was easier to bear than the secrets. Or something like that. Three cocktails ago, she'd made a mental note of it, but it was a tad scrambled now.

Ding ding ding.

Diana Atkins was rattling the glass of her porn star martini and demanding their attention. Thankfully, other than the staff over at the stunning art deco bar in the middle of the restaurant, they were the only diners left in the room.

'Ladies, I would like to say something.' She waited until everyone was tuned in. 'I woke up this morning feeling awful. I also had a dream that I had sex with my gynaecologist, but that's another story.'

Bernadette scanned the group. 'Anyone here married to a gynaecologist who's been acting suspiciously lately? Only with you lot...'

The hoots of laughter carried right over the sound of Celine Dion singing 'The Power of Love' in the background.

'Anywaaaaaay,' Diana drawled, reclaiming the floor. 'As I was saying, I woke up this morning feeling awful. Even though Kenneth was most definitely on my shit list, I knew I had to show face at his funeral, and I was dreading it. I couldn't stand to see Murray again, because he has wounded me to the core. And, also, I thought he might turn up with some young blonde on his arm to piss me off.'

'Turns out he left with a young blonde on his arm...' Danielle pointed out, rather unnecessarily.

'And yes, that did piss me off. I've said a silent prayer that there's an STD in his near future,' Diana said with an exaggerated purse of the lips. There was more laughter before she carried on. 'But the point is, it's turned out to be the best day I've had in ages. I haven't laughed more...'

'Or drank more,' Bernadette offered, but she was fairly sure she was projecting.

And she was also tipsily aware that she herself hadn't drunk this much since... since... well, ever. This was ten years' worth of Christmases, New Year, and birthdays combined. With a cherry on top.

'So I want to thank you all,' Diana said, raising her glass. 'To us.'

Around the table, they all joined the toast, before Annabel Stevenson took the reins.

'I would like to thank you all too. Ladies, you have soothed my soul today and reminded me that we're all human. Sometimes that's easy to forget.'

They were all nodding, taking on board the profound, spiritual message in her comment, when she added, 'But I am up for re-election next month, and can't afford a whiff of scandal or the rest of the hypocritical, misogynistic gits will have me replaced by someone from the Green party. So I would like to request that nothing that has been said tonight is ever repeated. I trust you all,' she paused to let that soak in. 'But you might get a non-disclosure agreement from my office just to be on the safe side.'

That set them all off again and this time it crossed Bernadette's mind that if Annabel's constituents saw her jokey side, it might make her even more popular. At least, Bernadette hoped that was a joke.

It was Danielle who raised her glass next. 'Well, first of all, I'd like to thank this restaurant for my Cheat Day chips,' she said, with a drum roll on the table. 'They'll keep me going for a whole seven days until the next time.'

'Glad we could be of service,' Marge piped up and Bernadette was pleased, because she'd been a little worried by how quiet she'd been for the last hour or so. Maybe she had had a difficult discussion with Clara. Or perhaps Marge was just one of those people with a smaller social battery and it was running low, as opposed to Bernadette, who had been accused by many of being plugged in to the National Grid.

Back to Danielle. 'And I'd also like to thank you all for making me feel like a far less shitty and stupid person than I have since I found out I had an affair with a married man because I fell for all his lies. And especially to you, Bernadette. I don't think there are many women who would embrace us the way that you have. Kenneth was a complete dick to let you go.'

The staff at the restaurant bar were now rolling their eyes every time they did a round of applause and a cheer, but they were too many porn star martinis in to take offence or stop.

It was Marge's turn next. 'Well, I would like to thank you all for making today eventful and eye-opening. And for embracing me in this group, despite the fact that I have undoubtedly been short, sharp and dismissive of you over the years, especially during the periods of your liaisons.'

Annabel shuddered. 'I've just remembered that you once put me on hold for twenty-seven minutes. I've never been able to listen to Ravel's "Boléro" since. I have to switch the TV off when Torvill and Dean come on, just in case.'

'I wholeheartedly apologise,' Marge said, with what was obviously mock contrition. Over dinner, they'd all swapped stories of their interactions with Marge, all the calls or visits they'd made to Kenneth's office, emails they'd sent, functions they'd attended in her presence, and the common theme had been her absolute surface professionalism and her unmistakable underlying disapproval. Bernadette was grateful for the indirect support. She truly wished she and Marge had got to know each other so much better over the decades, as she saw now that they could have been great allies and friends. But then, that was obviously the reason that Kenneth kept them apart. He was reckless, but he wasn't stupid.

Marge had more to add. 'But I'd just like to say that I too once made a very similar mistake with a man...'

Bernadette was sure she saw the tiniest flicker of understanding shoot between Marge and Clara, before Marge went on.

'So I just want to say sorry. I wasn't judging you... I think I was just trying to deal with my own guilt.'

There was a surprised silence, as they all absorbed the apologetic sentiment, before Danielle came in with words of wisdom. 'Nope, not buying it. You were totally judging us.'

And in a flurry of cackles, the moment, and Marge's confession was gone, and Bernadette was sure her new friend's shoulders rose several inches as the guilt lifted from them.

Bernadette was about to take her turn, when Clara got in there before her. After Marge, Clara had perhaps been the biggest surprise of the day. Bernadette had always thought that she was incredibly regal and perhaps a tad prim, and she may indeed be those things, but today she had also been unwaveringly kind, wise, candid and there was definitely a twinkle of humour in her eye too.

'Well, before I make a toast, I'd like to make a suggestion. In May, every year, I travel to London, to meet up with the girlfriends I went to university with, on the anniversary of our graduation. It's a central point because we are all scattered

across the globe. And in September every year, I travel to Monaco to meet up with my sisters on my mother's birthday...'

'Clara, are you making a toast, or just showing off about your travel plans, because my last holiday was to Palma Nova and it rained every day,' Danielle pouted.

'Bear with me, I'm getting to the point,' Clara insisted. 'Here, in Glasgow I have many friends...'

Annabel rolled her eyes. 'She's showing off again. I have three friends and one of them is my mother.'

'But,' Clara countered pointedly, 'none that I've ever been able to speak to candidly and frankly about Lester's behaviour. I've known Annabel for many years, which is why I joined your table when Lester was ignoring me today. It was my own little rebellion, but it has turned into so much more than that. I can't tell you how refreshing this has been to meet you all. I know you're all very busy people, but I wondered if you would consider making this an annual event. A gathering every year. Perhaps even on today's date, just to remind us of the fortuitousness of our meeting.'

Every head at the table turned to Bernadette, who was attempting to absorb the shock of the suggestion.

Today had been great. A real tonic. There was no denying that. But Clara's idea? It was outrageous.

'So what you're saying is...' Bernadette began, slowly, in disbelief, 'that you want to meet every year on the anniversary of the funeral of my ex-husband of thirty years...'

She paused, trying to format her thoughts. Definitely a few too many of those cocktails.

'To celebrate the fact that he was a terrible person...'

No one interrupted.

'And to mark the fact that today was the day that – with the exception of Clara and Marge – I confirmed my suspicions that the rest of you shagged him behind my back...'

You could hear a pin drop.

'All of which contributed to the ultimate destruction of my marriage. Do I have that right?'

'Well...' Clara began, obviously regretting the request, but Bernadette put her hand up to stop her.

'I think it's outrageous. And I think Kenneth would be utterly disgusted and appalled.'

Still tumbleweed.

'So I abso-bloody-lutely think that's the best possible reason for doing it. Great idea, Clara, and I'll see you all next year, ladies. Same time. Maybe not same place, because it's fecking extortionate here and I'm on a nurse's wage. But let's do it.' With that, Bernadette raised her glass, 'Here's to us.'

The five other members of their newly formed, exclusive club raised their glasses.

And Bernadette was absolutely positive that wherever Kenneth Manson was now, whatever halls of hell he was pacing, he would be raging just a little bit louder.

And that made her smile just a little bit wider.

10 P.M.–MIDNIGHT

29

BERNADETTE

'I was just about to bring this into Marge's room for you, Bernie,' Keli told her, handing over a mug of tea, with the logo 'World's Most Knackered Nurse' on it. 'How are you doing? I was on the phone to Caleb on my break and he told me you all had an eventful day.'

'It was definitely one I'll remember, that's for sure,' Bernadette said with a wry grimace.

When Bernadette had returned to the elderly ward, it had been right at the end of visiting hours and still bustling with activity, but the halls were quiet now, and most of the patients were fast asleep. Bernadette was in front of the nurses' station, and from there she could see that the overhead lights were out in all the multi-bed units, with just a few rays coming from the bedside lights of the patients who were reading or scrolling on phones or iPads. That would never have been allowed in the days when she was training. The ward sister had the lights out at 10 p.m. sharp, and wouldn't dream of allowing technology or communication devices of any kind on the ward. Not that there was that kind of thing in those days. A Sony Walkman had been cutting edge back then. Televisions were communal and wheeled in every morning, and the telephones were a luxury that patients could only use by coming out to the ward's wall-mounted payphone during set times. Changed days.

Bernadette loved her job, but more and more she'd been thinking that perhaps it was time for a change. Or reduced hours. Or at least perhaps she could take the baby step of not coming in every time they were short-staffed. She couldn't be bothered with all that social media stuff, but she'd downloaded Facebook years ago, and then Nina had added Instagram too. And if one more member of her family or one more pal sent her that moody music picture post about how people on their deathbeds never said they wished they could go back and work more, she was deleting them. Or blocking them. Or whatever it was called. She could take a hint – she worked too many long hours. And today, seeing how fragile life was, had definitely been the biggest hint ever that it was time to plan a new future. She just hoped that Jack felt the same. Was he ready to take the next step with her too? He'd brought it up many times in the first couple of years of their relationship and she'd always said they were fine as they were, her fear of getting into another binding relationship over-ruling the fact that she adored him. She'd always thought that he'd backed off to give her space and time, but that he still wanted the same thing. But did he? Had she left it too late and now he was the one who'd backed off? Going by his lack of communication lately, she was beginning to wonder. That was a problem for tomorrow. Today, her priority was the friend in the room across the hall.

'Keli, are you okay with me staying for a little while with Marge? She nodded off when Estelle went down to the cafe with our friend, Clara, but I just don't want her to wake up and be alone. She's been flitting in and out of sleep since I got here. I'll wait until Estelle comes back up and then I'll head off.'

Keli's expression was full of sympathy. 'We're making her as comfortable as we can. The palliative ward have said we can bring her down at nine o'clock in the morning, and she'll be well taken care of there too. I'm sorry, Bernadette – it's hard to watch a friend go through this.'

Bernadette contemplated that and it brought up so many mixed feelings for her. Sorrow. Sadness. An aching heart for a life that would be lost before its time and for the future that wouldn't exist.

'It is. But that's the thing, Keli – I've known Marge for over thirty years because she was my ex-husband's secretary, but we only talked properly after he died. At his funeral, actually. So we weren't really friends. Not true pals that hang out together and share each other's lives. But the saddest thing is that we were going to be. The last time we were together was a year ago tonight and we sat in Carlo's Cafe and vowed to be better at keeping in touch. We even talked about taking a trip over to Ireland too because she hasn't met Jack and she's never been there. Now I don't know why we didn't just do it. Marge was a bit of a loner, and I never seem to have enough hours in the day between this place and the grandkids and... It's all just excuses really. I could have found the time. We both could. We just didn't. I thought we would eventually get round to it, maybe this year, maybe next year. But now it's too late and I could kick myself.'

Bernadette heard her voice falter as she said that last line and swallowed back the emotion of it all. This wasn't about her, and she had no right to be anything except strong for Marge right now. But still... cancer was a bastard of a thing. And so was regret.

'If it's any consolation, hon,' Keli said, her voice oozing sympathy, 'I hear that so often on this ward. There's almost always regret. Sometimes it's the patients, sometimes it's the people that love them, but it's always there. I could see how happy Marge was that you were with her earlier, so if you haven't been there enough that's okay – what matters is that you're here now.'

Bernadette sniffed as she stepped forward and hugged Keli, who opened her arms and welcomed it. They stood like that for a moment, Bernadette soaking in the human comfort, before she was ready to let go and take a step back.

'Thanks, Keli. Ugh, how did you get so wise? It's supposed to be the old Jedi masters like me that are the profound ones.'

'It's my family,' Keli made light of it. 'You can't go to my mum's house for a cuppa without someone delivering at least one life lesson with every KitKat.'

Bernadette had met Keli's family several times and she knew exactly what she meant. Her mother, Gilda, was one of those naturally smart, strong women, a legal secretary who did so much for her community, and three of her four siblings were in the medical profession. They were just one of those families that cared about other people.

'Okay,' Bernadette said, blowing her cheeks out and changing her energy back to positive and light, 'I'm going to go back in and sit with Marge until Estelle comes back up, then I'll get off home.'

'You've got Nina's vow renewal tomorrow, haven't you? Caleb was telling me about it. So romantic.'

So much had happened today that Bernadette had put that to the back of her mind. Right now, all she wanted to do tomorrow morning was lie in bed and sleep, maybe watch some of those house renovation shows or old episodes of *Friends* – anything that would take her mind to a numb, happy place where the worst thing that could happen was a burst pipe.

But, of course, she wouldn't do that. Because even better than sleep, would be a morning with the people she loved. Hadn't today reminded her how priceless that was?

With more thanks to Keli, she took her tea back through into Marge's room, and saw that she was still sleeping. Bernadette went on to autopilot, switching on her bedside light, turning off the overhead ones, fixing Marge's blanket so that she'd be settled for the night.

When she sat down, she pulled her phone from her pocket and made sure it was on silent before checking her messages. One from Caleb, saying thanks again for coming in today and telling her that he and Stevie had opened a bottle of wine if she fancied joining them later. Another one from Nina saying how excited she was for tomorrow.

And finally, one from Jack.

Missing u. See u tomorrow. Hope you're having a goof fay.

That made her smile – he clearly hadn't had his specs on when he typed that and those big hands of his were as hopeless with the buttons as they were with the emojis and the xxxx's.

Miss you too, love. Let's talk tomorrow. Think it's time we made some plans. 🩶 x

It was, wasn't it? Was she ready? Was he? She'd started today with the serious thought of suggesting they make it official and get married. Wasn't four years long enough to be sure? It was for her, yet she was the one who'd been dragging her heels, refusing to commit because she was already once burned. She hadn't been ready to give up her life here, her work, her friends, her proximity to her family. Surely, though, they could figure out a way to make at least some of that happen now? Perhaps do some part-time shifts at a hospital in Ireland? Maybe rent her cottage here out as an Airbnb so she could afford to keep it, then she could still come back and forward to see the family every couple of weeks. It was only a forty-five-minute flight. That way, she was giving up her job here, but not her whole life.

'So serious.' The voice from the bed interrupted her thoughts and she looked up to see Marge was awake again, watching her, the corners of her pale lips quivering a little as they turned up.

Bernadette immediately snapped out of her malaise and went straight back to cheeriness. 'Ah, it's just me being dramatic, Marge. Can't decide if I'm coming or going. I woke up this morning thinking that I should propose. Can you believe that? You'd think I'd know better.'

'To your Irishman?'

Bernadette laughed. 'Ah yes, I forgot I'd bored your socks off about him before. Nearly four years we've been doing the long-distance thing for now and I'm wondering if it's time for one of us to make the move. He's born and bred there, so it makes more sense for me to go but... Och, I don't know, Marge. Didn't I put my life aside for a man once before, and look how that turned out. Once bitten, twice running a mile.'

'You were going to... take me to meet him.'

The trip they'd talked about taking last year. Marge remembered too. Bernadette's regret came flooding right back like a big bastard wave to drown her. Why the bugger hadn't they done it? Why hadn't she called Marge? Why hadn't Marge called her? Why had they left it too bloody late?

Bernadette had to clear her throat again. Jesus, what a heartbreak. But she knew too much about illness and too much about the straight-talking Marge Drummond to lie to her. 'I was, Marge. I'm so sorry we never did that. Would you still like to meet him?'

'I would indeed,' Marge whispered.

'Then, I tell you what, he's coming over here tomorrow. Our Nina is renewing her vows. I know – no idea what all that's about. In our day, one wedding to the same man was plenty. Too many in my case. Anyway, Jack is coming over tomorrow and he'll be here for a couple of days, so I'll bring him up to visit you if you'd like that? Only if you feel up to it.'

'I'd like that very much,' Marge whispered, then Bernadette saw her gaze move. 'Estelle?'

'She's gone downstairs to the cafe with Clara for a cuppa. That was a brave thing you did there, Marge, but your lass surprised us all.'

Bernadette had listened, incredulous, as Estelle had explained that she'd known for years that Lester Kelaney was her father. Tears had run down Marge's cheeks when she'd revealed that. 'I'm sorry,' Marge had whispered again.

'Mum, you have nothing to be sorry for. You were protecting me. And I'm glad that you did. Truly. I didn't want another dad. I had everything I could possibly need in the one I had.'

If it was possible to watch a weight rising from someone's heart, that was exactly what they'd seen. It was the forgiveness. Not Estelle forgiving Marge, but Marge forgiving herself. Bernadette had to fish into her pocket for her hanky yet again.

'She did.'

'You know, Marge, she's going to be okay. Clara will make sure of that. Whatever Estelle wants, she'll make it happen.'

'I know. But she's going to...' Marge paused and Bernadette could see that talking was taking it out of her. '...Be alone.'

Before Bernadette could reply, could reassure her, the door opened and Estelle came back in.

'I'm glad you're awake, Mum – I brought someone up to see you.'

30

MARGE

Marge wasn't sure if she was awake or asleep and dreaming because she could see Amber with Estelle, just the way that they'd been a thousand times when they'd come through her door. But this wasn't her door. This was the hospital. Wasn't it?

'Hi, Marge.' Amber's smile was beaming. 'Oh, I've missed your face.'

Marge felt her spirits soar. She'd adored this young woman from the first day she'd come into their home, so gregarious and always quick to laugh. She and Estelle had balanced each other perfectly – her more serious, thoughtful daughter and her spontaneous friend.

'And Bernadette. Twice in one day,' Amber quipped.

So Bernadette and Amber had met already. That could only be a good thing, Marge decided. More people to help Estelle when... She couldn't finish that thought.

'You have that chair,' Estelle said, pointing to the one that she'd been sitting in for what felt like weeks now. Or was it actually weeks? Marge had lost track of time. Amber sat in the chair and leaned forwards towards the bed.

'It's so good to see you,' Marge whispered, wondering if that was a flinch of sorrow crossing Amber's face. Perhaps not. It passed so quickly and now Amber was grinning again.

'How are you feeling, Marge? I'm so sorry you've been sick. Estelle was just telling me about it. I wish I'd been here to visit you.'

'That's okay,' Marge said softly, meaning it. 'You're here now.'

'I am. I only came up for a few minutes because it's late and I know you need your sleep, but I'm glad I got to see you.'

At the end of the bed, Estelle's finger grazed the sheet that was covering Marge's foot. 'Mum, I'll be back in a sec. I'm just going to let Keli know we're here and that I'll be heading home soon.'

'Okay.'

'I'll just nip to the loo while you're doing that,' Bernadette said, getting up from the chair.

Marge remembered what she'd been talking to Bernadette about before Estelle and Amber came in. 'Bernadette,' she said, then watched as Bernadette stopped at the door. Turned. 'You should go to Ireland. Maybe I'll still get there too one day.'

Bernadette obviously liked that suggestion because her eyes were shining. 'I think I will, Marge.'

She went on out of the door, leaving just Amber, who had reached over and placed her hand on Marge's forearm.

'Marge, I'm sorry about everything that happened with Estelle too. I was so stubborn. I should have listened to her, but listening has never been my strong point.'

Always so self-deprecating. And so strong. Marge remembered now that Amber came to Kenneth's funeral with her, even though she was exhausted with work and a baby and breastfeeding.

'Your boys?'

'Growing like weeds and they're gorgeous and funny and they give me new wrinkles every day from lack of sleep and worry. But they're great, Marge. I hear you're being moved to another ward tomorrow, so I was thinking if you would like me to, I could bring the boys along to visit.'

Marge remembered that Bernadette had said something similar – she was going to bring Jack up too. People were kind, weren't they? Caring. That sparked a thought that saddened her. Why had she waited so long to tell people where she was? Why had she not let anyone in? Shared what she was going through? She had no answers, but maybe it wasn't too late.

Marge nodded. 'I'd like that.'

Amber's eyes were glistening just like Bernadette's now, and Marge got the same feeling she'd had a moment ago. She had something to say. She couldn't quite think… Amber. Estelle. It came to her.

'You're friends again?'

She wished it was easier to talk, but she lost her strength as the day went on. She'd be better again in the morning. But in the meantime, she had more to say.

'Amber, take care of her. When I can't. Take care of her.'

Amber was crying now, and Marge felt terrible that she'd upset her. She watched as Amber used the sleeve of her jumper to quickly wipe her face.

'I will, Marge, I promise. And I'll take care of you too. I'll bring cakes tomorrow and I've got so many stories to tell you. And gossip. So much of the kind of gossip I used to tell you about, and you'd pretend you weren't interested, but I know you secretly were.'

Marge had such an urge to laugh, but it didn't escape her throat. She hoped Amber knew she was laughing on the inside, because she was so right in her recollection. The times Amber had sat at their kitchen table and told them all the ins and outs of who was dating who at college and then, later, all the playgroup mum dramas, and the gossip from her work. She had an endless stream of chat, and Marge had been amused by it all.

'And Ewan?' It was getting harder to force the words out now. She was getting tired.

'Ouch.' A big sigh. 'I think he's a work in progress. He still wants me to forgive him, but I don't know if I can.'

Before Marge could offer any thoughts on that, the door opened and Estelle and Bernadette came back in.

'Keli said we're fine for five more minutes, Mum, and then we'll get off and let you sleep. Unless you want me to stay? Craig's over visiting his brother in Edinburgh this weekend, so it would be no problem to sleep here. Keli says there's a rollout bed she can bring in for me…'

'No,' Marge managed to say. 'I'll. Be. Fine.' If she took a breath between each word, it was easier.

'Okay, Mum, if you're sure.' She'd come up to the side of the bed now and was stroking Marge's hair back like she used to do when she was playing hairdresser as a little girl. 'I love you, Mum.'

'Love. You.'

She felt a kiss on the top of her head, and she smiled. *Estelle.*

No, it was Ian.

'Hello, love,' he said, as he pushed a stray lock of hair back behind her ear. He had on her favourite jumper, the one that she'd bought him for Estelle's twenty-first birthday party. It was a pale blue colour and he'd made several jokes already about it matching his winter West of Scotland complexion. Marge didn't care. He was as handsome as she'd ever seen him.

He nudged the door open with his hip, because his hands were full, carrying the tray with two mugs of tea and a plate of his favourite biscuits.

'Come on, Marge. Just leave all that,' he said, pointing to the pile of paperwork that was in front of her on the kitchen table, waiting to be filed away. She liked things to be organised. Couldn't bear to leave a job half done. But... Well, what did it matter? If it were a choice of sitting in the garden on a mild, sunny day with Ian, or doing just about anything else, she was pulling her summer cardigan on and going with him.

She followed him out and took a seat at table they'd loved for years, the one that sat in the middle of the garden facing south. It was the perfect spot, even if she had to put her hand up to her face, and squint against the sun when she was looking at him.

'You told me you were pregnant right here, do you remember?'

She did. Every word of that conversation was etched on her brain. The day she'd thought she would lose him. Instead, she'd gained her future.

Marge nudged his shoulder with hers. 'And you walked down to that tree to think about it. The only swift decision you ever made in your life.'

'And the best one,' he said, as he always did.

It had been their standing joke throughout their marriage, mostly because it was true. He was a man of thought. Of consideration. He was never one for big romantic gestures, but there wasn't a time in their lives when she hadn't felt absolutely sure of him, and for Marge, that mattered so much more.

They sat in silence for a couple of minutes, as they often did, but Marge could sense that there was something on his mind.

'We're going to have to talk about it, my love,' he said eventually, and he didn't have to explain. She knew. It was the only subject they ever avoided, the only thing they never agreed on. 'She has a right to know.'

Marge felt the creeping sensation of dread wind its way around her body, and the red rash of heat rise up her neck.

'I agree. I do. But I just don't know if I can tell her.'

'Then I will,' he said gently, his hand reaching for hers. 'Not because I want to, but because it's the right thing to do.' Their fingers intertwined, as if they were two pieces of a puzzle, instinctively joining together to make one piece. 'If anything happens to us...' he went on.

'Nothing is going to happen to us,' Marge countered, refusing to consider that.

'I know. But if it does, she has to know that she has other people. A family. We have to give her that.'

Marge couldn't argue anymore because she knew he was right. 'When are you going to tell her?'

With a slow, gentle sigh, he stood up and she had to squint against the sun again to see his face. 'When the time is right. Don't worry about it any more, Marge. I've got this. I'll take care of you both.'

She didn't doubt him. She never did.

'Come on, love. Let's walk,' he said, gently pulling on her hand.

Marge thought about staying, about sitting for a moment longer, but the sun was moving and she didn't want to lose it. So she followed him, down the garden, towards the tree... But... she stopped. Something wasn't right.

The blue jumper. She'd bought that for Estelle's twenty-first. He'd only worn it that night. The night he died.

'Marge. Marge, can you hear me?' Bernadette's voice. Was she coming over today? Marge couldn't remember.

'Come on, love.' Ian was still waiting, still holding her hand, two steps ahead and just an arm length away.

'Amber, can you and go get Keli, please?' Bernadette again.

She could feel the gentle pull on her arm. He was getting impatient. The sun was going down behind the tree. Sunset. Their favourite time.

'Mum? Mum?' Estelle must be looking for her. She could hear her girl... why did she sound like she was crying?

'Estelle, please don't cry. I'm right here, darling.'

'Mum, please don't go. Please.'

Marge hesitated again. How could she leave her? She was her whole heart.

But Ian was waiting... And he'd made sure Estelle would have everything she needed to go on without them.

And that's why Marge knew it was time to go.

31

AMBER

Numb.

Just numb.

Amber put the three cups of coffee from the vending machine on the table in the deserted cafe, feeling like she was moving inside a bubble where there was no air and nothing could touch her – and she was glad of it because she knew the wave of grief that was sitting just outside the shell would drown her.

And that was nothing compared to the pain her friend must be feeling right now.

Exhaustion and sorrow were etched on Estelle's face and weariness was pressing down on her shoulders, as she stared at the table, so deep in thought that she didn't even realise that Amber had returned until she touched her friend's hand.

'How are you doing there, hon? Sorry. That might be the most stupid question I've ever asked.'

Estelle was saved from having to answer by the arrival of Bernadette, who had stayed behind up on the ward for a few minutes longer to speak to Keli.

She sat down now and Amber pushed the third cup towards her.

Bernadette smiled kindly and it struck Amber that other than a brief glimpse at a funeral, she'd never met this woman before this morning and yet now she'd be such a huge and comforting part of her story every time she thought back on today.

After Marge had died… Amber paused that thought, waiting for the pain from the punch to her gut to pass… Bernadette had taken care of them, sat with them, gently guided them through the next hour, and Amber would always be grateful for that care. She was grateful too that Estelle hadn't been alone, as Amber knew she'd been for weeks now. It was almost as if Marge waited until Estelle would have people there to take care of her. It was just the kind of thing she'd do for the daughter she loved so much.

Amber watched now as Bernadette handed a white bag, about the size of a normal shopping bag, and a small box over to Estelle.

'Here you go, love. Your mum's jewellery is in the box, and her handbag and shawl are in the bag. Keli will keep the rest of her personal effects safe and you can collect them when you're ready. Or I can bring them back to you. Whatever you want to do…'

'Thanks, Bernadette. My mum would be so thankful that you were there. I am too.'

The three of them sat with their own thoughts for a moment, before Estelle reached for the small box and opened it. Amber saw that inside was a fine gold chain and a simple gold band.

A tear dropped from Estelle's face on to the table as she slid the ring onto her own finger. 'You know, she never wore an engagement ring. I asked her once and she said that she had no need for it. That this was enough to remind her that she had everything.'

Amber and Bernadette stayed silent, letting Estelle work through her thoughts.

Estelle gently rubbed the thin piece of gold. 'I've heard people say this before and I didn't believe it, but in a way, I'm glad she didn't have to live like that any longer. She found it so difficult that she'd lost her independence and had to rely on others. She'd never complain, but I know she must have hated it.'

'Sometimes people are ready,' Bernadette said gently.

'I think that's it,' Estelle agreed. 'She was ready. And I know I sound like those sympathy cards or Instagram reels, but I honestly think she's in a better place. With my dad. The one I loved – not the other one.'

Her half-smile when she said that made Amber ache for her. 'He's the only one that matters.'

Estelle nodded. 'He is. I've always wondered... Actually, not wondered – I've always *known* that he left that letter for me deliberately. My dad wasn't a man who was careless with anything. To keep a copy of that letter in his desk... I think it was because he knew that if anything ever happened to him, I would find it there. I always thought it was his way of sparing Mum from having to tell me because he probably knew that it would be too hard for her to have that conversation. And he was right. I think he was looking out for me, even then. And now. Looking out for both me and Mum.'

'I think so,' Amber agreed. 'And you've got us too, Estelle. Do you want to come back to my place tonight? Stay over and let me take care of you?'

'Thank you...' Then she shook her head. 'But I called Craig from the ward, after Mum...' A pause. She didn't have to say the word. '...And he's on his way back from Edinburgh. He'll be home any time now so I'm going to go be with him. I've been at this hospital for so long that I just need to be in my own kitchen and in my own bed.'

'Then why don't I give you a lift home?' Bernadette offered. 'I don't want you to be driving. Not right now. And what about you, Amber? Did you drive here?'

Amber thought back to Wiki Taxi Driver, who was probably still out there, educating the unsuspecting passengers of Glasgow. 'No, I got a taxi. I'll call another one now.'

'Let me take you too,' Bernadette said kindly. Amber was about to object when she added, 'I think we could all do with the company for a little bit longer.'

A few minutes later, when they all got into Bernadette's car, Amber knew she'd been right. Going their separate ways would have felt too cold, too lonely. She'd seen so many scenes in television shows and movies that showed the end of someone's life, but it always cut before the next bit. This bit. When it was done and all that was left was shock and disbelief, and all the logistics of what to do next.

The dark roads were quiet as they travelled, swapping stories about Marge, moving between tears and sadness and laughter too.

They reached Estelle's house first, and as they pulled up to the old Georgian townhouse, a light went on in the hallway, then the door opened and Craig was there, standing in the doorway, waiting for her.

Amber got out, opened Estelle's door, waited for her to say her goodbyes to Bernadette. When Estelle climbed out, Amber wrapped her arms around her, the air gone from her lungs as she whispered, 'I'm so sorry. For everything.'

'Please don't be,' Estelle said, holding her tight. 'I really think that somehow my mum brought you back to me. She was so happy that you were there. Will you come over tomorrow? Help me with what comes next?'

'I wouldn't be anywhere else,' Amber promised, letting her go, then watching as she went up the path into Craig's arms. Amber raised her hand, and he did the same, letting them know that it was okay for them to go. He had her.

He had her.

Amber climbed back into the car, this time sitting in the front seat that Estelle had just left.

'Where to next?' Bernadette asked.

Amber gestured to the screen on Bernadette's dashboard. 'Shall I put it into the satnav?'

'I'm old school – just point me in the general direction.'

'If you just turn back on to Great Western Road,' she said, naming the main road nearby that stretched through the West End of the city, 'and head towards Hyndland Road, I'll direct you from there. And thanks for this, Bernadette.'

'It's no bother at all. How are you holding up there, love?' Bernadette asked as they pulled away from the kerb.

'Honestly, Bernadette, I have no idea. I'm devastated about Marge, worried about Estelle, and so incredibly thankful that I was with her tonight. What about you?'

Bernadette's soft chuckle was full of understanding. 'About the same.'

Amber exhaled, let her shoulders fall back on the seat. 'How do you deal with it all, Bernadette? In your job, you must see so much death, and pain, and heartache and terrible things. How do you manage to be happy when you see all that every day?'

Bernadette was still staring straight ahead, eyes on the road as she spoke. 'Because I see all the good things too. I see how much people care for each other. How scared they are when something is wrong, and then how relieved they are when we help. Every single day I see people realising how much they love someone, or getting a reality check that makes them remember what's important. I see parents who would do anything for their kids, and adults who want nothing more than for their elderly parents to be okay. I see all the goodness too... Although there was none of that with the bloke you came in with today, right enough,' she added, with a teasing dig that made Amber groan.

'I have no idea what you're talking about. I refuse to ever speak of it again.'

'That's probably wise, pet,' Bernadette agreed, before going back to her point. 'But then look at tonight. Look at the love between Marge and Estelle. I see that kind of care every day and, in my mind, that balances all the bad stuff out. Because at the end of the day, it's just the people we love that matter.'

'Oh, Jesus, Bernadette, I really wish I'd written that down.'

That made them both laugh, even as Amber replayed it in her mind.

It's just the people we love that matter.

'You'll have to direct me from here,' Bernadette said, as she turned the car onto Hyndland Road.

It's just the people we love that matter.

It was like a mantra, on repeat in her head, and Amber realised that was maybe because she had to hear it a few more times to get the message.

It's just the people we love that matter.

'If you could just turn left here, please,' she said, directing Bernadette down a side street, deserted except for two females, walking along the road, both laughing, one of the young women carrying her shoes with her free hand, despite the fact that it was probably minus two degrees outside, the other carrying what looked like a large white tray of chips. Just another Saturday night in February and Amber loved the sight of it.

'That used to be us,' Amber said, a memory popping into her head. 'Estelle would be the one in sensible shoes and I'd be the one with the blisters, carrying my heels. And Marge would wait up for us, and roll her eyes when she saw me.'

It's just the people we love that matter.

Amber wondered if Marge was watching her now, rolling her eyes.

'Just left here, Bernadette,' she said suddenly, realising where she was. 'The house with the blue door.'

Bernadette pulled into the space outside and Amber reached over to hug her.

'Thank you. For everything.'

'You're welcome, pet. Now on you go and get home.'

Amber let her go, climbed out, waved as she pulled away, and then stood for a moment, breathing in the cold air.

It's just the people we love that matter.

She walked up the path, but instead of pulling keys out of her bag, she knocked the door, not too loudly, so she wouldn't wake anyone inside that was sleeping.

No answer.

She was about to knock again when she heard footsteps, then the door opened and she met the eyes of the guy who was standing there.

'Hey.'

'Hey.'

'I was wondering if you still had space on that couch for me?'

THE NEXT MORNING…

32

BERNADETTE – 22 FEBRUARY 2026

For the second morning in a row, as Bernadette gradually transitioned from a dream-filled sleep to the semi-awake awareness of a new chilly morning, her gaze didn't fall on the empty space in the bed beside her. Or the light from the lamp post outside the window that was casting a beam through the still-dark morning. Nope. The first thing her eyes settled on was the pair of high-grade elastic, waist-to-knee, extra-firm control knickers that were draped over the chair in front of her dressing table.

And she groaned, just as she had yesterday.

She remembered having the brief thought last night that all she wanted to do this morning was lie in bed, sleep and watch feel good telly that would stop her mind from thinking about Jack, about Marge, about the past and about the absolutely exhausting twenty-four hours she'd just had. But now that she was awake, she knew the only thing that would make her feel better was to see Jack and her family. She just wished that Nina had given her a job to do this morning. Watch the kids. Check the flowers. Greet guests. Anything to take her mind off last night. But her daughter had insisted that everything was already organised, so all she had to do was get there.

It was probably just as well, because she wasn't sure how efficient she could be after only a few hours of fitful dozing.

When she'd got home last night, she hadn't been able to sleep. She'd thought about calling Nina to explain that Marge had passed away, but in the end, she'd decided not to. Marge wouldn't approve of that at all. Nina and Stuart knew Marge, but only as their dad's secretary and the person who'd helped them organise his funeral. Maybe later Bernadette would tell them everything else, but then again, she didn't want to bring her own sadness to a day that should be full of joy for her family.

Marge would be the very first person to say pull yourself together and stick to the plan, and she'd be right. Bernadette couldn't spoil her daughter's day, or be the cause of a cloud over a celebration of Nina and Gerry's marriage, just because she'd lost someone she cared about. There would be plenty of moments over the next days and weeks and months to think about Marge, to celebrate her life.

Instead, just after midnight, she'd called Clara and told her the news. Bernadette wasn't sure what would happen next – that was up to Estelle – but she had no doubt at all that whatever it was, Clara would take care of her and make sure that she was ok. Marge had known what she was doing when she'd trusted Clara to do the right thing.

When she'd hung up, she'd put a message on the group chat of the other women who had met every year on yesterday's date, since Kenneth's funeral.

One by one, they'd got back to her, and they'd ended up swapping messages into the early hours of the morning. They'd even made a plan. As soon as they knew the arrangements for the funeral, there would be a new gathering every year on the same date as before, but it would no longer be called Cheat Day. It would henceforth be known as Marge Day.

Bernadette hadn't called Jack, because much as his was the only voice she wanted to hear, she knew he'd be sleeping, and didn't want to wake him when he had an early flight this morning. Stuart lived closest to the airport, and he'd already offered to pick Jack up on the way to the hotel – the same one Nina had married in all those years ago.

She tried not to think about the last time they were there. Kenneth had been in a foul mood on Nina's wedding day, furious that she was defying him by marrying a man he didn't approve of. But, of course, he'd been the epitome of charm to the guests, the perfect host, who had schmoozed the guests he'd invited, made a show of plying them with the best champagne and sumptuous food, made a beautifully worded, sentimental speech that melted everyone's heart and left them all heading home that night thinking what a wonderful man he was. All bullshit. What they didn't see was that he'd told Bernadette that her clothes were awful, that her wedding tears embarrassed him, that her conversations with the guests were pathetic. They wouldn't know that she later found out he'd been sleeping with at least two of the women in attendance and when they'd got home that night, he'd gone into a full-scale rage and smashed every family picture on their walls.

That's what Bernadette had survived. It had sat with her since, in her fear of commitment, her reluctance to give up her power to any man again. Until now.

A buzzer on her phone sounded and she realised she must have left yesterday's alarm on repeat, because she had no memory of setting a new one before she finally fell asleep around 5 a.m. Unless... She wondered if divine intervention included a nudge from the heavens to get out of bed and get a move on. 'Okay, Marge, I hear you.'

Her phone buzzed again with a second nudge from an earthlier source. A text from Jack.

Landed. See you soon. Xx.

The kisses surprised her. Maybe after four years he was getting the hang of this long-distance affection stuff. The thought sent her right back to yesterday morning again and the one thing that had been on her mind, other than the prospect of getting into that underwear. Jack. Their future. What they'd had for the last four years had been enough for her, but she knew it wasn't any more. It was time for changes. Yesterday, she'd woken up contemplating whether she should ask him to make it more permanent and now she was sure she had the answer. It wasn't something for today, though. Today was about Nina and Gerry. But tonight she was going to speak to Jack, to tell him her thoughts. She was ready to be more than she was now. She was ready to give up her life here, and move to him, and together they could figure out the logistics of it all. That is, if he was ready too. If he didn't feel the same, she could be about to have her already fragile heart shattered but at least she would know. If Marge's death had taught her one thing, it was that she should make plans and do everything today, because she had no idea how many tomorrows there would be. And as Marge's final gift to Estelle had shown, there was power in knowing the full story.

Thinking about Estelle made her pick up the phone. She'd swapped numbers with Marge's daughter last night and now she wanted to check on her.

> Hello lovely. No need to respond, but I just wanted you to know I was thinking about you. Your mum told me many times over the years how wonderful you are and I was so glad to meet you and see just how right she was. We'll all miss her so very much, and we're here for you any time at all for anything you need, always. Sending much love and hugs to you, Bernadette x

Hopefully today Estelle would sleep and she would also let the people she loved take care of her. And Bernadette had a feeling that one of those people would be Amber. The love between them had been so obvious and it was more than just fate that they were in the same place at the same time. She replayed what Amber had said about coincidences being the universe's way of pointing you in the right direction. Bernadette couldn't agree more.

She put the phone back down on her bedside table, and, averting her eyes from the ominous shapewear knickers, she pushed back her white cotton duvet, ready now to face the day.

Half an hour later – twenty minutes to get showered, hair dried, put on some make-up, and then a full ten minutes to get the suction pants on – she was out of the door and into her car for the second time in under twenty-four hours. Nina had been right about the outfit though. The cream velvet dress did things to her body that could only be described as miraculous, and with the soft black jacket on top, Bernadette felt as fabulous as she ever had.

The clock had just clicked on to quarter to ten, when she pulled up outside the hotel. There were already many cars there: she spotted Stuart's convertible, with the roof up of course – he only got to take advantage of the wind in his hair in the summer, and even then, in this part of the world, that could be touch-and-go. Val's Jeep was there, parked squinty, with one wheel up on the kerb, as if she'd screeched to a halt and given chase to a criminal. Which, actually, probably wasn't out of the question for her pal. Behind it was Gerry's Range Rover. The irony of it all. The man Kenneth had disapproved of because he was a skint electrician had left the housing association he worked for, set up his own electrical business, grafted his socks off as he built it up to a team of ten, with a solid bank of major commercial contracts, and was probably now earning more than Kenneth ever had. Urgh, that would infuriate him. And the thought of that made Bernadette smile as she reached the doors, paused, took a breath, put all of the stresses and strains and sadnesses of yesterday out of her mind, and prepared to do everything she could to make Nina's celebration perfect.

When she was ready, she opened the door and stepped inside to a room filled with white flowers, rows of silver silk-covered chairs and with music from a string quartet in the corner. In the seats were so many people that she loved, and her depleted heart began to fill again as some of them spotted her and greeted her with warm smiles.

And there was Jack. Her handsome man was walking towards her now, his hand outstretched to hers. Over his shoulder, she could see Nina, her face beaming with happiness as she waved. And there was Gerry and the kids. And Val and her other pals, Sarah and Alice. And Stuart and Connor. And...

'You made it,' Jack said, and oh, his easy grin still made her stomach flip.

'I did.' Right, time to get this show on the road.

Although, it was starting to make her a bit uncomfortable that everyone in the room now seemed to be looking her way. The centre of attention was a place she always did her best to avoid. Nina had assured her that getting here at this time would make her the first to arrive. That suited Bernadette perfectly, because then she could blend into the background and be the person that just made sure everything ran like clockwork and everyone was having a good time. Clearly, there had been a miscommunication, because this was about as far from blending into the background as she could be.

'Bernadette, ma love, I wanted to speak to you...' Jack began, and Bernadette's face flushed. Why was everyone *still* staring at her?

'Jack, it'll need to wait to after the ceremony,' she said, hoping that she didn't sound too dismissive but deeply aware that apparently everyone was waiting to get started.

Nina was walking towards them now. 'Mum, there isn't going to be a ceremony.'

The first thought that went through Bernadette's mind was *Oh for the love of God, what now?* Followed by... Had they had a fight? Changed their minds? Had the celebrant not showed up? Was there a burst pipe?

And now that she was scanning the room for potential ceremony-ending disasters, there were more questions. Was that Caleb? And Stevie and Keli?

And over there – some of the women from the support group she ran. And... Bloody hell, Jack's family – his sons, Tadgh and Shay and their partners – were there too. Nina hadn't even mentioned that she'd invited them and Jack had kept quiet on them coming here from Ireland too.

Jack was speaking again. 'I know that you hate to be the centre of attention, ma love, so Nina came up with the vow renewal as a wee ruse, to put you off the scent.'

Oh no. Bernadette hated surprises. And now it felt like everyone was in on something she knew nothing about.

What scent? THE BLOODY SCENT OF WHAT?

'We knew if we suggested this' – his gaze went to Nina and Stuart, who were nodding in agreement – 'that you'd refuse, but I wanted all of our family and friends to be here, to share this. You deserve to be the centre of attention, Bernadette O'Brien. Today and every day.'

Bernadette had no idea if she was still standing, still there, or still in her bed and this was just another crazy dream, but if she wasn't mistaken, Jack Donovan, the love of her life, was now opening a tiny box and inside was a perfect emerald solitaire, perched on a gleaming gold band.

'I'm too old and these trousers are too damn tight to be doing the whole down on one knee thing...' Jack was saying now, with that unmistakable, lovable twinkle in his eye. 'But, Bernadette, I adore you. And I've come to truly believe that you are the most important thing in my life. That's why I've decided to make some changes. I've decided to sell my business so we can be together and spend the rest of our years enjoying our lives together. If you'll have me, that is. So Bernadette, ma love, I'll be forever grateful if you would do me the honour of becoming my wife.'

As Bernadette held her breath, she stared at him, this wonderful man, and she knew that all the other stuff, the past, the worries about the future, the decision about where they'd live and where she'd work... None of that mattered. And her turmoil over whether or not to take the next step had just been taken out of her hands.

It's just the people we love that matter.

She heard herself saying that to Amber last night, and she knew that now it was time to take her own advice. They'd work it out.

'Yes, Jack Donovan. I certainly will.'

As the room erupted into cheers and applause, Jack's face broke into the widest grin, as he flushed with relief. 'Oh thank the heavens for that, because if you'd said no, this next bit would be awkward. You see, we knew you'd never plan a big wedding, so the second part of the surprise is that there's a celebrant waiting at the end of that aisle...'

Bernadette's gaze followed his gesture, and yes, there was definitely a kindly faced woman in a suit standing there, next to Milo and Casey, who were being uncharacteristically still.

'And we'll need to do all the official paperwork later, but, Bernadette, in front of everyone we love, will you marry me right here and now?'

Yes, she hated surprises, but this...

Bernadette sent the question up to the other woman who'd been happy to always be in the background, to organise, to cope, to plan, to sort everything out for everyone else. If there was an afterlife, a heaven, a higher plane, then she knew that Marge Drummond was up there now, her steely eye taking in the scene, checking that everything was just the way it should be.

'I'd love to, Jack Donovan.'

As more cheers rang out, her friend, Stevie, stepped forward and music began to play that Bernadette recognised immediately. It was one of her and Jack's special songs. Gladys Knight. 'Best Thing That Ever Happened to Me'. Stevie's beautiful, melodic voice, stood in for Gladys, and she began to sing.

At that, Stuart held out his arm. 'Mum?'

Not to be outdone, Nina, on the other side, stepped forward too. 'We'd both like to walk you down the aisle.'

As she took her first step towards a new future that she couldn't wait to embrace, Bernadette said a silent thanks to the woman who had left this earth just a few hours before.

Thank you for reminding me to live for today.

And Bernadette knew with every beat of her overflowing heart that Marge would approve.

* * *

MORE FROM SHARI LOW

Another book from Shari Low is available to order now here:

https://mybook.to/ShariLow22

ABOUT THE AUTHOR

Shari Low is the #1, multi-million copy bestselling author of over 30 novels, including *One Day With You* and *One Moment in Time* and a collection of parenthood memories called *Because Mummy Said So*. She lives near Glasgow.

Download your exclusive bonus content from Shari Low here:

Visit Shari's website: www.sharilow.com

Follow Shari on social media:

- facebook.com/sharilowbooks
- x.com/sharilow
- instagram.com/sharilowbooks
- bookbub.com/authors/shari-low

ALSO BY SHARI LOW

My One Month Marriage

One Day In Summer

One Summer Sunrise

The Story of Our Secrets

One Last Day of Summer

One Day With You

One Moment in Time

One Christmas Eve

One Year After You

One Long Weekend

One Midnight With You

One Day and Forever

One More Day of Us

One Snowy Day

Just One More Day

The Carly Cooper Series

What If?

What Now?

What Next?

The Hollywood Trilogy (with Ross King)

The Rise

The Catch

The Fall

www.ingramcontent.com/pod-product-compliance
Ingram Content Group UK Ltd.
Pitfield, Milton Keynes, MK11 3LW, UK
UKHW040951030226
10470UKWH00041B/574